THE SAINT INTERVENES

FOREWORD BY
BRAD MENGEL

THE ADVENTURES OF THE SAINT

Enter the Saint (1930), *The Saint Closes the Case* (1930),
The Avenging Saint (1930), *Featuring the Saint* (1931),
Alias the Saint (1931), *The Saint Meets His Match* (1931),
The Saint Versus Scotland Yard (1932), *The Saint's Getaway* (1932),
The Saint and Mr Teal (1933), *The Brighter Buccaneer* (1933),
The Saint in London (1934), *The Saint Intervenes* (1934),
The Saint Goes On (1934), *The Saint in New York* (1935),
Saint Overboard (1936), *The Saint in Action* (1937),
The Saint Bids Diamonds (1937), *The Saint Plays with Fire* (1938),
Follow the Saint (1938), *The Happy Highwayman* (1939),
The Saint in Miami (1940), *The Saint Goes West* (1942),
The Saint Steps In (1943), *The Saint on Guard* (1944),
The Saint Sees It Through (1946), *Call for the Saint* (1948),
Saint Errant (1948), *The Saint in Europe* (1953),
The Saint on the Spanish Main (1955), *The Saint Around the World* (1956),
Thanks to the Saint (1957), *Señor Saint* (1958), *Saint to the Rescue* (1959),
Trust the Saint (1962), *The Saint in the Sun* (1963),
Vendetta for the Saint (1964), *The Saint on TV* (1968),
The Saint Returns (1968), *The Saint and the Fiction Makers* (1968),
The Saint Abroad (1969), *The Saint in Pursuit* (1970),
The Saint and the People Importers (1971), *Catch the Saint* (1975),
The Saint and the Hapsburg Necklace (1976), *Send for the Saint* (1977),
The Saint in Trouble (1978), *The Saint and the Templar Treasure* (1978),
Count On the Saint (1980), *Salvage for the Saint* (1983)

THE SAINT INTERVENES

LESLIE CHARTERIS

SERIES EDITOR: IAN DICKERSON

Published by Thomas & Mercer, Seattle

www.apub.com

ISBN-13: 9781477842720
ISBN-10: 1477842721

Cover design by David Drummond, www.salamanderhill.com

Printed in the United States of America

To H. H. Gibson,

Many years ago I resolved that you were one of the first people I must dedicate a book to. But time slips by, and it's sadly easy to lose touch with someone who lives hundreds of miles away. So this comes very late, but I hope not too late; because even though this may be a bad book, if I hadn't come under your guidance many years ago it would probably have been very much worse.

PUBLISHER'S NOTE

The text of this book has been preserved from the original edition and includes vocabulary, grammar, style, and punctuation that might differ from modern publishing practices. Every care has been taken to preserve the author's tone and meaning, allowing only minimal changes to punctuation and wording to ensure a fluent experience for modern readers.

FOREWORD TO THE NEW EDITION

"What's boodle?" you may ask yourself if you have picked up this volume of the adventures of Simon Templar, better known as the Saint. Looking at my handy dictionary, boodle is a term meaning loot, booty, or treasure. Well if that's the case this book is full of boodle. The Saint stories are some of the great adventure stories of all time. *Boodle* (later retitled *The Saint Intervenes*) is a collection of fourteen short stories where the Saint intervenes in fourteen crimes, sometimes helping the police, other times helping those the police cannot help.

The writings of Leslie Charteris have been a big influence on me and not just as a writer. The Saint showed me it was possible to fight crime and have a sense of humour. I remember a scene in one of the first Saint books I read where Simon and his merry men were hunting for an unknown criminal mastermind. Most writers would have made the hero refer to the unknown criminal as X, but Leslie Charteris and the Saint don't work that way. No, the mystery villain was referred to as Pongo. It was this unconventional thinking that I loved and try to bring to my own writing and my own personal life. It was that attitude that I was trying to express when I got my first (and so far only) tattoo. It's on my right arm and is the Saint stick figure—the same stick figure that once appeared at the end of each Saint book with the note, "Watch for the sign of the Saint, he will be back."

That's the mark of a great character: you know that he will be back in some form or another. The Saint appeared in books and short stories, in comics, on the radio and film and TV. The last official appearance of a character called the Saint was the 1997 film starring Val Kilmer and the novelisation by Burl Barer. That character was very different from the one that appeared in the book you are reading. Barer also wrote an all-new adventure of the classic Saint at the same time called *Capture the Saint*. And now there's a new TV show starring Adam Rayner in production.

If I look closely I can see the Saint's influence everywhere. There is a whole subgenre of gentleman adventurers with names like The Falcon, The Toff, The Baron, Captain Satan, and The Angel who were all inspired by the Saint. Even James Bond was influenced by Simon Templar.

In the world of paperback originals of the 1970s we have series like *The Arrow*, about a disgraced police officer who now steals from criminals, and *The Decoy*, about a former thief who investigates crimes for kicks. Both of these characters seem to have some Saintly DNA. The plot of the movie *Death Wish 3* is completely based on *The Saint in New York*.

In the TV series *White Collar*, Neil Caffrey and FBI agent Peter Burke provide a fresh twist on the relationship between Simon Templar and Scotland Yard Inspector Claud Eustace Teal (a relationship portrayed beautifully in this book's "The Man Who Liked Toys"). Nate Ford and his team in the TV series *Leverage* recreate the Saint's knack for outconning various conmen (see "The Ingenuous Colonel" and "The Mixture as Before" amongst others in this volume). *The Pretender* TV series is about a man who takes revenge on people who abuse their power and authority, something the Saint was known to undertake on occasion (see "The Sleepless Knight").

I could continue on with shows, books, comics, and movies that all owe a debt to Leslie Charteris and the Saint, but none of them really capture the magic of the original stories. Simon Templar is an amazing character—a modern day Robin Hood, a buccaneer relieving the ungodly of their ill-gotten boodle with a smile on his face and a quip on his lips. The Saint has an attitude towards life that never fails to lift my spirits.

So read on and enjoy. Trust me, this book is full of boodle.

—*Brad Mengel*

THE SAINT INTERVENES

THE INGENUOUS COLONEL

Lieutenant-Colonel Sir George Uppingdon, it must be admitted, was not a genuine knight; neither, as a matter of fact, was he a genuine colonel. This is not to say that he thought that sandbags contained the material for making mortar shells, or that an observation post was a species of flagpole on which inquisitive generals hung at half-mast. But his military experience was certainly limited to a brief period during the latter days of the war when conscription had gathered him up and set him to the uncongenial task of peeling potatoes at Aldershot.

Apart from that not inglorious interlude of strengthening the stomachs of the marching armies, his career had been far less impressive than the name he passed under seemed to indicate. Pentonville had housed him on one occasion, and he had also taken one short holiday at Maidstone.

Nevertheless, although the expensive public school which had taught him his practical arithmetic had long since erased his name from its register of alumni, he had never lost his well-educated and aristocratic bearing, and with the passing of time had added to it a magnificent pair of white moustachios which were almost as valuable to him in his career.

A slight tinge of the old-fashioned conservatism which characterized his style of dress clung equally limpet-like to the processes of his mind.

"These new-fangled stunts are all very well," he said doggedly. "But what happens to them? You work them once, and they receive a great deal of publicity, and then you can never use them again. How many of them will last as long as our tried and proved old friends?"

His companion on that occasion, an equally talented Mr Sidney Immelbern—whose real name, as it happens, was Sidney Immelbern—regarded him gloomily.

"That's the trouble with you, George," he said. "It's the one thing which has kept you back from real greatness. You can't get it into your head that we've got to move with the times."

"It has also kept me out of a great deal of trouble," said the Colonel sedately. "If I remember rightly, Sid, when you last moved with the times, it was to Wormwood Scrubs."

Mr Immelbern frowned. There were seasons when he felt that George Uppingdon's gentlemanly bearing had no real foundations of good taste.

"Well," he retorted, "your methods haven't made us millionaires. Here it's nearly two months since we made a touch, and we only got eight hundred from that Australian at Brighton."

Mr Immelbern's terse statement being irrefutable, a long and somewhat melancholy silence settled down upon the partnership.

Even by the elastic standards of the world in which they moved, it was an unusual combination. Mr Sidney Immelbern had none of the Colonel's distinguished style—he was a stocky man with an unrefined and slightly oriental face, who affected check tweeds of more than dashing noisiness and had an appropriate air of smelling faintly of stables.

But they had worked excellently together in the past, and only in such rare but human excesses of recrimination as that which has just been recorded did they fail to share a sublime confidence that their team technique would shine undimmed in brilliance through the future, as and when the opportunity arose.

The unfortunate part was that the opportunity did not arise. For close upon eight weeks it had eluded them with a relentlessness which savoured of actual malice. True, there had been an American at the Savoy who had seemed a hopeful proposition, but he had turned out to be one of those curious people who sincerely disapprove of gambling on principle, and an equally promising leather merchant from Leicester had been recalled home by an ailing wife a few hours before they would have made their kill.

The profession of confidence man requires capital—he must maintain a good appearance, invest lavishly in food and wine, and be able to wait for his profits. It was not surprising that Messrs Uppingdon and Immelbern should watch the dwindling of their resources with alarm, and at times give way to moments of spleen which in more prosperous days would never have smirched their mutual friendship.

But with almost sadistic glee their opportunity continued to elude them. The lounge of the Palace Royal Hotel, where they sat sipping their expensive drinks, was a scene of life and gaiety, but the spirit of the place was not reflected in their faces. Among the lunch-time cocktail crowd of big business men, young well-groomed men, and all their chosen women, there appeared not one lonely soul with the unmistakable air of a forlorn stranger in the city whom they might tactfully accost, woo from his glum solitude with lunch and friendship, and in due course mulct of a contribution to their exchequer proportionate to his means. Fortune, they felt, had deserted them for ever. Nobody loved them.

"It is," admitted Lieutenant-Colonel Uppingdon, breaking the silence, "pretty bloody."

"It is," concurred Mr Immelbern, and suddenly scowled at him. "What's that?" he added.

Somewhat vaguely, the Colonel was inclining his head. But the remarkable point was that he was not looking at Mr Immelbern.

"What is what?" he inquired, making sure of his ground.

"What's that you're staring at with that silly look on your face?" said Mr Immelbern testily.

"That young fellow who just came in," explained the Colonel. "He seemed to know me."Mr Immelbern glanced over the room. The only man whom he was able to bring within the limits of his partner's rather unsatisfactory description was just then sitting down at a table by himself a few places away—a lean and somehow dangerous-looking young man with a keen tanned face and very clear blue eyes. Instinctively Mr Immelbern groped around for his hat.

"D'you mean he's a fellow you swindled once?" he demanded hastily.

Uppingdon shook his head. "Oh, no. I'm positive about that. Besides, he smiled at me quite pleasantly. But I can't remember him at all."

Mr Immelbern relaxed slowly. He looked at the young man again with diminished apprehension. And gradually, decisively, a certain simple deduction registered itself in his practised mind.

The young man had money. There was no deception about that. Everything about him pointed unobtrusively but unequivocally towards that one cardinal fact. His clothes, immaculately kept, had the unostentatious seal of Savile Row on every stitch of them. His silk shirt had the cachet of St. James's. His shoes, brightly polished and unspotted by the stains of traffic, could never have been anything but custom made.

He had just given his order to the waiter, and while he waited for it to arrive he was selecting a cigarette from a thin case which to the lay eye might have been silver, but which Mr Immelbern knew beyond all doubt was platinum.

There are forms of instinct which soar beyond all physical explanations into the clear realms of clairvoyance. The homing pigeon wings its way across sightless space to the old roost. The Arabian camel finds the water-hole, and the pig detects the subterranean truffle. Even thus was the clairvoyance of Mr Immelbern.

If there was one thing on earth which he could track down it was money. The affinity of the pigeon for its roost, the camel for the water-hole, the pig for the truffle, were as nothing to the affinity of Mr Immelbern for dough. He was in tune with it. Its subtle emanations floated through the ether and impinged on psychic antennae in his system which operated on a superheterodyne circuit.

And while he looked at the young man who seemed to know Lieutenant-Colonel Uppingdon, that circuit was oscillating over all its tubes. He summarized his conclusions with an explicit economy of verbiage which Le Bruyère could not have pruned by a single syllable.

"He's rich," said Mr Immelbern.

"I wish I could remember where I met him," said the Colonel, frowning over his own train of thought. "I hate to forget a face."

"You doddering old fool!" snarled Mr Immelbern, smiling at him affectionately. "What do I care about your memory? The point is that he's rich, and he seemed to recognize you. Well, that saves a lot of trouble, doesn't it?"

The Colonel turned towards him and blinked. "What do you mean?"

"Will you never wake up?" moaned Mr Immelbern, extending his cigarette-case with every appearance of affability. "Here you've been sitting whining and moping for half an hour because we don't get a chance to make a touch, and when a chance does come along you can't see it. What do I care where you met the man? What do I care if you never met him? He nodded to you, and he's sitting two yards away—and you ask me what I mean!"

The Colonel frowned at him for a moment. He was, as we have explained, a born traditionalist. He never allowed himself to be carried away. He deliberated. He calculated. He explored. He would, but for the ever-present stimulus of Mr Immelbern, have done as little as any other traditionalist.

But gradually the frown faded, and a dignified smile took its place. "There may be something in what you say, Sid," he conceded.

"Go on," ordered Mr Immelbern crudely. "Hop it. And try to wake your ideas up a bit. If somebody threw a purse into your lap, you'd be asking me what it was."

Lieutenant-Colonel Uppingdon gave him an aristocratically withering look, and rose sedately from the table. He went over to where the young man sat and coughed discreetly.

"Excuse me, sir," he said, and the young man looked up from his idle study of the afternoon's runners at Sandown Park. "You must have thought me a trifle rude just now."

"Not at all," said the young man amiably. "I thought you were busy and didn't want to be bothered. How are things these days, George?"

The Colonel suppressed a start. The use of his Christian name implied an intimacy that was almost alarming, but the young man's pleasant features still struck no responsive chord in his memory.

"To tell you the truth," he said. "I'm afraid my eyes are not as good as they were. I didn't recognize you until you had gone by. Dear me! How long is it since I saw you last?"

The young man thought for a moment. "Was it at Biarritz about ten years ago?"

"Of course!" exclaimed Uppingdon delightedly—he had never been to Biarritz in his life. "By Gad, how the time does fly! I never thought I should have to ask when I last saw you, my dear—"

He broke off short, and an expression of shocked dismay overspread his face.

"Good Gad!" he blurted. "You'll begin to think there's something the matter with me. Have you ever had a lapse of memory like that?

I had your name on the tip of my tongue—I was just going to say it—and it slipped off! Wait—don't help me—didn't it begin with H?"

"I'm afraid not," said the young man pleasantly.

"Not either of your names?" pursued the Colonel hopefully.

"No."

"Then it must have been J."

"No."

"I mean T."

The young man nodded.

Uppingdon took heart. "Let me see, Tom—Thomson—Travers—Terrington—"

The other smiled. "I'd better save you the trouble. Templar's the name—Simon Templar."

Uppingdon put a hand to his head.

"I knew it!" He was certain that he had never met anyone named Simon Templar. "How stupid of me! My dear chap, I hardly know how to apologize. Damned bad form, not even being able to remember a fellow's name. Look here, you must give me a chance to put it right. What about joining us for a drink? Or are you waiting for somebody?"

Simon Templar shook his head.

"Splendid!" said the Colonel. "Splendid! Perfectly splendid!" He seized the young man's arm and led him across to where Mr Immelbern waited. "By Gad, what a perfectly splendid coincidence. Simon, you must meet Mr Immelbern. Sidney, this is an old friend of mine, Mr Templar. By Gad!"

Simon found himself ushered into the best chair, his drink paid for, his health proposed and drunk with every symptom of cordiality.

"By Gad!" said the Colonel, mopping his brow and beaming.

"Quite a coincidence, Mr Templar," remarked Immelbern, absorbing the word into his vocabulary.

"Coincidence is a marvellous thing," said the Colonel. "I remember when I was in Allahabad with the West Nottinghams, they had a quartermaster whose wife's name was Ellen. As a matter of fact, he wasn't really our quartermaster—we borrowed him from the Southwest Kents. Rotten regiment, the Southwest Kents. Old General Plushbottom was with them before he was thrown out of the service. His name wasn't really Plushbottom, but we called him Old General Plushbottom.

"The thing was a frightful scandal. He had a fight with a subaltern on the parade-ground at Poona—as a matter of fact, it was almost on the very spot where Reggie Carfew dropped dead of heart failure the day after his wife ran away with a bank clerk. And the extraordinary thing was that her name was Ellen too."

"Extraordinary," agreed the young man.

"Extraordinary!" concurred Mr Immelbern, and trod viciously on Uppingdon's toe under the table.

"That was a marvellous trip we had on the Bremen—I mean to Biarritz—wasn't it?" said the Colonel, wincing.

Simon Templar smiled. "We had some good parties, didn't we?"

"By Gad! And the casino!"

"The Heliopolis!"

"The races!" said the Colonel, seizing his cue almost too smartly, and moving his feet quickly out of range of Mr Immelbern's heavy heel.

Mr Immelbern gave an elaborate start. He pulled a watch from his waistcoat pocket and looked at it accusingly.

"By the way, Sir George," he interrupted with a faintly conspiratorial air. "I don't want to put you out at all, but it's getting a bit late."

"Late?" repeated the Colonel, frowning at him.

"You know," said Mr Immelbern mysteriously.

"Oh," said the Colonel, grasping the point.

Mr Immelbern turned to Simon.

"I'm really not being rude, Mr Templar," he explained, "but Sir George has important business to attend to this afternoon, and I had to remind him about it. Really, Sir George, don't think I'm butting in, but it goes at two o'clock, and if we're going to get any lunch—"

"But that's outrageous!" protested the Colonel indignantly. "I've only just brought Mr Templar over to our table, and you're suggesting that I should rush off and leave him!"

"Please don't bother about me," said Simon hastily. "If you have business to do—"

"My dear chap, I insist on bothering. The whole idea is absurd. I've put far too great a strain on your good nature already. This is preposterous. You must certainly join us in another drink. And in lunch. It's the very least I can do."

Mr Immelbern did not look happy. He gave the impression of a man torn between politeness and frantic necessity, frustrated by having to talk in riddles, and perhaps pardonably exasperated by the obtuseness of his companion.

"But really. Sir George—"

"That's enough," said the Colonel, raising his hand. "I refuse to listen to anything more. Mr Templar is an old friend of mine, and my guarantee should be good enough for you. And as far as you are concerned, my dear chap," he added, turning to Simon, "if you are not already engaged for lunch, I won't hear any other excuse."

Simon shrugged. "It's very kind of you. But if I'm in the way—"

"That," said the Colonel pontifically, "will do." He consulted his watch, drummed his fingers thoughtfully on the table for a moment, and said, "The very thing! We'll go right along to my rooms, and I'll have some lunch served there. Then Mr Immelbern and I can do our business as well without being rushed."

"But Sir George!" said Immelbern imploringly. "Won't you listen to reason? Look here, can I speak to you alone for a minute? Mr Templar will excuse us."

He grabbed the spluttering Colonel by the arm and dragged him away almost by main force. They retreated to the other end of the lounge.

"We'll get him," said the Colonel, gesticulating furiously.

"I know," said Mr Immelbern, beating his fist on the palm of his hand. "That is, if you don't scare him off with that imitation of a colonel. That stuff's so corny it makes me want to scream. Have you found out who he is?"

"No. I don't even recognize his name."

"Probably he's mistaken you for somebody else," said Mr Immelbern, appearing to sulk.

The Colonel turned away from him and marched back to the table, with Mr Immelbern following him glumly.

"Well, that's settled, by Gad," he said breezily. "If you've finished your drink, my dear fellow, we'll get along at once."

They went in a taxi to the Colonel's apartment, a small suite at the lower end of Clarges Street. Uppingdon burbled on with engaging geniality, but Mr Immelbern kept his mouth tightly closed and wore the look of a man suffering from toothache.

"How about some caviar sandwiches and a bottle of wine?" suggested the Colonel. "I can fix those up myself. Of if you'd prefer something more substantial, I can easily have it sent in."

"Caviar sandwiches will do for me," murmured Simon accommodatingly.

There was plenty of caviar, and some excellent sherry to pass the time while the Colonel was preparing the sandwiches. The wine was impeccable, and the quantity apparently unlimited. Under its soothing influence even the morose Mr Immelbern seemed to thaw slightly, although towards the end of the meal he kept looking at his watch and comparing it anxiously with the clock on the mantelpiece.

At a quarter to two he caught his partner's eye in one of the rare lulls in the Colonel's meandering flow of reminiscence.

"Well, Sir George," he said grimly, "if you can spare the time now—"

"Of course," said the Colonel brightly.

Mr Immelbern looked at their guest, and hesitated again.

"Er . . . to deal with our business."

Simon put down his glass and rose quickly. "I'll leave you to it," he said pleasantly. "Really, I've imposed on you quite long enough."

"Sit down, my dear chap, sit down," commanded the Colonel testily. "Dammit, Sidney, your suspicions are becoming ridiculous. If you go on in this way I shall begin to believe you suffer from delusions of persecution. I've already told you that Mr Templar is an old friend of mine, by Gad, and it's an insult to a guest in my house to suggest that you can't trust him. Anything we have to discuss can be said in front of him."

"But think, Sir George. Think of the risk."

"Nonsense," snorted the Colonel. "It's all in your imagination. In fact"—the idea suddenly appeared to strike him—"I'm damned if I don't tell him what it's all about."

Mr Immelbern opened his mouth, closed it again, and sank back wearily without speaking. His attitude implied that he had already exhausted himself in vain appeals to an obvious lunatic, and he was beginning to realize that it was of no avail. He could do no more.

"It's like this, my dear chap," said the Colonel, ignoring him. "All that this mystery amounts to—all that Immelbern here is so frightened of telling you—is that we are professional gamblers. We back racehorses."

"That isn't all of it," contradicted Mr Immelbern sullenly.

"Well, we have certain advantages. I, in my social life, am very friendly with a large number of racehorse owners.

Mr Immelbern is friendly with trainers and jockeys. Between the two of us, we sometimes have infallible information, the result of piecing together everything we hear from various sources, of times when the result of a certain race has positively been arranged. Then all we have to do is to make our bets and collect the money. That happens to be our business this afternoon. We have an absolutely certain winner for two o'clock race at Sandown Park, and in a few minutes we shall be backing it."

Mr Immelbern closed his eyes as if he could endure no more.

"That seems quite harmless," said Templar.

"Of course it is," agreed the Colonel. "What Immelbern is so frightened of is that somebody will discover what we're doing—I mean that it might come to the knowledge of some of our friends who are owners or trainers or jockeys, and then our sources of information would be cut off. But, by Gad, I insist on the privilege of being allowed to know when I can trust my own friends."

"Well, I won't give you away," Simon told him obligingly.

The Colonel turned to Immelbern triumphantly.

"There you are! So there's no need whatever for our little party to break up yet, unless Mr Templar has an engagement. Our business will be done in a few minutes. By Gad, damme, I think you owe Mr Templar an apology!"

Mr Immelbern sighed, stared at his fingernails for a while in grumpy silence, and consulted his watch again.

"It's nearly five to two," he said. "How much can we get on?"

"About a thousand, I think," said the Colonel judiciously.

Mr Immelbern got up and went to the telephone, where he dialled a number.

"This is Immelbern," he said, in the voice of a martyr responding to the curtain call for the lion-wrestling event. "I want two hundred pounds on Greenfly."

He heard his bet repeated, pressed down the hook, and dialled again.

"We have to spread it around to try and keep the starting price from shortening," explained the Colonel.

Simon Templar nodded, and leaned back with his eyes half-closed, listening to the click and tinkle of the dial and Immelbern's afflicted voice. Five times the process was repeated, and during the giving of the fifth order Uppingdon interrupted again.

"Make it two-fifty this time, Sidney," he said.

Mr Immelbern said, "Just a moment, will you hold on?" to the transmitter, covered it with his hand, and turned aggrievedly.

"I thought you said a thousand. That makes a thousand and fifty."

"Well, I thought Mr Templar might like to have fifty on."

Simon hesitated. "That's about all I've got on me," he said.

"Don't let that bother you, my dear boy," boomed Colonel Uppingdon. "Your credit's good with me, and I feel that I owe you something to compensate for what you've put up with. Make it a hundred if you like."

"But Sir George!" wailed Mr Immelbern.

"Dammit, will you stop whining 'But Sir George!'?" exploded the Colonel. "That settles it. Make it three hundred—that will be a hundred on for Mr Templar. And if the horse doesn't win I'll stand the loss myself."

A somewhat strained silence prevailed after the last bet had been made. Mr Immelbern sat down again and chewed the unlighted end of a cigar in morbid meditations. The Colonel twiddled his thumbs as if the embarrassment of these recurrent disputes was hard to shake off. Simon Templar lighted a cigarette and smoked calmly.

"Have you been doing this long?" he inquired.

"For about two years," said the Colonel. "By Gad, though, we've made money at it. Only about one horse in ten that we back doesn't romp home, and most of 'em are at good prices. Sometimes our money does get back to the course and spoils the price, but I'd rather have a winner at evens than a loser at ten to one any day. Why, I remember one race meeting we had at Delhi. That was the year when old Stubby Featherstone dropped his cap in the Ganges—he was the fella who got killed at Cambrai . . ."

He launched off on another wandering reminiscence, and Simon listened to him with polite attention. He had some thinking to do, and he was grateful for the gallant Colonel's willingness to take all the strain of conversation away from him. Mr Immelbern chewed his cigar in chronic pessimism until half an hour had passed, and then he glanced at his watch again, started up, and broke into the middle of one of his host's rambling sentences.

"The result ought to be through by now," he said abruptly. "Shall we go out and get a paper?"

Simon stood up unhurriedly. He had done his thinking. "Let me go," he suggested.

"That's awfully good of you, my dear boy. Mr Immelbern would have gone. Never mind, by Gad. Go out and see how much you've won. I'll open another bottle. Damme, we must have a drink on this, by Gad!"

Simon grinned and sauntered out, and as the doors closed behind him the eyes of the two partners met.

"Next time you say 'damme' or 'by Gad,' George," said Mr Immelbern, "I will knock your block off, so help me. Why don't you get some new ideas?"

But by that time Lieutenant-Colonel Sir George Uppingdon was beyond taking offence.

"We've got him," he said gleefully.

"I hope so," said Mr Immelbern, more cautiously.

"I know what I'm talking about, Sid," said the Colonel stubbornly. "He's a serious young fellow, one of these conservative chaps like myself—but that's the best kind. None of this dashing around, keeping up with the times, going off like a firework and fizzling out like a pricked balloon. I'll bet you anything you like, in another hour he'll be looking around for a thousand pounds to give us to put on tomorrow's certainty. His kind starts slowly, but it goes a lot further than any of your high-pressure Smart Alecs."

Mr Immelbern made a rude noise.

Simon Templar bought a *Star* at Devonshire House and turned without anxiety to the stop press. Greenfly had won the two o'clock at five to one.

As he strolled back towards Clarges Street he was smiling. It was a peculiarly ecstatic sort of smile, and as a matter of fact he had volunteered to go out and buy the paper, even though he knew what the result would be as certainly as Messrs Uppingdon and Immelbern knew it, for the sole and sufficient reason that he wanted to give that smile the freedom of his face and let it walk around. To have been compelled to sit around any longer in Uppingdon's apartment and sustain the necessary mask of gravity and sober interest without a breathing spell would have sprained every muscle within six inches of his mouth.

"Hullo, Saint," said a familiar sleepy voice beside him.

A hand touched his arm, and he turned quickly to see a big baby-faced man in a bowler hat of unfashionable shape, whose jaws moved rhythmically like those of a ruminating cow.

"Hush," said the Saint. "Somebody might hear."

"Is there anybody left who doesn't know?" asked Chief Inspector Teal sardonically.

Simon Templar nodded slowly.

"Strange as it may seem, there is. Believe it or not, Claud Eustace, somewhere in this great city—I wouldn't tell you where for anything—there are left two trusting souls who don't even recognize my name. They have just come down from their hermits' caves in the mountains of Ladbroke Grove, and they haven't yet heard the news.

"The Robin Hood of modern crime," said the Saint oratorically, "the scourge of the ungodly, the defender of the faith—what are the newspaper headlines?—has come back to raise hell over the length and breadth of England—and they don't know."

"You look much too happy," said the detective suspiciously. "Who are these fellows?"

"Their names are Uppingdon and Immelbern, if you want to know—and you've probably met them before. They have special information about racehorses, and I am playing my usual role of the Sucker who does not Suck too long. At the moment they owe me five hundred quid."

Chief Inspector Claud Eustace Teal's baby blue eyes looked him over thoughtfully. And in Chief Inspector Teal's mind there were no illusions. He did not share the ignorance of Messrs Uppingdon and Immelbern. He had known the Saint for many years, and had heard that he was back.

He knew that there was going to be a fresh outbreak of buccaneering through the fringes of London's underworld, exactly as there had been so many times before; he knew that the feud between them was going to start again, the endless battle between the gay outlaw and the guardian of the Law; and he knew that his troubles were at the beginning of a new lease of life. And yet one of his rare smiles touched his mouth for a fleeting instant.

"See that they pay you," he said, and went on his portly and lethargic way.

Simon Templar went back to the apartment on Clarges Street. Uppingdon let him in, and even the melancholy Mr Immelbern was moved to jump up as they entered the living-room.

"Did it win?" they chorused.

The Saint held out the paper. It was seized, snatched from hand to hand, and lowered reverently while an exchange of rapturous glances took place across its columns.

"At five to one," breathed Lieutenant-Colonel Uppingdon.

"Five thousand quid," whispered Mr Immelbern.

"The seventh winner in succession."

"Eighty thousand quid in four weeks."

The Colonel turned to Simon.

"What a pity you only had a hundred pounds on," he said, momentarily crestfallen. Then the solution struck him, and he brightened. "But how ridiculous! We can easily put that right. On our next coup, you shall be an equal partner. Immelbern, be silent! I have put up with enough interference from you. Templar, my dear boy, if you care to come in with me next time—"

The Saint shook his head. "I'm sorry," he said. "I don't mind a small gamble now and again, but for business I only bet on certainties."

"But this is a certainty!" cried the Colonel.

Simon frowned. "Nothing," he said gravely, "is a certainty until you know the result. A horse may drop dead, or fall down, or be disqualified. The risk may be small, but it exists. I eliminate it." He gazed at them suddenly with a sober intensity which almost held them spellbound. "It sounds silly," he said, "but I happen to be psychic."

The two men stared back at him.

"Wha . . . what?" stammered the Colonel.

"What does that mean?" demanded Mr Immelbern, more grossly.

"I am clairvoyant," said the Saint simply. "I can foretell the future. For instance, I can look over the list of runners in a newspaper and close my eyes, and suddenly I'll see the winners printed out in my mind, just as if I was looking at the evening edition. I don't know how it's done. It's a gift. My mother had it."

The two men were gaping at him dubiously. They were incredulous, wondering if they were missing a joke and ought to laugh politely, and yet something in the Saint's voice and the slight uncanny widening of his eyes sent a cold supernatural draught creeping up their spines.

"Haw!" ejaculated the Colonel uncertainly, feeling that he was called upon to make some sound, and the Saint smiled distantly. He glanced at the clock on the mantelpiece.

"Let me show you. I wasn't going to make any bets today, but since I've started I may as well go on."

He picked up his lunch edition, which he had been reading in the Palace Royal lounge, and studied the racing entries on the back page. Then he put down the paper and covered his eyes. For several seconds there was a breathless silence, while he stood there with his head in his hands, swaying slightly, in an attitude of terrific concentration.

Again the supernatural shiver went over the two partners, and then the Saint straightened up suddenly, opened his eyes, and rushed to the telephone.

He dialled his number rather slowly. He had watched the movements of Mr Immelbern's fingers closely, on every one of the gentleman's five calls, and his keen ears had listened and calculated every click of the returning dial. It would not be his fault if he got the wrong number.

The receiver at the other end of the line was lifted. The voice spoke.

"Baby Face," it said hollowly.

Simon Templar drew a deep breath, and a gigantic grin of bliss deployed itself over his inside. But outwardly he did not bat an eyelid.

"Two hundred pounds on Baby Face for Mr Templar," he said, and the partners were too absorbed with other things to notice that he spoke in a very fair imitation of Mr Immelbern's deep rumble.

He turned back to them, smiling. "Baby Face," he said, with the quietness of absolute certitude, "will win the three o'clock race at Sandown Park."

Lieutenant-Colonel Uppingdon fingered his superb white moustachios.

"By Gad!" he said.

Half an hour later the three of them went out together for a newspaper. Baby Face had won—at ten to one.

"Haw!" said the Colonel, blinking at the result rather dazedly.

On the face of Mr Immelbern was a look of almost superstitious awe. It is difficult to convey what was in his mind at that moment. Throughout his life he had dreamed of such things. Horseflesh was the one true love of his un-romantic soul. The fashions of Newmarket ruled his clothes, the scent of stables hung around him like a subtle perfume; he might, in prosperous times, have been a rich man in his illegal way, if all his private profits had not inevitably gravitated on to the backs of unsuccessful horses as fast as they came into his pocket.

And in the secret daydreams which coil through even the most phlegmatic bosom had always been the wild impossible idea that if by some miracle he could have the privilege of reading the next day's results every day for a week, he could make himself a fortune that would free him for the rest of his life from the sordid labours of the confidence game and give him the leisure to perfect that infallible racing system with which he had been experimenting ever since adolescence.

And now the miracle had come to pass, in the person of that debonair and affluent young roan who did not even seem to realize the potential millions which lay in his strange gift.

"Can you do that every day?" he asked huskily.

"Oh, yes," said the Saint.

"In every race?" said Mr Immelbern hoarsely.

"Why not?" said the Saint. "It makes racing rather a bore, really, and you soon get tired of picking up the money."

Mr Immelbern gulped. He could not conceive what it felt like to get tired of picking up money. He felt stunned.

"Well," said the Saint casually, "I'd better be buzzing along—"

At the sound of those words something came over Lieutenant-Colonel Sir George Uppingdon. It was, in its way, the turning of a worm. He had suffered much. The gibes of Mr Immelbern still rankled in his sedate aristocratic breast. And Mr Immelbern was still goggling in a half-witted daze—he who had boasted almost naggingly of his accessibility to new ideas.

Lieutenant-Colonel Sir George Uppingdon took the Saint's arm, gently but very firmly.

"Just a minute, my dear boy," he said, rolling the words succulently round his tongue. "We must not be old-fashioned. We must move with the times. This psychic gift of yours is truly remarkable. There's a fortune in it. Damme, if somebody threw a purse into Immelbern's lap, he'd be asking me what it was. Thank God, I'm not so dense as that, by Gad. My dear Mr Templar, my dear boy, you must—I positively insist—you must come back to my rooms and talk about what you're going to do with this gift of yours. By Gad."

Mr Immelbern did not come out of his trance until halfway through the bargaining that followed.

It was nearly two hours later when the two partners struggled somewhat short-windedly up the stairs to a dingy one-roomed office off the Strand. Its furniture consisted of a chair, a table with a telephone on it, and a tape machine in one corner. It had not been swept for weeks, but it served its purpose adequately.

The third and very junior member of the partnership sat on the chair with his feet on the table, smoking a limp cigarette and turning the pages of *Paris Plaisirs*. He looked up in some surprise not unmixed with alarm at the noisy entrance of his confederates—a pimply youth with a chin that barely contrived to separate his mouth from his sallow neck.

"I've made our fortunes!" yelled Mr Immelbern, and, despite the youth's repulsive aspect, embraced him.

A slight frown momentarily marred the Colonel's glowing benevolence.

"What d'you mean—*you've* made our fortunes?" he demanded. "If it hadn't been for me—"

"Well, what the hell does it matter?" said Mr Immelbern. "In a couple of months we'll all be millionaires."

"How?" asked the pimply youth blankly.

Mr Immelbern broke off in the middle of an improvised hornpipe.

"It's like this," he explained exuberantly. "We've got a sike—sidekick—"

"Psychic," said the Colonel.

"A bloke who can tell the future. He puts his hands over his eyes and reads the winners off like you'd read them out of a paper. He did it four times this afternoon. We're going to take him in with us. We had a job to persuade him—he was going off to the South of France tonight—can you imagine it, a bloke with a gift like that going away while there's any racing here? We had to give him five hundred quid advance on the money we told him we were going to make for him to make him put it off. But it's worth it. We'll start tomorrow, and if this fellow Templar—"

"Ow, that's 'is nane, is it?" said the pimply youth brightly. "I wondered wot was goin' on."

There was a short puzzled silence.

"How do you mean—what was going on?" asked the Colonel at length.

"Well," said the pimply youth, "when Sid was ringing up all the afternoon, practic'ly every rice—"

"What d'you mean?" croaked Mr Immelbern. "I rang up every race?"

"Yes, an' I was givin' you the winners, an' you were sayin', 'Two 'undred pounds on Baby Face for Mr Templar'—'Four 'undred pounds on Cellophane for Mr Templar'—gettin' bigger an' bigger all the time an' never givin' 'im a loser—well, I started to wonder wot was 'appening."

The silence that followed was longer, much longer, and there were things seething in it for which the English language has no words.

It was the Colonel who broke it.

"It's impossible," he said dizzily. "I know the clock was slow, because I put it back myself, but I only put it back five minutes, and this fellow was telephoning ten minutes before the times of the races."

"Then 'e must 'ave put it back some more while you wasn't watchin' 'im," said the pimply youth stolidly.

The idea penetrated after several awful seconds.

"By Gad!" said Lieutenant-Colonel Sir George Uppingdon in a feeble voice.

Mr Immelbern did not speak. He was removing his coat and rolling up his sleeves, with his eyes riveted yearningly on the Colonel's aristocratic block.

THE UNFORTUNATE FINANCIER

INTRODUCTION

It will have been noticed by the connoisseur that the Saint stories of the older vintages contained considerably more physical violence than most of the later brews. I don't mean by this that there are conspicuously fewer citizens at large whose principal ambition is to inflict upon the Saint some grave form of bodily damage. Nor do I mean that, when these citizens attempt to gratify such hearty yearnings, the Saint has lost any of his gusto for the pop of guns or the exhilarating impact of a well-placed poke on the proboscis. Such healthy joys as those can never lose their charm. But I do mean that he has meanwhile been developing an appreciation for other, perhaps even more artistically satisfying, methods of making miserable the lives of the Ungodly.

As an example of this more ethereal technique I am offering the following story, which gave me more childish pleasure than I can modestly talk about.

—Leslie Charteris (1939)

"The secret of success," said Simon Templar profoundly, "is never to do anything by halves. If you try to touch someone for a tenner, you probably get snubbed, but if you put on a silk hat and a false stomach and go into the City to raise a million-pound loan, people fall over each other in the rush to hand you blank cheques. The wretched little thief who pinches a handful of silver spoons gets shoved into clink through a perfect orgy of congratulations to the police and the magistrates, but the bird who swindles the public of a few hundred thousands legally, gets a knighthood. A sound buccaneering business has to be run on the same principles."

While he could not have claimed any earth-shaking originality for the theme of his sermon, Simon Templar was in the perhaps rarer position of being able to claim that he practised what he preached. He had been doing it for so long, with so much diligence and devotion, that the name of the Saint had passed into the Valhalla of all great names: it had become a household word, even as the name of Miss Amelia Bloomer, an earlier crusader, was absorbed into the tongue that Shakespeare did not live long enough to speak—but in a more romantic context. And if there were many more sharks in the broad lagoons of technically legal righteousness who knew him better by his chosen *nom de guerre* than by his real name, and who would not even have recognized him had they passed him in the street, that minor degree of anonymity was an asset in the Saint's profession which more than compensated him for the concurrent gaps in his publicity.

Mr Wallington Titus Oates was another gentleman who did nothing by halves.

He was a large red-faced man who looked exactly like a City alderman or a master butcher, with a beefy solidity about him which disarmed suspicion. It was preposterous, his victims thought, in the early and expensive stages of their ignorance, that such an obvious rough diamond, such a jovial hail-fellow-well-met, such an almost startlingly lifelike reincarnation of the cartoonist's figure of John Bull, could be a practitioner of cunning and deceit. Even about his rather unusual names he was delightfully frank.

If he had been an American he would certainly have called himself Wallington T. Oates, and the "T" would have been shrouded in a mystery that might have embraced anything from Thomas to Tamerlane. In the more reserved manner of the Englishman, who does not have a Christian name until you have known him for twenty-five years, he might without exciting extraordinary curiosity have been known simply as W. T. Oates. But he was not. His cards were printed W. Titus Oates, and he was not even insistent on the preliminary "W." He was, in fact, best pleased to be known as plain Titus Oates, and would chortle heartily over his chances of tracing a pedigree back to the notorious inventor of the Popish Plot who was whipped from Aldgate to Newgate and from Newgate to Tyburn some three hundred years ago.

But apart from the fact that some people would have given much to apply the same discouraging treatment to Mr Wallington Titus Oates, he had little else in common with his putative ancestor. For although the better-known Titus Oates stood in the pillory outside the Royal Exchange before his dolorous tour, it is not recorded that he was interested in the dealing within; whereas the present Stock Exchange was Mr Wallington Titus Oates's happy hunting ground.

If there was anything that W. Titus Oates understood from "A" to whatever letters can be invented after "Z," it was the manipulation of shares. Bulls and bears were his domestic pets. Mergers and debentures were his bedfellows. It might almost be said that he danced contangos in his sleep. And it was all very profitable—so profitable that Mr Oates possessed not only three Rolls-Royces but also a liberal allowance of pocket-money to spend on the collection of postage stamps which was his joy and relaxation.

This is not to be taken to mean that Mr Oates was known in the City as a narrow evader of the law. He was, on the contrary, a highly respected and influential man, for it is one of the sublime subtleties of the laws of England that whilst the manipulation of the form of racehorses is a hideous crime, to be rewarded with expulsion from the most boring clubs and other forms of condign punishment, the manipulation of share values is a noble and righteous occupation by which the large entrance fees to such clubs may commendably be obtained, provided that the method of juggling is genteel and smooth. Mr Oates's form as a juggler was notably genteel and smooth, and the ambition of certain citizens to whip Mr Oates at a cart's tail from Aldgate to Newgate was based not so much on the knowledge of any actual fraud as on the fact that the small investments which represented their life savings had on occasion been skittled down the market in the course of Mr Oates's important operations, which every right-thinking person will agree was a very unsporting and un-British attitude to take.

The elementary principles of share manipulation are, of course, simplicity itself. If large blocks of a certain share are thrown on the market from various quarters, the word goes around that the stock is bad, the small investor takes fright and dashes in to cut his losses, thereby making matters worse, and the price of the share falls according to the first law of supply and demand. If, on the other hand, there is heavy buying in a certain share, the word goes around that it is a "good thing," the small speculator jumps in for a quick profit, adding his weight to the snowball, and the price goes up according to the same law. This is the foundation system on which all speculative operators work, but Mr Oates had his own ways of accelerating these reactions.

"Nobody can say that Titus Oates ain't an honest man," he used to say in the very exclusive circle of confederates who shared his confidence and a reasonable proportion of his profits. "P'raps I am a bit smarter than some of the others, but that's their funeral. You don't know what tricks they get up to behind the scenes, but nobody knows what tricks I get up to, either. It's all in the day's work."

He was thinking along the same lines on a certain morning, while he waited for his associates to arrive for the conference at which the final details of the manoeuvre on which he was working at that time would be decided. It was the biggest manipulation he had attempted so far, and it involved a trick that sailed much closer to the wind than anything he had done before, but it has already been explained that he was not a man who did things by halves. The economic depression which had bogged down the market for many months past, and the resultant steadfast refusal of stocks to soar appreciably however stimulated by legitimate and near-legitimate means, had been very bad for his business as well as others. Now, envisaging the first symptoms of an upturn, he was preparing to cash in on it to an extent that would compensate for many months of failure, and with so much lost ground to make up he had no time for half measures. Yet he knew that there were a few tense days ahead of him.

A discreet knock on his door, heralding the end of thought and the beginning of action, was almost a relief. His new secretary entered in answer to his curt summons, and his eyes rested on her slim figure for a moment with unalloyed pleasure—she was a remarkably beautiful girl with natural honey-golden hair and entrancing blue eyes which in Mr

Oates's dreams had been known to gaze with Dietrich-esque yearning upon his unattractive person.

"Mr Hammel and Mr Costello are here," she said.

Mr Oates beamed.

"Bring them in, my dear." He rummaged thoughtfully through his pockets and produced a crumpled five-pound note, which he pushed towards her. "And buy yourself some silk stockings when you go out to lunch—just as a little gift from me. You've been a good gal. Some night next week, when I'm not working so hard, we might have dinner together, eh?"

"Thank you, Mr Oates," she said softly, and left him with a sweet smile which started strange wrigglings within him.

When they had dinner together he would make her call him Titus, he thought, and rubbed his hands over the romantic prospect. But before that happy night he had much to do, and the entrance of Hammel and Costello brought him back to the stern consideration of how that dinner and many others, with silk stockings and orchids to match, were to be paid for.

Mr John Hammel was a small rotund gentleman whose rimless spectacles gave him a benign and owlish appearance, like somebody's very juvenile uncle. Mr Costello was longer and much more cadaverous, and he wore a pencil-line of hair across his upper-lip with a certain undercurrent of self-consciousness which might have made one think that he went about in the constant embarrassing fear of being mistaken for Clark Gable. Actually their resemblance to any such harmless characters was illusory—they were nearly as cunning as Mr Oates himself, and not even a trifle less unscrupulous.

"Well, boys," said Mr Oates, breaking the ice jovially, "I found another good thing last night."

"Buy or sell?" asked Costello alertly.

"Buy," said Mr Oates. "I bought it. As far as I can find out, there are only about a dozen in the world. The issue was corrected the day after it came out."

Hammel helped himself to a cigar and frowned puzzledly.

"What is this?"

"A German five-pfennig with the "Befreiungstag" overprint inverted and spelt with a 'P' instead of a 'B,'" explained Mr Oates. "That's a stamp you could get a hundred pounds for any day."

His guests exchanged tolerant glances. While they lighted their Partagas they allowed Mr Oates to expatiate on the beauties of his acquisition with all the extravagant zeal of the rabid collector, but as soon as the smokes were going Costello recalled the meeting to its agenda.

"Well," he said casually, "Midorients are down to 25."

"24," said Mr Oates. "I rang up my brokers just before you came in and told them to sell another block. They'll be down to 23 or 22 after lunch. We've shifted them pretty well."

"When do we start buying?" asked Hammel.

"At 22. And you'll have to do it quickly. The wires are being sent off at lunch-time tomorrow, and the news will be in the papers before the Exchange closes."

Mr Oates paced the floor steadily, marshalling the facts of the situation for an audience which was already conversant with them.

The Midorient Company owned large and unproductive concessions in Mesopotamia. Many years ago its fields had flowed with seemingly inexhaustible quantities of oil of excellent quality, and the stock had paid its original holders several thousand times over. But suddenly, on account of those abstruse and unpredictable geological causes to which such things are subject, the supply had petered out. Frenzied drilling had failed to produce results. The output had dropped to a paltry few hundred barrels which sufficed to pay dividends of two per cent on the stock—no more, and, as a slight tempering of the wind to the shorn stockholders, no less. The shares had adjusted their market value accordingly. Drilling had continued ever since, without showing any improvement, and indeed the shares had depreciated still further during the past fortnight as a result of persistent rumours that even the small output which had for a long while saved the stock from becoming entirely derelict was drying up—rumours which, as omniscient chroniclers of these events, we are able to trace back to the ingenious agency of Mr Titus Oates.

That was sufficient to send the moribund stock down to the price at which Messrs Oates, Costello, and Hammel desired to buy it. The boom on which they would make their profit called for more organization, and involved the slight deception on which Mr Oates was basing his gamble.

Travelling in Mesopotamia at that moment there was an English tourist named Ischolskov, and it is a matter of importance that he was there entirely at Mr Oates's instigation and expense. During his visit he had contrived to learn the names of the correspondents of the important newspapers and news agencies in that region, and at the appointed time it would be his duty to send off similarly worded cablegrams, signed with the names of these correspondents, which would report to London that the Midorient Company's engineers had struck oil again—had, in fact, tapped a gigantic gusher of petroleum that would make the first phenomenal output of the Midorient Oil Fields look like the dribbling of a baby on its bib.

"Let's see," said Mr Oates, "this is Tuesday. We buy today and tomorrow morning at 22 or even less. The shares start to go up tomorrow afternoon. They will go up more on Thursday. By Friday morning they ought to be around 45—they might even go to 50. They'll hang fire there. The first boom will be over, and people will be waiting for more information."

"What about the directors?" queried Hammel.

"They'll get a wire too, of course, signed by the manager on the spot. And don't forget I'm a director. Every penny I have is tied up in that company—it's my company, lock, stock, and barrel. They'll call a special meeting, and I know exactly what they're going to do about it. Of course they'll cable the manager for more details, but I can arrange to see that his reply doesn't get through to them before Friday lunch."

Costello fingered his wispy moustache.

"And we sell out on Friday morning," he said.

Mr Oates nodded emphatically.

"We do more than sell out. We sell short, and unload twice as much stock as we're holding. The story'll get all over England over the week-end, and when the Exchange opens on Monday morning the shares'll be two a penny. We make our profit both ways."

"It's a big risk," said Hammel seriously.

"Well, I'm taking it for you, ain't I?" said Mr Oates. "All you have to do is to help me to spread the buying and selling about, so it don't look too much like a one-man deal. I'm standing to take all the knocks. But it can't go wrong. I've used Ischolskov before—I've got too much on him for him to try and double-cross me, and besides he's getting paid plenty. My being on the Midorient board makes it watertight. I'm taken in the same as the rest of 'em, and I'm hit as hard as they are. You're doing all the buying and selling from now on—there won't be a single deal in my name that anyone can prove against me. And whatever happens, don't sell till I give you the wire. I'll be the first to know when the crash is coming, and we'll hold out till the last moment."

They talked for an hour longer, after which they went out to a belated but celebratory lunch.

Mr Oates left his office early that afternoon, and therefore he did not even think of the movements of his new secretary when she went home. But if he had been privileged to observe them, he would have been very little wiser, for Mr Oates was one of the numerous people who knew the Saint only by name, and if he had seen the sinewy sunburned man who met her at Piccadilly Circus and bore her off for a cocktail he might have suffered a pang of jealousy, but he would have had no cause for alarm.

"We must have Bollinger champagne cocktail, Pat," said the Saint, when they were settled in Oddenino's. "The occasion calls for one. There's a wicked look in your eye that tells me you have some news. Have you sown a few more wild Oates?"

"Must you?" she protested weakly.

"Shall we get him an owl?" Simon suggested.

"What for?" asked Patricia unguardedly.

"It would be rather nice," said the Saint reflectively, "to get Titus an owl."

Patricia Holm shuddered.

Over the cocktails and stuffed olives, however, she relented.

"It's started," she said. "Hammel and Costello had a long conference after lunch, but I'd heard enough before they went out."

She told him every detail of the discussion that had taken place in Mr Titus Oates's private office, and Simon Templar smiled approval as he listened. Taken in conjunction with what he already knew, the summaries of various other conversations which she had reported to him, it left him with the whole structure of the conspiracy clearly catalogued in his mind.

"You must remember to take that microphone out of his office first thing in the morning," he remarked. "It might spoil things if Titus came across it, and I don't think you'll need to listen any more . . . Here, where did you get that from?"

"From sowing my wild Oates," said Patricia angelically, as the waitress departed with a five-pound note on her tray.

Simon Templar regarded her admiringly.

"Darling," he said at length, "there are no limits to your virtues. If you're as rich as it appears, you can not only buy me some more Bollinger, but you can take me to dinner at the Caprice as well."

On the way to the restaurant he bought an *Evening Standard* and opened it at the table.

"Midorients closed at 21," he said. "It looks as if we shall have to name a ward in our Old Age Home for Retired Burglars after Comrade Oates."

"How much shall we make if we buy and sell with him?" asked the girl.

The Saint smiled.

"I'm afraid we should lose a lot of money," he said. "You see, Titus isn't going to sell."

She stared at him, mystified, and he closed the menu and laughed at her silently.

"Did you by any chance hear Titus boasting about a stamp he bought for his collection last night?" he asked, and she nodded. "Well, old darling, I'm the guy who sold it to him. I never thought I should sink to philatelism even in my dotage, but in this case it seemed the best way to work. Titus is already convinced that I'm the greatest stamp-sleuth in captivity, and when he hears about the twopenny blue Mauritius I've discovered for him he will be fairly purring through the town. I don't see any reason why our Mr Oates should go unpunished for his sins and make a fortune out of this low swindle. He collects stamps, but I've got an even better hobby. I collect queer friends." The Saint was lighting a cigarette, and his blue eyes danced over the match. "Now listen carefully while I tell you the next move."

Mr Wallington Titus Oates was gloating fruitily over the closing prices on the Friday evening when his telephone bell rang.

He had reason to gloat. The news story provided by the cablegrams of Mr Ischolskov had been so admirably worded that it had hit the front page of every afternoon edition the previous day and a jumpy market had done the rest. The results exceeded his most optimistic estimates. On the Wednesday night Midorients had closed at 32, and dealings in the street had taken them up to 34. They opened on Thursday morning at 38, and went to 50 before noon. One lunch edition ran a special topical article on fortunes made in oil, the sun shone brilliantly, England declared for 537 for six wickets in the first Test, all the brokers and jobbers felt happy, and Midorients finally went to 61 at the close. Moreover, in the evening paper which Mr Oates was reading there could not be found a breath of suspicion directed against the news which had caused the boom. The Midorient directors had issued a statement declaring that they were awaiting further details, that their manager on the spot was a reliable man not given to hysterical exaggerations, and that for the moment they were satisfied that prosperity had returned to an oilfield which, they pointed out, had merely been suffering a temporary set-back. Mr Oates had had much to do with the wording of the statement himself, and if it erred somewhat on the side of optimism, the error could not by any stretch of imagination have been described as criminal misrepresentation.

And when Mr Oates picked up his receiver and heard what it had to say, his cup was filled to overflowing.

"I've got you that twopenny blue," said a voice which he recognized. "It's a peach! It must be one of the most perfect specimens in existence—and it'll cost you nine hundred quid!"

Mr Oates gripped the receiver, and his eyes lighted up with the unearthly fire which illuminates the state of the collector when he sees a coveted trophy within his grasp. It was, in its way, a no less starkly primitive manifestation than the dilating nostrils of a bloodhound on the scent.

"Where is it?" barked Mr Oates, in the baying voice of the same hound. "When can I see it? Can you bring it over? Have you got it yourself? Where is it?"

"Well, that's the snag, Mr Oates," said the Saint apologetically. "The owner won't let it go. He won't even let it out of his safe until it's paid for. He says he's got to have a cheque in his pocket before he'll let me take it away. He's a crotchety old bird, and I think he's afraid I might light a cigarette with it or something."

Mr Oates fairly quivered with suppressed emotion.

"Well, where does he live?" he yelped. "I'll settle him. I'll go round and see him at once. What's his name? What's the address?"

"His name is Dr Jethero," Simon answered methodically, "and he lives at 105 Matlock Gardens, Notting Hill. I think you'll catch him there—I've only just left him, and he said nothing about going out."

"Dr Jethero—105—Matlock—Gardens—Notting—Hill," repeated Mr Oates, reaching for a message pad and scribbling frantically.

"By the way," said the Saint. "I said he was crotchety, but you may think he's just potty. He's got some sort of a bee in his bonnet about people trying to get in and steal his stamp, and he told me that if you want to call and see him you've got to give a password."

"A password?" bleated Mr Oates.

"Yes. I told him that everybody knew Titus Oates, but apparently that wasn't good enough for him. If you go there you've got to say, 'I was whipped from Aldgate to Newgate, and from Newgate to Tyburn.' Can you remember that?"

"Of course," said Mr Oates indignantly. "I know all about that. Titus Oates was an ancestor of mine. Come and see me in the morning, my dear boy—I'll have a present waiting for you. Good-bye."

Mr Oates slammed back the receiver and leapt up as if unleashed. Dithering with ecstasy and excitement, he stuffed his note of the address into his pocket, grabbed a cheque-book, and dashed out into the night.

The taxi ride to his destination seemed interminable, and when he got there he was in such a state of expectant rapture that he flung the driver a pound note and scurried up the steps without waiting for change. The house was one of those unwieldly Victorian edifices with which the west of London is encumbered against all hopes of modern development, and in the dim street lighting he did not even notice that all the windows were barred, nor would he have been likely to speculate upon the reason for that peculiar feature if he had noticed it.

The door was opened by a white-coated man, and Mr Oates almost bowled him over as he dashed past him into the hall.

"I want Dr Jethero," he bayed. "I'm Titus Oates!"

The man closed the door and looked at him curiously.

"Mr Titus Oates, sir?"

"Yes!" roared the financier impatiently. "Titus Oates. Tell him I was whipped from Aldgate to Newgate, and from Newgate to Tyburn. And hurry up!"

The man nodded perfunctorily, and edged past him at a cautious distance of which Mr Oates was too wrought up to see the implications.

"Yes, sir. Will you wait in here a moment, sir?"

Mr Oates was ushered into a barely furnished distempered room and left there. With an effort he fussed himself down to a superficial calm—he was Titus Oates, a power in the City, and he must conduct himself accordingly. Dr Jethero might misunderstand a blundering excitement. If he was crotchety, and perhaps even potty, he must be handled with tact. Mr Oates strode up and down the room, working off his overflow of excitement. There was a faint characteristic flavour of iodoform in the air, but Mr Oates did not even notice that.

Footsteps sounded along the hall, and the door opened again. This time it admitted a grey-bearded man who also wore a white coat. His keen spectacled eyes examined the financier calmly. Mr Oates mustered all his self-control.

"I am Titus Oates," he said with simple dignity.

The grey-bearded man nodded.

"You wanted to see me?" he said, and Mr Oates recalled his instructions again.

"Titus Oates," he repeated gravely. "I was whipped from Aldgate to Newgate, and from Newgate to Tyburn."

Dr Jethero studied him for a moment longer, and glanced towards the door, where the white-coated attendant was waiting unobtrusively—Mr Oates had not even noticed the oddity of that.

"Yes, yes," he said soothingly. "And you were pilloried in Palace Yard, weren't you?"

"That's right," said Mr Oates eagerly. "And outside the Royal Exchange. They put me in prison for life, but they let me out at the Revolution and gave me my pension back."

Dr Jethero made clucking noises with his tongue.

"I see. A very unfortunate business. Would you mind coming this way, Mr Oates?"

He led the way up the stairs, and Mr Oates followed him blissfully. The whole rigmarole seemed very childish, but if it pleased Dr Jethero, Mr Oates was prepared to go to any lengths to humour him. The white-coated attendant followed Mr Oates. Dr Jethero opened the door of a room on the second floor and stood aside for Mr Oates to pass in. The door had a barred grille in its upper panels through which the interior of the room could be observed from the outside, an eccentricity which Mr Oates was still ready to accept as being in keeping with the character of his host.

It was the interior of the room into which he was shown that began to place an excessive strain on his adaptability. It was without furnishings of any kind, unless the thick kind of mattress in one corner could be called furnishings, and the walls and floor were finished in some extraordinary style of decoration which made them look like quilted upholstery.

Mr Oates looked about him, and turned puzzledly to his host.

"Well," he said, "where's the stamp?"

"What stamp?" asked Dr Jethero.

Mr Oates's laboriously achieved restraint was wearing thin again.

"Don't you understand? I'm Titus Oates. I was whipped from Aldgate to Newgate, and from Newgate to Tyburn. Didn't you hear what I said?"

"Yes, yes, yes," murmured the doctor peaceably. "You're Titus Oates. You stood in the pillory and they pelted you with rotten eggs."

"Well," said Mr Oates, "what about the stamp?"

Dr Jethero cleared his throat.

"Just a minute, Mr Oates. Suppose we go into that presently. Would you mind taking off your coat and shoes?"

Mr Oates gaped at him.

"This is going too far," he protested. "I'm Titus Oates. Everybody knows Titus Oates. You remember—the Popish Plot—"

"Mr Oates," said the doctor sternly, "will you take off your coat and shoes?"

The white-coated attendant was advancing stealthily towards him, and a sudden vague fear seized on the financier. Now he began to see the reason for the man's extraordinary behaviour. He was not crotchety. He was potty. He was worse—he must be a raving lunatic. Heaven knew what he would be doing next. A wild desire to be away from number 105 Matlock Gardens gripped Mr Oates—a desire that could not even be quelled by the urge to possess a twopenny blue Mauritius in perfect preservation.

"Never mind," said Mr Oates liberally. "I'm not really interested. I don't collect stamps at all. I'm just Titus Oates. Everyone knows me. I'm sure you'll excuse me—I have an appointment—"

He was edging towards the door, but Dr Jethero stood in the way.

"Nobody's going to hurt you, Mr Oates," he said, and then he caught the desperate gleam in Mr Oates's eye, and signed quickly to the attendant.

Mr Oates was seized suddenly from behind in a deft grip. Overcome with terror, he struggled like a maniac, and he was a big man, but he was helpless in the expert hands that held him. He was tripped and flung to the floor, and pinioned there with practised skill. Through whirling mists of horror he saw the doctor coming towards him with a hypodermic syringe, and he was still yelling feebly about the Popish Plot when the needle stabbed into his arm . . .

Dr Jethero went downstairs and rang up a number which he had been given.

"I've got your uncle, Mr Tombs," he announced. "He gave us a bit of trouble, but he's quite safe now."

Simon Templar, who had found the name of Tombs a convenient alias before, grinned invisibly into the transmitter.

"That's splendid. Did he give you a lot of trouble?"

"He was inclined to be violent, but we managed to give him an injection, and when he wakes up he'll be in a strait-jacket. He's really a most interesting case," said the doctor with professional enthusiasm. "Quite apart from the delusion that he is Titus Oates, he seems to have some extraordinary hallucination about a stamp. Had you noticed that before?"

"I hadn't," said the Saint. "You may be able to find out some more about that. Keep him under observation, doctor, and call me again on Monday morning."

He rang off and turned gleefully to Patricia Holm, who was waiting at his elbow.

"Titus is in safe hands," he said. "And now I've got a call of my own to make."

"Who to?" she asked.

He showed her a scrap of paper on which he had jotted down the words of what appeared to be a telegram.

> *Amazing discovery stop have reason to believe boom may be based on genuine possibilities stop do not on any account sell without hearing from me.*

"Dicky Tremayne's in Paris, and he'll send it for me," said the Saint. "A copy goes to Albert Costello and John Hammel tonight—I just want to make sure that they follow Titus down the drain. By the way, we shall clear about twenty thousand if Midorients are still at 61 when they open again tomorrow morning."

"But are you sure Jethero won't get into any trouble?" she said.

Simon Templar nodded.

"Somehow I feel that Titus will prefer to keep his mouth shut after I've had a little chat with him on Monday," he said, and it is a matter of history that he was absolutely right.

THE NEWDICK HELICOPTER

A WORD . . .

". . . there was my short story *The Newdick Helicopter*, which centered on the fact that nobody when I wrote it had yet made a true helicopter work. (They had only gotten as far as autogyros, which are not quite the same thing.) Now helicopters are as common as moths once were, and my story, in which a character accidentally invented them, is as unreadable as Jules Verne's *From the Earth to the Moon* unless you read the date first."

—Leslie Charteris (1965)

"I'm afraid," said Patricia Holm soberly, "you'll be getting into trouble again soon."

Simon Templar grinned, and opened another bottle of beer. He poured it out with a steady hand, unshaken by the future predicted for him.

"You may be right, darling," he admitted. "Trouble is one of the things that sort of happen to me, like other people have colds."

"I've often heard you complaining about it," said the girl sceptically.

The Saint shook his head.

"You wrong me," he said. "Posterity will know me as a maligned, misunderstood, ill-used victim of a cruel fate. I have tried to be good. Instinctive righteousness glows from me like an inward light. But nobody gives it a chance. What do you suggest?"

"You might go into business."

"I know. Something safe and respectable, like manufacturing woollen combinations for elderly ladies with lorgnettes. We might throw in a pair of lorgnettes with every suit. You could knit them, and I'd do the fitting—the fitting of the lorgnettes, of course." Simon raised his glass and drank deeply. "It's an attractive idea, old darling, but all these schemes involve laying out a lot of capital on which you have to wait such a hell of a long time for a return. Besides, there can't be much of a profit in it. On a rough estimate, the amount of wool required to circumnavigate a fifty-four inch bust—"

Monty Hayward, who was also present, took out a tobacco-pouch and began to fill his pipe.

"I had some capital once," he said reminiscently, "but it didn't do me much good."

"How much can you lend me?" asked the Saint hopefully.

Monty brushed stray ends of tobacco from his lap and tested the draught through his handiwork cautiously.

"I haven't got it anymore, but I don't think I'd lend it to you if I had," he said kindly. "Anyway, the point doesn't arise, because a fellow called Oscar Newdick has got it. Didn't I ever tell you about that?"

The Saint moved his head negatively, and settled deeper into his chair.

"It doesn't sound like you, Monty. D'you mean to say you were hornswoggled?"

Monty nodded.

"I suppose you might call it that. It happened about six years ago, when I was a bit younger and not quite so wise. It wasn't a bad swindle on the whole, though." He struck a match and puffed meditatively. "This fellow Newdick was a bloke I met on the train coming down from the office. He used to get into the same compartment with me three or four times a week, and naturally we took to passing the time of day—you know the way one does. He was an aeronautical engineer and a bit of an inventor, apparently. He was experimenting with autogyros, and he had a little one-horse factory near Walton where he was building them. He used to talk a lot of technical stuff about them to me, and I talked technical stuff about make-up and dummies to him—I don't suppose either of us understood half of what the other was talking about, so we got on famously."

With his pipe drawing satisfactorily, Monty possessed himself of the beer-opener and executed a neat flanking movement towards the source of supply.

"Well, one day this fellow Newdick asked me if I'd like to drop over and have a look at his autogyros, so the following Saturday afternoon I hadn't anything particular to do and I took a run out to his aerodrome to see how he was getting along. All he had there was a couple of corrugated-iron sheds and a small field which he used to take off from and land at, but he really had got a helicopter effect which he said he'd made himself. He told me all about it and how it worked, which was double-Dutch to me, and then he asked if I'd like to go up in it. So I said 'Thank you very much, I should simply hate to go up in it.' You know what these things look like—an ordinary aeroplane with the wings taken off and just a sort of large fan business to hold you up in the air—I never have thought they looked particularly safe even when they're properly made, and I certainly didn't feel like risking my neck in this home-made version that he'd rigged up out of old bits of wood and angle iron. However, he was so insistent about it and seemed so upset when I refused that eventually I thought I'd better gratify the old boy and just keep on praying that the damn thing wouldn't fall to pieces before we got down again."

The Saint sighed.

"So that's what happened to your face," he remarked, in a tone of profound relief. "If you only knew how that had been bothering me—"

"My mother did that," said Monty proudly. "No—we didn't crash. In fact, I had a really interesting flight. Either it must have been a very good machine, or he was a very good flier, because he made it do almost everything except answer questions. I don't know if you've ever been up in one of these autogyros—I've never been up in any other make, but this one was certainly everything that he claimed for it. It went up exactly like going up in a lift, and came down the same way. I never have known anything about the mechanics of these things, but after having a ride in this bus of his I couldn't help feeling that the Air

Age had arrived—I mean, anyone with a reasonable-sized lawn could have kept one of 'em and gone tootling off for week-ends in it."

"And therefore," said the Saint reproachfully, "when he asked you if you'd like to invest some money in a company he was forming to turn out these machines and sell them at about twenty pounds a time, you hauled out your cheque-book and asked him how much he wanted."

Monty chuckled good-humouredly.

"That's about it. The details don't really matter, but the fact is that about three weeks later I'd bought about five thousand quid's worth of shares."

"What was the catch?" Simon asked, and Monty shrugged.

"Well, the catch was simply that this helicopter wasn't his invention at all. He had really built it himself, apparently, but it was copied line for line from one of the existing makes. There wasn't a thing in it that he'd invented. Therefore the design wasn't his, and he hadn't any right at all to manufacture it. So the company couldn't function. Of course, he didn't put it exactly like that. He told me that he'd 'discovered' that his designs 'overlapped' the existing patents—he swore that it was absolutely a coincidence, and nearly wept all over my office because his heart was broken because he'd found out that all his research work had already been done before. I said I didn't believe a word of it, but that wasn't any help towards getting my money back. I hadn't any evidence against him that I could have brought into a court of law. Of course he'd told me that his design was patented and protected in every way, but he hadn't put any of that in writing, and when he came and told me the whole thing was smashed he denied it. He said he told me he was getting the design patented. I did see a solicitor about it afterwards, but he told me I hadn't a chance of proving a deliberate fraud. Newdick would probably have been ticked off in court for taking my money without reasonable precautions, but that wouldn't have brought any of it back."

"It was a private company, I suppose," said the Saint.

Monty nodded.

"If it had been a public one, with shares on the open market, it would have been a different matter," he said.

"What happened to the money?"

"Newdick had spent it—or he said he had. He told me he'd paid off all the old debts that had run up while he was experimenting, and spent the rest on some manufacturing plant and machinery for the company. He did give me about six or seven hundred back, and told me he'd work like hell to produce another invention that would really be original so he could pay me back the rest, but that was the last I heard of him. He's probably caught several other mugs with the same game since then." Monty grinned philosophically, looked at the clock, and got up. "Well, I must be getting along. I'll look in and see you on Saturday—if you haven't been arrested and shoved in clink before then."

He departed after another bottle of beer had been lowered, and when he had gone Patricia Holm viewed the Saint doubtfully. She had not missed the quiet attention with which he had followed Monty Hayward's narrative, and she had known Simon Templar a long time. The Saint had a fresh cigarette slanting from the corner of his mouth, his hands were in his pockets, and he was smiling at her with a seraphic innocence which was belied by every facet of the twinkling tang of mockery in his blue eyes.

"You know what I told you," she said.

He laughed.

"About getting into trouble? My darling, when will you stop thinking these wicked thoughts? I'm taking your advice to heart. Maybe there is something to be said for going into business. I think I should look rather fetching in a silk hat and a pair of white spats with pearl buttons, and you've no idea how I could liven up a directors' meeting if I set my mind to it."

Patricia was not convinced.

She was even less convinced when the Saint went out the next morning. From his extensive wardrobe he had selected one of his most elegant suits, a creation in light-hued saxony of the softest and most expensive weave—a garment which could by no possible chance have been worn by a man who had to devote his day to honest toil. His tie was dashing, his silk socks would have made a Communist's righteous indignation swell to bursting point, and over his right eye he had tilted a brand new Panama which would have made one wonder whether the strange shapeless headgear of the same breed worn by old gents whilst pottering around their gardens could conceivably be any relation whatsoever of such a superbly stylish lid. Moreover he had taken out the car which was the pride of his stable—the new cream and red Hirondel which was in itself the hallmark of a man who could afford to pay five thousand pounds for a car and thereafter watch a gallon of petrol blown into smoke every three or four miles.

"Where's the funeral?" she asked, and the Saint smiled blandly.

"I'm a young sportsman with far more money than sense, and I'm sure Comrade Newdick will be pleased to see me," he said, and kissed her.

Mr Oscar Newdick was pleased to see him—Simon Templar would have been vastly surprised if he hadn't been. That aura of idle affluence which the Saint could put on as easily as he put on a coat was one of his most priceless accessories, and it was never worn for any honest purpose.

But this Mr Oscar Newdick did not know. To him, the arrival of such a person was like an answer to prayer. Monty Hayward's guess at Mr Newdick's activities since collecting five thousand pounds from him was fairly accurate, but only fairly. Mr Newdick had not caught several other mugs, but only three, and one of them had only been induced to invest a paltry three hundred pounds. The helicopter racket had been failing in its dividends, and the past year had not shown a single pennyworth of profit. Mr Newdick did not believe in accumulating pennies; when he made a touch, it had to be a big one, and he was prepared to wait for it—the paltry three-hundred-pound investor had been an error of judgment, a young man who had grossly misled him with fabulous accounts of wealthy uncles, which when the time came to make the touch had been discovered to be the purest fiction—but recently the periods of waiting had exceeded all reasonable limits. Mr Newdick had travelled literally thousands of miles on the more prosperous suburban lines in search of victims—the fellow-passenger technique really was his own invention, and he practised it to perfection—but many moons had passed since he brought a prospective investor home from his many voyages.

When Simon Templar arrived, in fact, Mr Newdick was gazing mournfully over the litter of spars and fabric and machinery in one of his corrugated-iron sheds, endeavouring to estimate its value in the junk market. The time had come, he was beginning to feel, when that particular stock-in-trade had paid the last percentage that could be squeezed out of it; it had rewarded him handsomely for his initial investment, but now it was obsolete. The best solution appeared to be to turn it in and concentrate his varied talents on some other subject. A fat insurance policy, of course, followed by a well-organized fire, would have been more profitable, but a recent sensational arson trial and the consequent publicity given to such schemes made him wary of taking that way out. And he was engrossed in these uninspiring meditations when the bell in his "office" rang and manna fell from heaven.

Mr Oscar Newdick, it must be acknowledged, did not instantly recognize it as manna. At first he thought it could only be the rate collector, or another summons for his unpaid electric light bill. He tiptoed to a grimy window which looked out on the road, with intent to escape rapidly across the adjacent fields if his surmise proved correct, and it was thus that he saw the imposing automobile which stood outside.

Mr Newdick, a man of the world, was wise to the fact that rate collectors and servers of summonses rarely arrived at their grim work in five-thousand-pound Hirondels, and it was with an easy conscience, if not yet admixed with undue optimism, that he went to open the door.

"Hullo, old bean," said the Saint.

"Er . . . hullo," said Mr Newdick.

"I blew in to see if you could tell me anything about your jolly old company," said the Saint.

"Er . . . yes," said Mr Newdick. "Er . . . why don't you come inside?"

His hesitation was not due to any bashfulness or even to offended dignity. Mr Newdick did not mind being called an old bean. He had no instinctive desire to snub wealthy-looking young men with five-thousand-pound Hirondels who added jollity to his old company. The fact was that he was just beginning to recognise the manna for what it was, and his soul was suffering from the same emotions as those which had afflicted the Israelites in their time when they contemplated the miracle.

The Saint came in. Mr Newdick's "office" was a small, roughly-fashioned cubicle about the size of a telephone booth, containing a small table littered with papers and overlaid with a thin film of dust—it scarcely seemed in keeping with the neatly engraved brass plate on the door which proclaimed it to be the registered offices of the Newdick Helicopter Company, Limited, but his visitor did not seem distressed by it.

"What did you want to know?" asked Mr Newdick.

Simon observed him to be a middle-aged man of only vaguely military appearance, with sharp eyes that looked at him unwaveringly.

That characteristic alone might have deceived most men, but Simon Templar had moved in disreputable circles long enough to know that the ability to look another man squarely in the eye is one of the most fallacious indices of honesty.

"Well," said the Saint amiably, tendering a platinum cigarette-case, "the fact is that I'm interested in helicopters. I happen to have noticed your little place several times recently when I've been passing, and I got the idea that it was quite a small show, and I wondered if there might by any chance be room for another partner in it."

"You mean," repeated Mr Newdick, checking back on the incredible evidence of his ears, "that you wanted to take an interest in the firm?"

Simon nodded.

"That was the jolly old idea," he said. "In fact, if the other partners felt like selling out, I might take over the whole blinkin' show. I've got a good deal of time on my hands, and I like pottering about with aeroplanes and what not. A chap's got to do something to keep out of mischief, what? Besides, it doesn't look as if you were doing a lot of business here, and I might be able to wake the jolly old place up a bit. Sort of aerial roadhouse, if you know what I mean. Dinners—drinks—dancing—pretty girls . . . What?"

"I didn't say anything," said Mr Newdick.

"All right. What about it, old bean?"

Mr Newdick scratched his chin. The notion of manna had passed into his cosmogony. It fell from Heaven. It was real. Miracles happened. The world was a brighter, rosier place.

"One of your remarks, of course," he said, "is somewhat uninformed. As a matter of fact, we are doing quite a lot of business. We have orders, negotiations, tenders, contracts . . ." The elegant movement of one hand, temporarily released from massaging his chin, indicated a whole field of industry of which the uninitiated were in ignorance. "However," he said, "if your proposition were attractive enough, it would be worth hearing."

Simon nodded.

"Well, old bean, who do I put it to?"

"You may put it to me, if you like," said Mr Newdick. "I am Oscar Newdick."

"I see. But what about the other partners, Oscar, old sprout?"

Mr Newdick waved his hand.

"They are largely figureheads," he explained. "A few friends with very small interests—just enough to meet the technical requirements of a limited company. The concern really belongs to me."

Simon beamed.

"Splendid!" he said. "Jolly good! Well, well, well, dear old Newdick, what d'you think it's worth?"

"There is a nominal share value of twenty-five thousand pounds," said Mr Newdick seriously. "But, of course, they are worth far more than that. Far more . . . I very much doubt," he said, "whether fifty thousand would be an adequate price. My patents alone are worth more than fifty thousand pounds. Sixty thousand pounds would scarcely tempt me. Seventy thousand would be a poor price. Eighty thousand—"

"Is quite a lot of money," said the Saint, interrupting Mr Newdick's private auction.

Mr Newdick nodded.

"But you haven't seen the place yet—or the machines we turn out. You ought to have a look round, even if we can't do business."

Mr Newdick suffered a twinge of horror at the thought even while he uttered it.

He led the Saint out of his "office" to the junk shed. No one who had witnessed his sad survey of that collection of lumber a few minutes before would have believed that it was the same man who now gazed on it with such enthusiasm and affection.

"This," said Mr Newdick, "is our workshop. Here you can see the parts of our machines in course of construction and assembly. Those lengths of wood are our special longerons. Over there are stays and braces . . ."

"By Jove!" said the Saint in awe. "I'd no idea helicopters went in for all those things. They must be quite dressed up when you've finished with them, what? By the way, talking of longerons, a girlfriend of mine has the neatest pattern of step-ins . . ."

Mr Newdick listened patiently.

Presently they passed on to the other shed. Mr Newdick opened the doors as reverently as if he had been unveiling a memorial.

"And this," he said, "is the Newdick helicopter."

Simon glanced over it vacuously, and looked about him.

"Where are all your workmen today?" he asked.

"They are on holiday," said Mr Newdick, making a mental note to engage some picturesque mechanics the next day. "An old custom of the firm. I always give them a full day's holiday on the anniversary of my dear mother's death." He wiped away a tear and changed the subject. "How would you like to take a flight?"

"Jolly good idea," agreed the Saint.

The helicopter was wheeled out, and while it was warming up, Simon revealed that he was also a flier and possessed a licence for helicopters. Mr Newdick complimented him gravely. They made a ten-minute flight, and when they had landed again the Saint remained in his seat.

"D'you mind if I try her out myself?" he said. "I won't ask you to take the flight with me."

The machine was not fitted with dual control, but it was well insured. Mr Newdick only hesitated a moment. He was very anxious to please.

"Certainly," he said. "Give her a thorough test yourself, and you'll see that she's a good bus."

Simon took the ship off and climbed towards the north. When Mr Newdick's tiny aerodrome was out of sight he put the helicopter through every test he could think of, and the results amazed him even while they only confirmed the remarkable impression he had gained while Mr Newdick was flying it.

When he saw the London Air Park below him he shut off the engine and came down in a perfect vertical descent which set him down outside the Cierva hangars. Simon climbed out and buttonholed one of the company's test pilots.

"Would you like to come on a short hop with me?" he asked. "I want to show you something."

As they walked back towards the Newdick helicopter, the pilot studied it with a puzzled frown.

"Is that one of our machines?" he said.

"More or less," Simon told him.

"It looks as if it had been put together wrong," said the pilot worriedly. "Have you been having trouble with it?"

The Saint shook his head.

"I think you'll find," he answered, "that it's been put together right."

He demonstrated what he meant, and when they returned, the test pilot took the machine up again himself and tried it a second time. Other test pilots tried it. Engineers scratched their heads over it and tried it. Telephone calls were made to London. A whole two hours passed before Simon Templar dropped the machine beside Mr

Newdick's sheds and relieved the inventor of the agonies of anxiety which had been racking him.

"I was afraid you'd killed yourself," said Mr Newdick with emotion: and, indeed, the thought that his miraculous benefactor might have passed away before being separated from his money had brought Mr Newdick out in several cold sweats.

The Saint grinned.

"I just buzzed over to Reading to look up a friend," he said untruthfully. "I like your helicopter. Let us go inside and talk business."

When he returned to Patricia, much later that day, he was jubilant but mysterious. He spent most of the next day with Mr Newdick, and half of the Saturday which came after, but he refused to tell her what he was doing. It was not until that evening, when he was pouring beer once more for Monty Hayward, that he mentioned Mr Newdick again, and then his announcement took her breath away.

"I've bought that helicopter company," he said casually.

"You've what?" spluttered Monty.

"I've bought that helicopter company and everything it owns," said the Saint, "for forty thousand pounds."

They gaped at him for a while in silence, while he calmly continued with the essential task of opening bottles.

"The man's mad," said Patricia finally. "I always thought so."

"When did you do this?" asked Monty.

"We fixed up the last details of the deal today," said the Saint. "Oscar is due here at any minute to sign the papers."

Monty swallowed beer feverishly.

"I suppose you wouldn't care to buy my shares as well?" he suggested.

"Sure, I'll buy them," said the Saint affably. "Name your price. Oscar's contribution gives me a controlling interest, but I can always handle a bit more. As ordered by Patricia, I'm going into business.

The machine is to be re-christened the Templar helicopter. I shall go down to history as the man who put England in the air. Bevies of English beauty, wearing their Templar longerons—stays, braces, and everything complete—"

The ringing of his door-bell interrupted the word-picture and took him from the room before any of the questions that were howling through their bewildered minds could be asked.

Mr Newdick was on the mat, beaming like a delighted fox. Simon took his hat and umbrella, took Mr Newdick by the arm, and led him through into the living-room.

"Boys and girls." he said cheerfully, "this is our fairy godmother, Mr Oscar Newdick. This is Miss Holm, Oscar, old toadstool, and I think you know Mr Hayward—"

The inventor's arm stiffened under his hand, and his smile had vanished. His face was turning pale and nasty.

"What's the game?" he demanded hoarsely.

"No game at all, dear old garlic-blossom," said the Saint innocently. "Just a coincidence. Mr Hayward is going to sell me his shares, too. Now, all the papers are here, and if you'll just sign on the dotted line—"

"I refuse!" babbled Newdick wildly. "It's a trap!"

Simon stepped back and regarded him blandly.

"A trap, Oscar? What on earth are you talking about? You've got a jolly good helicopter, and you've nothing to be ashamed of. Come now, be brave. Harden the Newdick heart. There may be a wrench at parting with your brainchild, but you can cry afterwards. Just a signature or two on the dotted line, and it's all over. And there's a cheque for forty thousand pounds waiting for you . . ."

He thrust a fountain-pen into the inventor's hand, and, half-hypnotized, Mr Newdick signed. The Saint blotted the signatures carefully and put the agreements away in a drawer, which he locked. Then he handed Mr Newdick a cheque. The inventor grasped it weakly and stared at the writing and figures on it as if he expected them to fade away under his eyes. He had the quite natural conviction that his brain had given way.

"Th-thank you very much," he said shakily, and was conscious of little more than an overpowering desire to remove himself from those parts—to camp out on the doorstep of a bank and wait there with his head in his hands until morning, when he could pass the cheque over the counter and see crisp banknotes clicking back to him in return to prove that his sanity was not entirely gone. "Well, I must be going," he gulped out, but the Saint stopped him.

"Not a bit of it, Oscar," he murmured. "You don't intrude. In fact, you ought to be the guest of honour. Your class as an inventor really is A.1. When I showed the Cierva people what you'd done, they nearly collapsed."

Mr Newdick blinked at him in a painful daze.

"What do you mean?" he stammered.

"Why, the way you managed to build an autogyro that would go straight up and down. None of the ordinary ones will, of course—the torque of the vanes would make it spin round like a top if it didn't have a certain amount of forward movement to hold it straight. I can only think that when you got hold of some Cierva parts and drawings and built it up yourself, you found out that it didn't go straight up and down as you'd expected and thought you must have done something wrong. So you set about trying to put it right—and somehow or other you brought it off. It's a pity you were in such a hurry to tell Mr Hayward that everything in your invention had been patented before, Oscar, because if you'd made a few more inquiries you'd have found that it hadn't." Simon Templar grinned, and patted the stunned man kindly on the shoulder. "But everything happens for the best, dear old bird, and when I tell you that the Cierva people have already made me an offer of a hundred thousand quid for the invention you've just sold me, I'm sure you'll stay and join us in a celebratory bottle of beer."

Mr Oscar Newdick swayed slightly, and glugged a strangling obstruction out of his throat.

"I . . . I don't think I'll stay," he said. "I'm not feeling very well."

"A dose of salts in the morning will do you all the good in the world," said the Saint chattily, and ushered him sympathetically to the door.

THE PRINCE OF CHERKESSIA

Of the grey hairs which bloomed in the thinning thatch of Chief Inspector Claud Eustace Teal, there were at least a couple of score which he could attribute directly to an equal number of encounters with the Saint. Mr Teal did not actually go so far as to call them by name and celebrate their birthdays, for he was not by nature a whimsical man, but he had no doubts about their origin.

The affair of the Prince of Cherkessia gave him the forty-first—or it may have been the forty-second.

His Highness arrived in London without any preliminary publicity, but he permitted a number of reporters to interview him at his hotel after his arrival. The copy which he provided had a sensation value which no self-respecting news editor could ignore.

It started before the assembled pressmen had drunk more than half the champagne which was provided for them in the Prince's suite, which still stands as a record for any reception of that type. It was started by a cub reporter, no more ignorant than the rest, but more honest about it, who had not been out on that kind of assignment long enough to learn that the serious business of looking for a story is not supposed to mar the general conviviality while there is anything left to drink.

"Where," asked this revolutionary spirit brazenly, with his mouth full of *foie gras*, "is Cherkessia?"

The Prince raised his Mephistophelian eyebrows. "You," he replied, with faint contempt, "would probably know it better as Circassia."

At the sound of his answer a silence spread over the room. The name rang bells, even in journalistic heads. The cub gulped down the rest of his sandwich without tasting it, and one reporter was so far moved as to put down a glass which was only half empty.

"It is a small country between the Caucasus Mountains and the Black Sea," said the Prince. "Once it was larger, but it has been eaten away by many invaders. The Turks and the Russians have robbed us piecemeal of most of our lands—although it was the Tartars themselves who gave my country its name, from their word *Chertkess*, which means 'robbers.' That ancient insult was long since turned to glory by my ancestor Schamyl, whose name I bear, and in the paltry lands which are still left to me the proud traditions of our race are carried on to this day."

The head of the reporter who had put down his glass was buzzing with vague memories.

"Do you still have beautiful Circassians?" he asked hungrily.

"Of course," said the Prince. "For a thousand years our women have been famed for their beauty. Even today, we export many hundreds annually to the most distinguished harems in Arabia—a royal tax on these transactions," added the Prince, with engaging simplicity, "has been of great assistance to our national budget."

The reporter swallowed, and retrieved his glass hurriedly, and the cub who had started it all asked, with bulging eyes, "What other traditions do you have, Your Highness?"

"Among other things," said the Prince, "we are probably the only people today among whom the *droit de seigneur* survives. That is to say that every woman in my country belongs to me, if and when I choose to take her, for as long as I choose to keep her in my palace."

"And do you still exercise that right?" asked another journalist, with ecstatic visions of headlines floating through his mind.

The Prince smiled, as he might have smiled at the naivety of a child.

"If the girl is sufficiently attractive—of course. It is a divine right bestowed upon my family by Mohammed himself. In my country it is considered an honour to be chosen, and the marriageable value of any girl on whom I bestow my right is greatly increased by it."

From that moment the reception was a historic success, and the news that one reason for the Prince's visit was to approve the final details of a new one-hundred-thousand-pound crown which was being prepared for him by a West End firm of jewellers was almost an anti-climax.

Chief Inspector Teal read the full interview in his morning paper the following day. He was so impressed with its potentialities that he made a personal call on the Prince that afternoon.

"Is this really the interview you gave, Your Highness?" he asked, when he had introduced himself, "or are you going to repudiate it?"

Prince Schamyl took the paper and read it through. He was a tall well-built man with a pointed black beard and twirled black moustaches like a seventeenth-century Spanish grandee. When he had finished reading he handed the paper back with a slight bow, and fingered his moustaches in some perplexity.

"Why should I repudiate it?" he inquired. "It is exactly what I said."

Teal chewed for a moment on the spearmint which even in the presence of royalty he could not deny himself, and then he said, "In that case, Your Highness, would you be good enough to let us give you police protection?"

The Prince frowned puzzledly. "But are not all people in this country protected by the police?"

"Naturally," said Teal. "But this is rather a special case. Have you ever heard of the Saint?"

Prince Schamyl shrugged. "I have heard of several."

"I don't mean that kind of saint," the detective told him grimly. "The Saint is the name of a notorious criminal we have here, and something tells me that as soon as he sees this interview he'll be making plans to steal this crown you're buying. If I know anything about him, the story that you make some of your money out of selling girls to harems, and that you exercise this *droit de seigneur*, whatever that is, would be the very thing to put him on your tracks."

"But, please," said the Prince in ingenuous bewilderment, "what is wrong with our customs? My people have been happy with them for hundreds of years."

"The Saint wouldn't approve of them," said Teal with conviction, and realized the hopelessness of entering upon a discussion of morals with such a person. "Anyhow, sir, I'd be very much obliged if you would let us give you a special guard until you take your crown out of the country."

The Prince shook his head, as if the incomprehensible customs of England baffled him to speechlessness.

"In my country there are no notorious criminals," he said, "because as soon as a criminal is known he is beheaded.

However, I shall be glad to help you in any way I can. The crown is to be delivered here tomorrow, and you may place as many guards in my suite as you think necessary."

The news that four special detectives had been detailed to guard the Prince of Cherkessia's crown was published in an evening paper which Simon Templar was reading at a small and exclusive dinner at which the morning paper's interview was also discussed.

"I knew you wouldn't be able to resist it," said Patricia Holm fatalistically, "directly I saw the headlines. You're that sort of idiot."

Simon looked at her mockingly. "Idiot?" he queried. "My dear Pat, have you ever known me to be anything but sober and judicious?"

"Often," said his lady candidly. "I've also known you to walk into exactly the same trap. I'll bet you anything you like that Teal made up the whole story just to get a rise out of you, and the Prince'll turn out to be another detective with a false beard."

"You'd lose your money," said the Saint calmly. "Teal is as worried about it as you are, and if you like to drop in at Vazey's on Bond Street or make discreet inquiries at the Southshire Insurance Company, you'll find that that crown genuinely is costing a hundred thousand pounds and is insured for the same amount. It's rather pleasant to think that the Southshire will have to stand the racket, because their ninety per cent underwriter is a very scaly reptile named Percy Quiltan, whose morals are even more repulsive than Prince Schamyl's. And the Prince's are bad enough . . . No, Pat, you can't convince me that that tin hat isn't legitimate boodle, and I'm going to have it."

A certain Peter Quentin, who was also present, sighed, and turned the sigh into a resigned grin. "But how d'you propose to do it?" he asked.

The Saint's blue eyes turned on him with an impish twinkle. "I seem to remember that you retired from this business some months ago, Peter," he murmured. "A really respectable citizen wouldn't be asking that question with so much interest. However, since your beautiful wife is away—if you'd like to lend a hand, you could help me a lot."

"But what's the plan?" insisted Patricia.

Simon Templar smiled. "We are going to dematerialize ourselves," he said blandly. "Covetous but invisible, we shall lift the crown of Cherkessia from under Claud Eustace's very nose, and put it on a shelf in the fourth dimension."

She was no wiser when the party broke up some hours later. Simon informed her that he and Peter Quentin would be moving into Prince Schamyl's hotel to take up residence there for a couple of days. But she knew that they would not be there under their own names, and the rest of his plan remained wrapped in the maddening mystery with which the Saint's sense of the theatrical too often required him to tantalize his confederates.

Chief Inspector Teal would have been glad to know even as little as Patricia, but the evidence which came before him was far less satisfactory. It consisted of a plain postcard, addressed to Prince Schamyl, on which had been drawn a skeleton figure crowned with a rakishly tilted halo. A small arrow pointed to the halo, and at the other end of the arrow was written in neat copperplate the single word: "Thursday."

"If the Saint says he's coming on Thursday, he's coming on Thursday," Teal stated definitely, in a private conference to which he was summoned when the card arrived.

Prince Schamyl elevated his shoulders and spread out his hands. "I do not attempt to understand your customs, Inspector. In my country, if we require evidence, we beat the criminal with rods until he provides it."

"You can't do that in this country," said Teal, as if he wished you could. "That postcard wouldn't be worth tuppence in a court of law—not with the sort of lawyers the Saint could afford to engage. We couldn't prove that he sent it. We know it's his trade-mark, but the very fact that everybody in England knows the same thing would be the weakest point in our case. The prosecutor could never make the jury believe that a crook as clever as the Saint is supposed to be would send out a warning that could be traced back to him so easily.

"The Saint knows it, and he's been trading on it for years—it's the strongest card in his hand. If we arrested him on evidence like that, he'd only have to swear that the card was a fake—that some other crook had sent it out as a blind—and he could make a fool of anyone who tried to prove it wasn't. Our only chance is to catch him more or less red-handed. One of these days he'll go too far, and I'm only hoping it'll be on Thursday."

Teal thumbed the pages of a cheap pocket diary, although he had no need to remind himself of dates.

"This is Wednesday," he said. "You can say that Thursday begins any time after midnight. I'll be here at twelve o'clock myself, and I'll stay here till midnight tomorrow."

Mr Teal was more worried than he would have cared to admit. The idea that even such a satanic ingenuity as he knew the Saint to possess could contrive a way of stealing anything from under the eyes of a police guard who had been forewarned that he was coming for it was obviously fantastic. It belonged to sensational fiction, to the improbable world of Arsène Lupin.

Arsène Lupin would have disguised himself as Chief Inspector Teal or the Chief Commissioner, and walked out with the crown under his arm. But Teal knew that such miracles of impersonation only happened in the romances of unscrupulous and reader-cheating authors. And yet he knew the Saint too well, he had crossed swords too often with that amazing brigand of the twentieth century, to derive any solid consolation from that thought.

When he came back to the hotel that night, he checked over his defences as seriously as if he had been guarding the premier of a great European power from threatened assassination. There were men posted at the entrances of the hotel and one at a strategic point in the lobby which covered the stairs and lifts. A Flying Squad car stood outside. Every member of the hotel staff who would be serving the Prince during the next twenty-four hours had been investigated.

A burly detective paced the corridor outside the Prince's suite, and two more equally efficient men were posted inside. Teal added himself to the last number. The one-hundred-thousand-pound crown of Cherkessia reposed in a velvet-lined box on a table in the sitting-room of the suite—Teal had unsuccessfully attempted more than once to induce Prince Schamyl to authorize its removal to a safe-deposit or even to Scotland Yard itself.

"Where is the necessity?" inquired the Prince blankly. "You have your detectives everywhere. Are you afraid that they will be unable to cope with this absurd criminal?"

Teal had no answer. He was afraid—there was a gloomy premonition creeping around his brain that the Saint could not have helped foreseeing all his precautions, and therefore must have discovered a loophole long in advance. That was the reason why he had studiously withheld even a rumour of the Saint's threat from the Press, for he had his own stolid vanity. But he could not tell the Prince that.

He glowered morosely at the private detective who had been added to the contingent by the Southshire Insurance Company, a brawny broken-nosed individual with a moustache like the handlebars of a bicycle, who was pruning his nails with a penknife in the corner. He began to ask himself whether those battered and belligerently whiskered features could by any feat of make-up have been imposed with putty and spirit gum on the face of the Saint or any of his known associates, and then the detective looked up and encountered his devouring stare with symptoms of such pardonable alarm that Teal hastily averted his eyes.

"Surely," said the Prince, who still appeared to be striving to get his bearings, "if you are really anticipating an attack from this criminal, and he is so well known to you, his movements are being watched?"

"I wish I could say they were," said Teal glumly. "As soon as that postcard arrived I went after him myself, but he appears to have left the country. Anyhow, he went down to Hanworth last night, where he keeps an aeroplane, and went off in it, and he hasn't been back since. Probably he's only fixing up an alibi—"

Even as he uttered the theory, the vision of a helicopter flashed into his mind. The hotel was a large tall building, with a spacious roof garden—with the latest type of whirly-bird it might have been possible to land and take off there. Teal had a sudden wild desire to post more detectives on the roof—even to ask for special planes to patrol the skies over the hotel. He laughed himself out of the planes, but he went downstairs and picked up one of the men he had posted in the lobby.

"Go up and watch the roof," he ordered. "I'll send someone to relieve you at eight o'clock."

The man nodded obediently and went off, but he gave Teal a queer look in parting which made the detective realize how deeply the Saint superstition had got into his system. The realization did not make Mr Teal any better pleased with himself, and his manner when he returned to the royal suite was almost surly.

"We'd better watch in turns," he said. "There are twenty-four hours to go, and the Saint may be banking on waiting until near the end of the time when we're all tired and thinking of giving it up."

Schamyl yawned. "I am going to bed," he said. "If anything happens, you may inform me."

Teal watched the departure of the lean black-hawk figure, and wished he could have shared the Prince's tolerant boredom with the whole business. One of the detectives who watched the crowd, at a sign from Teal, curled up on the settee and closed his eyes. The private watchdog of the Southshire Insurance lolled back in his chair; very soon his mouth fell open, and a soporific buzzing emanated from his throat and caused his handlebar moustaches to vibrate in unison.

Chief Inspector Teal paced up and down the room, fashioning a wedge of chewing gum into endless intricate shapes with his teeth and tongue. The exercise did not fully succeed in soothing his nerves. His brain was haunted by memories of the buccaneer whom he knew only too well—the rakish carving of the brown handsome face, the mockery of astonishingly clear blue eyes, the gay smile that came so easily to the lips, the satirical humour of the gentle dangerous voice.

He had seen all those things too often ever to forget them—had been deceived, maddened, dared, defied, and outwitted by them in too many adventures to believe that their owner would ever be guilty of an empty hoax. And the thought that the Saint was roving at large that night was not comforting. The air above Middlesex had literally swallowed him up, and he might have been anywhere between Berlin and that very room.

When the dawn came Teal was still awake. The private detective's handlebars ceased vibrating with a final snort. The officer on the couch woke up, and the one who had kept the night watch took his place. Teal himself was far too wrought up to think of seizing his own chance to rest. Ten o'clock arrived before the Prince's breakfast, and Schamyl came through from his bedroom as the waiter was laying the table.

He peered into the box where the crown was packed, and stroked his beard with an ironical glint in his eyes.

"This is very strange, Inspector," he remarked. "The crown has not been stolen! Can it be that your criminal has broken his promise?"

With some effort, Teal kept his retort to himself. While the Prince attacked his eggs with a healthy appetite, Teal sipped a cup of coffee and munched on a slice of toast. For the hundredth time he surveyed the potentialities of the apartment. The bedroom and the sitting-room opened on either side of a tiny private hall, with the bathroom in between. The hall had a door into the corridor, outside which another detective was posted; there was no other entrance or exit except the open windows overlooking Hyde Park, through which the morning sun was streaming. The possibility of secret panels or passages was absurd.

The furniture was modernistically plain, expensive, and comfortable. There was a chesterfield, three armchairs, a couple of smaller chairs, a writing desk, the centre table on which breakfast was laid, and a small side table on which stood the box containing the crown of Cherkessia. Not even a very small thief could have secreted himself in or behind any of the articles. Nor could he plausibly slip through the guards outside.

Therefore, if he was to make good his boast, it seemed as if he must be inside already, and Teal's eyes turned again to the moustached representative of the Southshire Insurance Company. He would have given much for a legitimate excuse to seize the handlebars of that battle-scarred sleuth, one in each hand, and haul heftily on them, and he was malevolently deliberating whether such a manoeuvre could be justified in the emergency when the interruption came.

It was provided by Peter Quentin, who stood at another window of the hotel vertically above the Prince's suite, dangling a curious egg-shaped object at the end of a length of cotton. When it hung just an inch above Schamyl's window, he took up a yard of slack and swung the egg-shaped object cautiously outwards. As it started to swing back, he dropped the slack, and the egg plunged through the Prince's open window and broke the cotton in the jerk that ended its trajectory.

Chief Inspector Teal did not know this. He only heard the crash behind him, and swung round to see a pool of milky fluid spreading around a scattering of broken glass on the floor. Without stopping to think he made a dive towards it, and a gush of dense black smoke burst from the milky pool like a flame and struck him full in the face.

He choked and gasped, and groped around in a moment of utter blindness. In another instant the whole room was filled with the jet-black fog. The shouts and stumblings of the other men in the room came to him as if through a film of cotton-wool as he lumbered sightlessly towards the table where the crown had stood. He cannoned into it and ran over its surface with frantic hands. The box was not standing there any longer. In a sudden panic of fear he dropped to his knees and began to feel all over the floor around the table . . .

He had already made sure that the box had not been knocked over on to the floor in the confusion, when the smoke in his lungs forced him to stagger coughing and retching to the door. The corridor outside was black with the same smoke, and in the distance he could hear the tinkling of fire alarms. A man collided with him in the blackness, and Teal grabbed him in a vicious grip.

"Tell me your name," he snarled.

"Mason, sir," came the reply, and Teal recognized the voice of the detective he had posted in the corridor.

His chest heaved painfully.

"What happened?"

"I don't know, sir. The door . . . opened from the inside . . . one of those damn smoke-bombs thrown out . . . started all this. Couldn't see . . . any more, sir."

"Let's get some air," gasped Teal.

They reeled along the corridor for what seemed to be miles before the smoke thinned out, and after a while they reached a haven where an open corridor window reduced it to no more than a thin grey mist. Red-eyed and panting, they stared at one another.

"He's done it," said Teal huskily.

That was the bitter fact he had to face, and he knew without further investigation, even without the futile routine search that had to follow, that he would never see the crown of Cherkessia again.

The other members of the party were blundering down towards them through the fog. The first figure to loom up was that of Prince Schamyl himself, cursing fluently in an incomprehensible tongue, and after him came the form of the Southshire Insurance Company's private bloodhound.

Teal's bloodshot eyes glared at that second apparition insanely through the murk. Mr Teal had suffered much; he was not feeling himself, and in the last analysis he was only human. That is the only explanation this chronicle can offer for what he did. For with a kind of strangled grunt, Chief Inspector Claud Eustace Teal lurched forward and took hold of the offensive handlebar moustaches, one in each determined hand.

"Perhaps now you'll tell me how you did it," said Patricia Holm.

The Saint smiled. He had arrived only twenty minutes before, fresh as a daisy, at the hotel in Paris where he had arranged to meet her, and he was unpacking.

From a large suitcase he had taken a small folding table, which was a remarkable thing for him to have even in his frequently eccentric luggage. He set it up before her, and placed on it a velvet-lined wooden box. The table was somewhat thicker in the top than most tables of that size, as if it might have contained a drawer, but she could not see any drawer.

"Watch," he said.

He touched a concealed spring somewhere in the side of the table—and the box vanished. Because she was watching it closely, she saw it go. It simply fell through the trapdoor into the hollow thickness of the top, and a perfectly fitted panel sprang up to fill the gap again. But it was all done in a split second, and even when she examined the top of the table closely it was hard to see the edges of the trapdoor. She shook the table, but nothing rattled. For all that any ordinary examination could reveal, the top might have been a solid block of mahogany.

"It was just as easy as that," said the Saint, with the air of a conjuror revealing a treasured illusion. "The crown never even left the room until I was ready to take it away. Fortunately the Prince hadn't actually paid for the crown. It was still insured by Vazey's themselves, so the Southshire Insurance Company's cheque will go direct to them—which saves me a certain amount of extra work. All I've got to do now is to finish off my alibi, and the job's done."

"But, Simon," pleaded the girl, "when Teal grabbed your moustaches—"

"Teal didn't grab my moustaches," said the Saint with dignity. "Claud Eustace would never have dreamed of doing such a thing. I shall never forget the look on that bird's face when the moustaches were grabbed, though. It was a sight I hope to treasure to my dying day, no matter how long postponed."

He had unpacked more of the contents of his large bag while he was talking, and at that moment he was laying out on the bed a pair of imperially curled moustachios to which was connected an impressively pointed black beard. Patricia's eyes suddenly opened wide.

"Good Lord!" she gasped. "You don't mean to say you kidnapped the Prince and pretended to be *him*?"

Simon Templar shook his head.

"I always was the Prince of Cherkessia—didn't you know?" he said innocently, and all at once Patricia began to laugh.

THE TREASURE OF TURK'S LANE

There was a morning when Simon Templar looked up from his newspaper with a twinkle of unholy meditation in his blue eyes and a rather thoughtful smile barely touching the corners of his mouth, and to the privileged few who shared all his lawless moods there was only one deduction to be drawn when the Saint looked up from his newspaper in just that thoughtful and unholy way.

"I see that Vernon Winlass has bought Turk's Lane," he said.

Mr Vernon Winlass was a man who believed in Getting Things Done. The manner of doing them did not concern him much, so long as it remained strictly within the law; it was only results which could be seen in bank accounts, share holdings, income tax returns, and the material circumstances of luxurious living, and with these things Mr Winlass was very greatly and wholeheartedly concerned.

This is not to say that he was more avaricious than any other business man, or more unscrupulous than any other financier. In his philosophy, the weakest went to the wall: the careless, the timid, the foolish, the simple, the hesitant paid with their misfortunes for the rewards that came naturally to those of sharper and more aggressive talents.

And in setting up that elementary principle for his only guiding standard, Mr Winlass could justifiably claim that after all he was only demonstrating himself to be the perfect evolutionary product of a civilization whose honours and amenities are given only to people who Get Things Done, whether they are worth doing or not—with the notable exception of politicians, who, of course, are exempted by election even from that requirement.

Simon Templar did not like Mr Winlass, and would have considered him a legitimate victim for his illegitimate talents, on general principles that were only loosely connected with one or two things he had heard about Mr Winlass's methods of Getting Things Done; but although the idea of devoting some time and attention to that hard-headed financier simmered at the back of his mind in a pleasant warmth of enthusiasm, it did not actually boil over until the end of the same week, when he happened to be passing Turk's Lane on his return from another business affair.

Turk's Lane is, or was, a narrow cul-de-sac of small two-storey cottages. That description is more or less as bald and unimaginative as anything a hard-headed financier would have found to say about it. In actual fact it was one of those curious relics of the past which may sometimes be discovered in London, submerged among tall modern buildings and ordered squares as if a new century had grown up around it without noticing its existence any more than was necessary to avoid treading on it.

The passer-by who wandered into that dark lane at night might have fancied himself magically transported back over two centuries. He would have seen the low ceilings and tiny leaded windows of oak-beamed houses, the wrought-iron lamps glowing above the lintels of the narrow doors, the worn cobblestones gleaming underfoot, the naphtha flares flickering on a riot of foodstuffs spread out in unglazed shop fronts, and he might have thought himself spirited away into the market street of a village that had survived there unaltered from the days when Kensington was a hamlet three miles from London and there was a real Knights' Bridge across the Serpentine where it now flows through sanitary drainpipes to the Thames.

Mr Winlass did not think any of these things, but he saw something far more interesting to himself, which was that Turk's Lane stood at the back of a short row of shabby early Victorian houses which were for sale. He also saw that the whole of Turk's Lane—except for the two end houses, which were the freehold property of the occupants—was likewise for sale, and that the block comprising these properties totalled an area of about half an acre, which is quite a small garden in the country, but which would allow plenty of space to erect a block of modern apartments with running hot and cold water in every room for the tenancy of fifty more sophisticated and highly civilized Londoners.

He also saw that this projected building would have an impressive frontage on a most respectable road in a convenient situation which the westward trend of expansion was annually raising in value, and he bought the row of shabby early Victorian houses and the whole of Turk's Lane except the two end cottages, and called in his architects.

Those two cottages which had not been included in the purchase were the difficulty.

"If you don't get those two places the site's useless," Mr Winlass was told. "You can't build a block of flats like you're proposing to put up with two old cottages in the middle."

"Leave it to me," said Mr Winlass. "I'll Get It Done."

Strolling into Turk's Lane on this day when the ripeness of Mr Winlass for the slaughter was finally made plain to him, Simon Templar learned how it was Getting Done.

It was not by any means the Saint's first visit to that picturesque little alley. He had an open affection for it, as he had for all such pathetic rear-guards of the forlorn fight against dull mechanical modernity, and he had at least one friend who lived there.

Dave Roberts was a cobbler. He was an old grey-haired man with gentle grey eyes, known to every inhabitant of Turk's Lane as "Uncle Dave," who had plied his trade there since the oldest of them could remember, as his father and grandfather had done before him. It might almost be said that he was Turk's Lane, so wholly did he belong to the forgotten days that were preserved there. The march of progress to which Mr Vernon Winlass belonged had passed him by.

He sat in his tiny shop and mended the boots and shoes of the neighbourhood for microscopical old-world prices; he had a happy smile and a kind word for everyone; and with those simple things, unlike Mr Vernon Winlass, his philosophy began and ended and was well content. To such pioneers as Mr Winlass he was, of course, a dull reactionary and a stupid bumpkin, but to the Saint he was one of the few and dwindling relics of happier and cleaner days, and many pairs of Simon's own expensive shoes had gone to his door out of that queer affection rather than because they needed repairing.

Simon smoked a cigarette under the low beamed ceiling in the smell of leather and wax, while Dave Roberts wielded his awl under a flickering gas-jet and told him of the things that were Happening in Turk's Lane.

"Ay, sir, Tom Unwin over the road, he's going. Mr Winlass put him out o' business. Did you see that new shop next to Tom's? Mr Winlass started that up, soon as he'd got the tenants out. Sold exactly the same things as Tom had in his shop for a quarter the price—practically give 'em away, he did. 'Course, he lost money all the time, but he can afford to. Tom ain't hardly done a bit o' business since then. 'Well,' Tom says to himself, "if this goes on for another couple o' months I'll be broke,' so in the end he sells out to Mr Winlass, an' glad to do it. I suppose I'll be the next, but Mr Winlass won't get me out if I can help it."

The Saint looked across the lane at the garish makeshift shop-front next door to Tom Unwin's store, and back again to the gentle old man straining his eyes under the feeble light.

"So he's been after you, has he?" he said.

"Ay, he's been after me. One of his men come in my shop the other day. 'Your place is worth five thousand pounds,' he says. 'We'll give you seven thousand to get out at once, an' Mr Winlass is being very generous with you,' he says. Well, I told him I didn't want to get out. I been here, man an' boy, for seventy years now, an' I wasn't going to get out to suit him. 'You realize,' he says, 'your obstinacy is holding up an important an' valuable piece of building?'—'Begging your pardon, sir,' I says, 'you're holding me up from mending these shoes.'—'Very well,' this chap says, 'if you're so stupid you can refuse two thousand pounds more than your place is worth, you're going to be glad to take two thousand less before you're much older, if you don't come to your senses quick,' he says, 'and them's Mr Winlass's orders,' he says."

"I get it," said the Saint quietly. "And in a day or two you'll have a Winlass shoe repair shop next door to you, working for nothing."

"They won't do work like I do," said Dave Roberts stolidly. "You can't do it, not with these machines. What did the Good Lord give us hands for, if it wasn't that they were the best tools in the world? . . . But I wouldn't be surprised if Mr Winlass tried it. But I wouldn't sell my house to him. I told this fellow he sent to see me: 'My compliments to Mr Winlass,' I says, 'and I don't think much of his orders, nor the manners of anybody that carries 'em out. The way you talk to me,' I says, 'isn't the way to talk to any self-respecting man, an' I wouldn't sell you my house, not now after you've threatened me that way,' I says, 'not if you offered me seventy thousand pounds.' An' I tells him to get out o' my shop an' take that message to Mr Winlass."

"I see," said the Saint.

Dave Roberts finished off his sewing and put the shoe down in its place among the row of other finished jobs.

"I ain't afraid, sir," he said. "If it's the Lord's will that I go out of my house, I suppose He knows best. But I don't want Mr Winlass to have it, an' the Lord helps them that helps themselves."

The Saint lighted a cigarette and stared out of the window.

"Uncle Dave," he said gently, "would you sell me your house?"

He turned round suddenly, and looked at the old man. Dave Robert's hand had fallen limply in his lap, and his eyes were blinking mistily.

"You, sir?" he said.

"Me," said the Saint. "I know you don't want to go, and I don't know whether it's the Lord's will or not, but I know that you're going to have to. And you know it too. Winlass will find a way to get you out. But I can get more out of him than you could. I know you don't want money, but I can offer you something even better. I know a village out of London where I can buy you a house almost exactly like this, and you can have your shop and do your work there without anybody troubling you again. I'll give you that in exchange, and however much money there is in this house as well."

It was one of those quixotic impulses that often moved him, and he uttered it on the spur of the moment with no concrete plan of campaign in his mind. He knew that Dave Roberts would have to go, and that Turk's Lane must disappear, make room for the hygienic edifice of mass-production cubicles which Mr Vernon Winlass had planned. He knew that, whatever he himself might wish, that individual little backwater must take the way of all such pleasant places, to be superseded by the vast white cube of Crescent Court, the communal sty which the march of progress demands for its armies. But he also knew that Mr Vernon Winlass was going to pay more than seven thousand pounds to clear the ground for it.

When he saw Patricia Holm and Peter Quentin later that night, they had no chance to mistake the light of unlawful resolution on his face.

"Brother Vernon hasn't bought the whole of Turk's Lane," he announced, "because I've got some of it."

"Whatever for?" asked Patricia.

"For an investment," answered the Saint virtuously. "Crescent Court will be built only by kind permission of Mr Simon Templar, and my permission is going to cost money."

Peter Quentin helped himself to some Peter Dawson.

"We believe you," he said dryly. "What's the swindle?"

"You have a mind like Claud Eustace Teal," said the Saint offensively. "There is no swindle. I am a respectable real estate speculator, and if you had any money I'd sue you for slander. But I don't mind telling you that I am rather interested to know what hobby Vernon Winlass has in his spare moments. Go out and do some sleuthing for me in the morning, Peter, and I'll let you know some more."

In assuming that even such a hard-headed business man as Mr Vernon Winlass must have some simple indulgence, Simon Templar was not taking a long chance. Throughout the ages, iron-gutted captains of industry had diverted themselves with rare porcelain, pewter, tram tickets, Venetian glass, first editions, second mortgages, second establishments, dahlias, stuffed owls, and such-like curios. Mr Wallington Titus Oates, of precious memory, went into slavering raptures at the sight of pieces of perforated paper bearing the portraits of stuffed-looking monarchs and the magic words of "Postage Two Pence." Mr Vernon Winlass, who entrenched himself during business hours behind a storm battalion of secretaries, under-secretaries, assistant secretaries, messengers, clerks, managers, and office-boys, put aside all his business and opened wide his defences at the merest whisper of old prints.

"It's just an old thing we came across when we were clearing out our old house," explained the man who had successfully penetrated these fortified frontiers—his card introduced him as Captain Tombs, which was an alias out of which Simon Templar derived endless amusement. "I took it along to Busby's to find out if it was worth anything, and they seemed to get quite excited about it. They told me I'd better show it to you."

Mr Winlass nodded.

"I buy a good many prints from Busby's," he said smugly. "If anything good comes their way, they always want me to see it."

He took the picture out of its brown paper wrapping and looked at it closely under the light. The glass was cracked and dirty, and the frame was falling apart and tied up with wire, but the result of his inspection gave him a sudden shock. The print was a discovery—if he knew anything at all about these things, it was worth at least five hundred pounds. Mr Winlass frowned at it disparagingly.

"A fairly good specimen of a rather common plate," he said carelessly. "I should think it would fetch about ten pounds."

Captain Tombs looked surprised. "Is that all?" he grumbled. "The fellow at Busby's told me I ought to get anything from three hundred up for it."

"Ah-hum," said Mr Winlass dubiously. He peered at the print again, and raised his eyes from it in an elaborate rendering of delight. "By Jove," he exclaimed, "I believe you're right. Tricky things, these prints. If you hadn't told me that, I might have missed it altogether. But it looks as if—if it is a genuine . . . Well!," said Mr Winlass expansively, "I almost think I'll take a chance on it. How about two hundred and fifty?"

"But the fellow at Busby's—"

"Yes, yes," said Mr Winlass testily. "But these are not good times for selling this sort of thing. People haven't got the money to spend. Besides, if you wanted to get a price like that, you'd have to get the picture cleaned up—get experts to certify it—all kinds of things like that. And they all cost money. And when you'd done them all, it mightn't prove to be worth anything. I'm offering to take a gamble on it and save you a lot of trouble and expense."

Captain Tombs hesitated, and Mr Winlass pulled out a cheque-book and unscrewed his fountain pen.

"Come, now," he urged genially. "I believe in Getting Things Done. Make up your mind, my dear chap. Suppose we split it at two-seventy-five—or two hundred and eighty—"

"Make it two hundred and eighty-five," said Captain Tombs reluctantly, "and I suppose I'd better let it go."

Mr Winlass signed the cheque with the nearest approach to glee that he would ever be able to achieve while parting with money in any quantity, and he knew that he was getting the print for half its value. When Captain Tombs had gone, he set it up against the inkwell and fairly gloated over it. A moment later he picked up a heavy paper-knife and attacked it with every evidence of ferocity.

But the scowl of pained indignation which darkened his brow was directed solely against the cracked glass and the dilapidated frame. The picture was his new-born babe, his latest ewe lamb, and it was almost inevitable that he should rise against the vandal disfigurement of its shabby trappings as a fond mother would rise in wrath against the throwing of mud pies at her beloved offspring. When the horrible cradle that had sheltered it was stripped away and cast into the waste-basket, he set up the print again and gloated over it from every angle. After a long time he turned it over to stow it safely in an envelope—and it was when he did this that he noticed the writing on the back.

The reactions of an equally inevitable curiosity made him carry the picture over to the window to read the almost indecipherable scrawl. The ink was rusty with age, the spidery hand angular and old-fashioned, but after some study he was able to make out the words.

To my wife, On this day 16 Aprille did I lodge in ye haufe of one Thomaf Robertf a cobbler and did hyde under hyf herthe in Turkes Lane ye feventy thoufande golde piecef wich

I stole of Hyf Grace ye Duke. Finde them if thif letre come to thee and Godes blefsynge, John.

None of the members of Mr Winlass's staff, some of whom had been with him through ten years of his hard-headed and dignified career, could remember any previous occasion when he had erupted from his office with so much violence. The big limousine which wafted him to Turk's Lane could not travel fast enough for him: he shuffled from one side of the seat to the other, craning forward to look for impossible gaps in the traffic, and emitting short nasal wuffs of almost canine impatience.

Dave Roberts was not in the little shop when Mr Winlass walked in. A freckle-faced pug-nosed young man wearing the same apron came forward.

"I want to see Mr Roberts," said Winlass, trembling with excitement, which he was trying not to show.

The freckle-faced youth shook his head.

"You can't see Mr Roberts," he said. "He ain't here."

"Where can I find him?" barked Winlass.

"You can't find him," said the youth phlegmatically. "He don't want to be found. Want your shoes mended, sir?"

"No, I do not want my shoes mended!" roared Winlass, dancing in his impatience. "I want to see Mr Roberts. Why can't I find him? Why doesn't he want to be found? Who the hell are you, anyhow?"

"I do be Mr Roberts's second cousin, sir," said Peter Quentin, whose idea of dialects was hazy but convincing. "I do have bought Mr Roberts's shop, and I'm here now, and Mr Roberts ain't coming back, sir, that's who I be."

Mr Winlass wrenched his features into a jovial beam.

"Oh, you're Mr Roberts's cousin, are you?" he said, with gigantic affability. "How splendid! And you've bought his beautiful shop. Well, well. Have a cigar, my dear sir, have a cigar."

The young man took the weed, bit off the wrong end, and stuck it into his mouth with the band on—a series of motions which caused Mr Winlass to shudder to his core. But no one could have deduced that shudder from the smile with which he struck and tendered a match.

"Thank 'ee, sir," said Peter Quentin. "Now, sir, can I mend thy shoes?"

He admitted afterwards to the Saint that the strain of maintaining what he fondly believed to be a suitable patois was making him a trifle light-headed, but Mr Vernon Winlass was far too preoccupied to notice his aberrations.

"No, my dear sir," said Mr Winlass, "my shoes don't want mending. But I should like to buy your lovely house."

The young man shook his head.

"I ain't a-wanting to sell 'er, sir."

"Not for seven thousand pounds?" said Mr Winlass calculatingly.

"Not for seven thousand pounds, sir."

"Not even," said Mr Winlass pleadingly, "for eight thousand?"

"No, sir."

"Not even," suggested Mr Winlass, with an effort which caused him acute pain, "if I offered you nine thousand?"

The young man's head continued to shake.

"I do only just have bought 'er, sir. I must do my work somewhere. I wouldn't want to sell my house, not if you offered me ten thousand for 'er, that I wouldn't."

"Eleven thousand," wailed Mr Winlass, in dogged anguish.

The bidding rose to sixteen thousand five hundred before Peter Quentin relieved Mr Winlass of further torture and himself of further lingual acrobatics. The cheque was made out and signed on the spot, and in return Peter attached his signature to a more complicated document which Mr Winlass had ready to produce from his breast pocket, for Mr Vernon Winlass believed in Getting Things Done.

"That's splendid," he boomed, when the formalities had been completed. "Now then, my dear sir, how soon can you move out?"

"In ten minutes," said Peter Quentin promptly, and he was as good as his word.

He met the Saint in a neighbouring hostelry and exhibited his trophy. Simon Templar took one look at it, and lifted his tankard.

"So perish all the ungodly," he murmured. "Let us get it to the bank before they close."

It was three days later when he drove down to Hampshire with Patricia Holm to supervise the installation of Uncle Dave Roberts in the cottage which had been prepared for him. It stood in the street of a village that had only one street, a street that was almost an exact replica of Turk's Lane set down in a valley between rolling hills. It had the same oak-beamed cottages, the same wrought-iron lamps over the lintels to light the doors by night, the same rows of tiny shops clustering face to face with their wares spread out in unglazed windows, and the thundering main road traffic went past five miles away and never knew that there was a village there.

"I think you'll be happy here, Uncle Dave," he said, and he did not need an answer in words to complete his reward.

It was a jubilant return journey for him, and they were in Guildford before he recollected that he had backed a very fast outsider at Newmarket. When he bought a paper he saw that that also had come home, and they had to stop at the Lion for celebrations.

"There are good moments in this life of sin, Pat," he remarked, as he started up the car again, and then he saw the expression on her face, and stared at her in concern. "What's the matter, old darling—has that last Dry Sack gone to your head?"

Patricia swallowed. She had been glancing through the other pages of *The Evening Standard* while he tinkered with the ignition, and now she folded the sheet down and handed it to him.

"Didn't you promise Uncle Dave whatever money there was in his house as well as that cottage?" she asked.

Simon took the paper and read the item she was pointing to.

TREASURE TROVE IN LONDON EXCAVATION
WINDFALL FOR WINLASS

The London clay, which has given up many strange secrets in its time, yesterday surrendered a treasure which has been in its keeping for 300 years.

Twenty thousand pounds is the estimated value of a hoard of gold coins and antique jewellery discovered by workmen engaged in demolishing an old house in Turk's Lane, Brompton, which is being razed to make way for a modern apartment building.

The owner of the property, Mr Vernon Winlass—

The Saint had no need to read any more, and as a matter of fact he did not want to. For several seconds he was as far beyond the power of speech as if he had been born dumb.

And then, very slowly, the old Saintly smile came back to his lips.

"Oh, well, I expect our bank account will stand it," he said cheerfully, and turned the car back again towards Hampshire.

THE SLEEPLESS KNIGHT

INTRODUCTION

Quite naturally, it seems to me, concurrently with the broadening conception of poetic justice which we were just discussing, there has been a shifting of the Saint's chief interest from common crime towards deeper waters.

That is not to say that the time-honoured themes of embezzlement, drug trafficking, blackmail, burglary, and the Blunt Instrument no longer amuse him. Far from it. But there is a measurable waning of the naïve exuberance which once found such simple villainies the completely satisfying and unsurpassable objectives of a buccaneer's attention. He has come to be aware of large issues, of a lurking background of bigger and beastlier dragons.

This story deals with what you might call a transitional or intermediate size of dragon, and may therefore be read just as beneficially by students of evolution as by missionaries, bartenders, grocers, actuaries, and manufacturers of patent corset fastenings—a most happy state of affairs, in my opinion.

—Leslie Charteris (1939)

If a great many newspaper clippings and references to newspapers find their way into these chronicles, it is simply because most of the interesting things that happen find their way into newspapers, and it is in these ephemeral sheets that the earnest seeker after unrighteousness will find many clues to his quest.

Simon Templar read newspapers only because he found collected in them the triumphs and anxieties and sins and misfortunes and ugly tyrannies which were going on around him, as well as the results of races in which chosen horses carried samples of his large supply of shirts, not because he cared anything about the posturing of Trans-Atlantic fliers or the flatulence of international conferences. And it was solely through reading a newspaper that he became aware of the existence of Sir Melvin Flager.

It was an unpleasant case, and the news item may as well be quoted in full.

JUDGE CENSURES TRANSPORT COMPANY
Driver's Four Hours' Sleep a Week
"MODERN SLAVERY"—Mr Justice Goldie.

Scathing criticisms of the treatment of drivers by a road transport company were made by Mr Justice Goldie during the trial of Albert Johnson, a lorry driver, at Guildford Assizes yesterday.

Johnson was charged with manslaughter following the death of a cyclist whom he knocked down and fatally injured near Albury on March 28th.

Johnson did not deny that he was driving to the danger of the public, but pleaded that his condition was due to circumstances beyond his control.

Police witnesses gave evidence that the lorry driven by Johnson was proceeding in an erratic manner down a fairly wide road at about 30 miles an hour. There was a cyclist in front of it, travelling in the same direction, and a private car coming towards it.

Swerving to make way for the private car, in what the witness described as "an unnecessarily exaggerated manner," the lorry struck the cyclist and caused fatal injuries.

The police surgeon who subsequently examined Johnson described him as being "apparently intoxicated, although there were no signs of alcohol on his breath.

"I was not drunk," said Johnson, giving evidence on his own behalf. "I was simply tired out. We are sent out on long journeys and forced to complete them at an average speed of over 30 miles an hour including stops for food and rest.

"Most of our work is done at night, but we are frequently compelled to make long day journeys as well.

"During the week when the accident occurred, I had only had four hours' sleep.

"It is no good protesting, because the company can always find plenty of unemployed drivers to take our places."

Other employees of the Flager Road Transport Company, which employs Johnson, corroborated his statement.

"This is nothing more or less than modern slavery," said

Mr Justice Goldie, directing the jury to return a verdict of Not Guilty.

"It is not Johnson, but Sir Melvin Flager, the managing director of the company, who ought to be in the dock.

"You have only to put yourselves in the position of having gone for a week on four hours' sleep, with the added strain of driving a heavy lorry throughout that time, to be satisfied that no culpable recklessness of Johnson's was responsible for this tragedy.

"I would like to see it made a criminal offence for employers to impose such inhuman conditions on their employees."

Sir Melvin Flager was not unnaturally displeased by this judicial comment, but he might have been infinitely more perturbed if he had known of the Saint's interest in the case.

Certain readers of these chronicles may have reached the impression that Simon Templar's motives were purely selfish and mercenary, but they would be doing him an injustice. Undoubtedly his exploits were frequently profitable, and the Saint himself would have been the first to admit that he was not a brigand for his health, but there were many times when only a very small percentage of his profits remained in his own pocket, and many occasions when he embarked on an episode of lawlessness with no thought of profit for himself at all.

The unpleasantness of Sir Melvin Flager gave him some hours of quite altruistic thought and effort.

"Actually," he said, "there's only one completely satisfactory way to deal with a tumour like that. And that is to sink him in a barrel of oil and light a fire underneath."

"The Law doesn't allow you to do that," said Peter Quentin pensively.

"Very unfortunately, it does not," Simon admitted, with genuine regret. "All the same, I used to do that sort of thing without the sanction of the Law, which is too busy catching publicans selling a glass of beer after hours to do anything about serious misdemeanours, anyway . . . But I'm afraid you're right, Peter—I'm much too notorious a character these days, and Chief Inspector Claud Eustace Teal isn't the bosom pal he was. We shall have to gang warily, but nevertheless, we shall certainly have to gang."

Peter nodded approvingly. Strangely enough, he had once possessed a thoroughly respectable reverence for the Law, but several months of association with the Saint had worked irreparable damage on that bourgeois inhibition.

"You can count me in," he said, and the Saint clapped him on the back.

"I knew it without asking you, you old sinner," he said contentedly. "Keep this next week-end free for me, brother, if you really feel that way—and if you want to be specially helpful you can push out this afternoon with a false beard tied round your ears and try to rent a large garage from which yells of pain cannot be heard outside."

"Is that all?" Peter asked suspiciously. "What's your share going to be—backing losers at Hurst Park?"

The Saint shook his head.

"Winners," he said firmly. "I always back winners. But I'm going to be busy myself. I want to get hold of a gadget. I saw it at a motor show once, but it may take me a couple of days to find out where I can buy one."

As a matter of fact it took him thirty-six hours and entailed a good deal of travelling and expense. Peter Quentin found and rented the garage which the Saint had demanded a little more quickly, but the task was easier and he was used to Simon Templar's eccentric commissions.

"I'm getting so expert at this sort of thing, I believe I could find you a three-humped camel overnight if you wanted it," Peter said modestly, when he returned to announce success.

Simon grinned.

The mechanical details of his scheme were not completed until the Friday afternoon, but he added every hour and penny spent to the private account which he had with Sir Melvin Flager, of which that slave-driving knight was blissfully in ignorance.

It is barely possible that there may survive a handful of simple unsophisticated souls who would assume that since Mr Justice Goldie's candid criticisms had been pronounced in open court and printed in every newspaper of importance, Sir Melvin Flager had been hiding his head in shame, shunned by his erstwhile friends and treated with deferential contempt even by his second footman. To these unfledged innocents we extend our kindly sympathy, and merely point out that nothing of the sort had happened. Sir Melvin Flager, of course, did not move in the very Highest Society, for an uncle of his on his mother's side still kept and served in a fried-fish shop near the Elephant and Castle, but the society in which he did move did not ostracize him. Once the first statement-seeking swarm of reporters had been dispersed, he wined and dined and diverted himself and ran his business exactly the same as he had done before, for the business and social worlds have always found it remarkably easy to forgive the trespasses of a man whose prices and entertainments are respectively cheaper and better than others.

On that Friday night Sir Melvin Flager entertained a small party to dinner, and took them on to a revue afterwards. Conscience had never troubled him personally, and his guests were perfectly happy to see a good show without worrying about such sordid trifles as how the money that paid for their seats was earned. His well-laden lorries roared through the night with red-eyed men at the wheel to add to his fortune, and Sir Melvin Flager sat in his well-upholstered seat and roared with carefree laughter at the antics of the comedian, forgetting all about his business until nearly the end of the first act, when a programme girl handed him a sealed envelope. Flager slit it open and read the note.

One of our lorries has had another accident. Two killed. Afraid it may be bad for us if this comes out so soon after the last one. May be able to square it, but must see you first. Will wait in your car during the interval.

It was in his business manager's handwriting, and it was signed with his business manager's name.

Sir Melvin Flager tore the note into small pieces and dumped it in the ashtray before him. There was a certain forced quality about his laughter for the next five minutes, and as soon as the curtain came down he excused himself to his guests and walked down the line of cars parked in a side street adjoining the theatre. He found his own limousine, and peered in at the back.

"You there, Nyson?" he growled.

"Yes, sir."

Flager grunted, and opened the door. It was rather dark inside the car, and he could only just make out the shape of the man who sat there.

"I'll fire every damned driver I've got tomorrow," he swore, as he climbed in. "What the devil do they think I put them on the road for—to go to sleep? This may be serious."

"You've no idea how serious it's going to be, brother," said the man beside him.

But the voice was not the voice of Mr Nyson, and the mode of address was not that which Sir Melvin Flager encouraged from his executives. For a moment the managing director of the Flager Road Transport Company did not move, and then he leaned sideways to stare more closely at his companion. His eyes were growing accustomed to the dark, but the movement did not help him at all, for with a sudden shock of fear he saw that the man's features were completely covered by a thin gauzy veil which stretched from his hat-brim down to his coat collar.

"Who the hell are you?" rasped Flager uncertainly.

"On the whole, I think it would be better for you not to know," said the Saint calmly.

Another man had climbed into the driver's seat, and the car vibrated almost imperceptibly as the engine started up. But this second man, although he wore a chauffeur's peaked cap, had a silhouette that in no way resembled that of the chauffeur whom Sir Melvin Flager employed.

Under his touch the car began to edge out of the line, and as he saw the movement Flager came back to life. In the stress of the moment he was unable to form a very clear idea of what was happening, but instinct told him that it was nothing to which he wanted to lend his tender person.

"Well, you won't kidnap me!" he shouted, and lashed out wildly at the veiled face of the man beside him.

Which was the last thing he knew about for the next half-hour, for his desperate swing was still far from its mark when a fist like a ball of iron struck him cleanly on the point of the jaw and lifted him back on to the cushions in a dreamless slumber.

When he woke up, his first impulse was to clasp his hands to his painfully singing head, but when he tried to carry it out his wrists refused to move—they felt as if they were anchored to some solid object. Blinking open his eyes, he looked down at them. They were handcuffed to what appeared to be the steering wheel of a car.

In another second the memory of what had happened to him before he fell asleep returned. He began to struggle frantically, but his body refused to respond, and he saw that a broad leather strap like the safety belt of an aeroplane had been passed around his waist and fastened in front of his abdomen, locking him securely to his seat. Wildly he looked about him, and discovered that he was actually sitting in the driving seat of a lorry. He could see the hood in front of him, and, beyond it, a kind of white screen which seemed vaguely familiar.

The feeling that he had been plunged into some fantastic nightmare seized him, and he let out a stifled yell of fright.

"That won't help you," said a cool voice at his side, and Flager jerked his head round to see the veiled face of the unknown man who had sat at his side in the car.

"Damn you!" he raved. "What have you done to me?"

He was a large fleshy man, with one of those fleshy faces which look as if their owner had at some time invited God to strike him pink, and had found his prayer instantaneously answered. Simon Templar, who did not like large fleshy men with fleshy pink faces, smiled under his mask.

"So far, we haven't done very much," he said. "But we're going to do plenty."

The quietness of his voice struck Flager with a sudden chill, and instinctively he huddled inside his clothes. Something else struck him as unusual even as he did so, and in another moment he realized what it was. Above the waist, he had no clothes on at all—the whole of his soft white torso was exposed to the inclemency of the air.

The Saint smiled again.

"Start the machine, Peter," he ordered, and Flager saw that the chauffeur who had driven the car was also there, and that he was similarly masked.

A switch clicked over, and darkness descended on the garage. Then a second switch clicked, and the white screen in front of the lorry's bonnet lighted up with a low whirring sound. Bewildered but afraid, Flager looked up and saw a free moving picture show.

The picture was of a road at night, and it unrolled towards him as if it had been photographed from behind the headlights of a car that was rushing over it. From time to time, corners, cross-roads, and the lights of other traffic proceeding in both directions swept up towards him—the illusion that he was driving the lorry in which he sat over that road was almost perfect.

"What's this for?" he croaked.

"You're taking the place of one of your own drivers for the week-end," answered the Saint. "We should have preferred to do it out on the road under normal working conditions, but I'm afraid you would have made too much noise. This is the best substitute we were able to arrange, and I think it'll work all right. Do you know what it is?"

Flager shook his head.

"I don't care what it is! Listen here, you—"

"It's a gadget for testing people's ability to drive," said the Saint smoothly. "When I turn another switch, the steering wheel you have there will be synchronized with the film. You will then be driving over the road yourself. So long as you keep on the road and don't try to run into the other traffic, everything will be all right. But directly you make a movement that would have taken you off the road or crashed you into another car—or a cyclist, brother—the film will stop for a moment, a red light will light up on top of the screen, and I shall wake you up like this."

Something swished through the air, and a broad stinging piece of leather which felt like a razor strop fell resoundingly across Sir Melvin's well-padded shoulders.

Flager gave a yelp of anguish, and the Saint laughed softly.

"We'll start right away," he said. "You know the rules and you know the penalties—the rules are only the same as your own employees have to obey, and the penalties are really much less severe. Wake up, Flager—you're off!"

The third switch snapped into place, and Flager grabbed blindly at the steering wheel. Almost at once the picture faltered, and a red light glowed on top of the screen.

Smack! came the leather strop across his shoulders.

"Damn you!" bellowed Flager. "What are you doing this for?"

"Partly for fun," said the Saint. "Look out—you're going to hit that car!"

Flager did hit it, and the strop whistled through the darkness and curled over his back. His shriek tortured the echoes, but Simon was without mercy.

"You'll be in the ditch in a minute," he said. "No . . . Here comes a corner . . . Watch it! . . . Nicely round, brother, nicely round. Now mind you don't run into the back of this cart—you've got plenty of room to pass . . . Stick to it . . . Don't hit the cyclist . . . You're going to hit him . . . Mind the fence—you're heading straight for it—look out . . . Look out!"

The strop whacked down again with a strong and willing arm behind it as the red light sprang up again.

Squealing like a stuck pig, Sir Melvin Flager tore the lorry back on to its course.

"How long are you keeping this up for?" he sobbed.

"Until Monday morning," said the Saint calmly. "And I wish it could be a month. I've never seen a more responsive posterior than you have. Mind the cyclist."

"But you're making me drive too fast!" Flager almost screamed. "Can't you slow the machine up a bit?"

"We have to average over thirty miles an hour," answered the Saint remorselessly. "Look out!"

Sir Melvin Flager passed into a nightmare that was worse than anything he had thought of when he first opened his eyes. The mechanical device which he was strapped to was not quite the same as the cars he was used to, and Simon Templar himself would have been ready to admit that it might be more difficult to drive. Time after time the relentless leather lashed across his shoulderblades, and each time it made contact he let loose a howl of pain which in itself was a reward to his tormentors.

After a while he began to master the steering, and long periods went by when the red light scarcely showed at all. As these intervals of immunity lengthened, Flager shrugged his aching back and began to pluck up courage. These lunatics who had kidnapped him, whoever they were, had taken a mean advantage of him at the start. They had fastened him to an unfamiliar machine and promptly proceeded to shoot it through space at forty-five miles an hour: naturally he had made mistakes. But that could not go on for ever. He had got the hang of it at last, and the rest of it seemed more or less plain sailing. He even had leisure to ponder sadistically on what their fate would be when they let him go and the police caught them, as they undoubtedly would be caught. He seemed to remember that the cat-o'-nine-tails was the punishment invariably meted out by the Law for crimes of violence. Well, flogging him with that leather strop was a crime of violence. He brooded savagely over various tales he had heard of the horrors of that punishment . . .

Whack!

The red light had glowed, and the strop had swung home again. Flager pulled himself together with a curse. It was no good getting careless now that he had mastered the machine. But he was beginning to feel tired. His eyes were starting to ache a little with the strain of keeping themselves glued watchfully to the movie screen ahead. The interminable unwinding of that senseless road, the whirr of the unseen projector, the physical effort of manipulating the heavy steering wheel, the deadly monotony of the task, combined with the heavy dinner he had eaten and a long sequence of other dinners behind it to produce a sensation of increasing drowsiness. But the unwinding of the road never slackened speed, and the leather strop never failed to find its mark every time his wearying attention caused him to make a mistake.

"You're getting careless about your corners," the Saint warned him tirelessly. "You'll be in the ditch at the next one. Lookout!"

The flickering screen swelled up and swam in his vision. There was nothing else in the world—nothing but that endlessly winding road uncoiling out of the darkness, the lights of other traffic that leapt up from it, the red light above the screen, and the smack of the leather strop across his shoulders. His brain seemed to be spinning round like a top inside his head when at last, amazingly, the screen went black and the other bulbs in the garage lighted up.

"You can go to sleep now," said the Saint.

Sir Melvin Flager was incapable of asking questions. A medieval prisoner would have been no more capable of asking questions of a man who released him from the rack. With a groan he slumped back in his seat and fell asleep.

It seemed as if he had scarcely closed his eyes when he was roused again by someone shaking him. He looked up blearily and saw the strange chauffeur leaning over him.

"Wake up," said Peter Quentin. "It's five o'clock on Saturday morning, and you've got a lot more miles to cover."

Flager had no breath to dispute the date. The garage lights had gone out again, and the road was starting to wind out of the screen again.

"But you told me I could sleep!" he moaned.

"You get thirty-five minutes every night," Peter told him pitilessly. "That averages four hours a week, and that's as much as you allowed Albert Johnson. Look out!"

Twice again Flager was allowed to sleep, for exactly thirty-five minutes; four times he watched his two veiled tormentors change places, a fresh man taking up the task while the other lay down on the very comfortable bed which had been made up in one corner and slept serenely. Every three hours he had five minutes' rest and a glass of water, every six hours he had ten minutes' rest, a cup of coffee, and a sandwich. But the instant that those timed five or ten minutes had elapsed, the projector was started up again, the synchronization switch was thrown over, and he had to go on driving.

Time ceased to have any meaning. When, after his first sleep, he was told that it was only five o'clock on Saturday morning, he could have believed that he had been driving for a week; before his ordeal was over, he felt as if he had been at the wheel for seven years. By Saturday night he felt he was going mad; by Sunday morning he thought he was going to die; by Sunday night he was a quivering wreck. The strop fell on his shoulders many times during the last few hours, when the recurrent sting of it was almost the only thing that kept his eyes open, but he was too weary even to cry out . . .

And then, at the end of what might have been centuries, Monday morning dawned outside, and the Saint looked at his watch and reversed the switches.

"You can go to sleep again now," he said for the last time, but Sir Melvin Flager was asleep almost before the last word was out of his mouth.

Sunken in the coma of utter exhaustion, Flager did not even feel himself being unstrapped and unhandcuffed from his perch; he did not feel the clothes being replaced on his inflamed back, nor did he even rouse as he was carried into his own car and driven swiftly away.

And then again he was being shaken by the shoulder, woken up. Whimpering, he groped for the steering wheel—and did not find it. The shaking at his shoulder went on.

"All right," he blubbered. "All right, I'm trying to do it. Can't you let me sleep a little—just once . . ."

"Sir Melvin! Sir Melvin!"

Flager forced open his bloodshot eyes. His hands were free. He was sitting in his own car, which was standing outside his own house. It was his valet who was shaking him.

"Sir Melvin! Try to wake up, sir. Where have you been? Are you ill, sir?"

Flager found strength to move his head from one side to the other.

"No," he said. "I just want to sleep."

And with a deep groan he let his swollen eyelids droop again, and sank back into soothing abysses of delicious rest.

When he woke up again he was in his own bedroom. For a long time he lay without moving, wallowing in the heavenly comfort of the soft mattress and cool linen, savouring the last second of sensual pleasure that could be squeezed out of the most beautiful awakening that he could remember.

"He's coming round," said a low voice at last, and with a sigh Flager opened his eyes.

His bed seemed to be surrounded with an audience such as a seventeenth-century monarch might have beheld at a levee. There was his valet, his secretary, his doctor, a nurse, and a heavy and stolid man of authoritative appearance who held an unmistakable bowler hat. The doctor had a hand on his pulse, and the others stood by expectantly.

"All right, Sir Melvin," said the physician. "You may talk for a little while now, if you want to, but you mustn't excite yourself. This gentleman here is a detective who wants to ask you a few questions."

The man with the bowler hat came nearer.

"What happened to you, Sir Melvin?" he asked.

Flager stared at him for several seconds. Words rose to his lips, but somehow he did not utter them.

"Nothing," he said at length. "I've been away for the week-end, that's all. What the devil's all this fuss about?"

"But your back, Sir Melvin!" protested the doctor. "You look as if you'd had a terrible beating—"

"I had a slight accident," snapped Flager. "And what the devil has it got to do with you, sir, anyway? Who the devil sent for all of you?"

His valet swallowed.

"I did, Sir Melvin," he stammered. "When I couldn't wake you up all day yesterday—and you disappeared from the theatre without a word to anybody, and didn't come back for two days—"

"And why the devil shouldn't I disappear for two days?" barked Flager weakly. "I'll disappear for a month if I feel like it. Do I pay you to pry into my movements? And can't I sleep all day if I want to without waking up to find a lot of quacks and policemen infesting my room like vultures? Get out of my house, the whole damned lot of you! Get out, d'you hear?"

Somebody opened the door, and the congregation drifted out, shaking its heads and muttering, to the accompaniment of continued exhortations in Flager's rasping voice.

His secretary was the last to go, and Flager called him back.

"Get Nyson on the telephone," he ordered. "I'll speak to him myself."

The secretary hesitated for a moment, and then picked up the bedside telephone and dialled the number dubiously.

Flager took the instrument as soon as his manager answered.

"Nyson?" he said. "Get in touch with all our branch depots immediately. From now on, all our drivers will be on a forty-hour week, and they get a twenty per cent rise as from the date we took them on. Engage as many more men as you need to make up the schedules."

He heard Nyson's incredulous gasp over the line.

"I beg your pardon. Sir Melvin—did you say—"

"Yes, I did!" snarled Flager, "You heard me all right. And after that, you can find out if that cyclist Johnson killed left any dependents. I want to do something for them . . ."

His voice faded away, and the microphone slipped through his fingers. His secretary looked at him quickly, and saw that his eyes were closed and the hemispherical mound of his abdomen was rising and falling rhythmically.

Sir Melvin Flager was asleep again.

THE UNCRITICAL PUBLISHER

Even the strongest men have their weak moments.

Peter Quentin once wrote a book. Many young men do, but usually with more disastrous results. Moreover he did it without saying a word to anyone, which is perhaps even more uncommon, and even the Saint did not hear about it until after the crime had been committed.

"Next time you're thinking of being rude to me," said Peter Quentin, on that night of revelation, "please remember that you're talking to a budding novelist whose work has been compared to Dumas, Tolstoy, Conan Doyle, and others."

Simon Templar choked over his highball.

"Only pansies bud," he said severely. "Novelists fester. Of course, it's possible to be both."

"I mean it," insisted Peter seriously. "I was keeping it quiet until I heard the verdict, and I had a letter from the publishers today."

There was no mistaking his earnestness, and the Saint regarded him with affectionate gloom. His vision of the future filled him with overwhelming pessimism. He had seen the fate of other young men—healthy, upright young men who had had a book published.

He had seen them tread the downhill path of pink shirts, velvet coats, long hair, quill pens, cocktail parties, and beards, until finally they sank into the awful limbos of Bloomsbury and were no longer visible to the naked eye. The prospect of such a doom for anyone like Peter Quentin, who had been with him in so many bigger and better crimes, cast a shadow of great melancholy across his spirits.

"Didn't Kathleen try to stop you?" he asked.

"Of course not," said Peter proudly. "She helped me. I owe—"

"—it all to her," said the Saint cynically. "All right. I know the line. But if you ever come out with 'My Work' within my hearing, I shall throw you under a bus . . . You'd better let me see this letter. And order me some more Old Curio while I'm reading it—I need strength."

He took the document with his fingertips, as if it were unclean, and opened it out on the bar. But after his first glance at the letter-head his twinkling blue eyes steadied abruptly, and he read the epistle through with more than ordinary interest.

Dear Sir,

We have now gone into your novel THE GAY ADVENTURER, *and our readers report that it is very entertaining and ably written, with the verve of Dumas, the dramatic power of Tolstoy, and ingenuity of Conan Doyle.*

We shall therefore be delighted to set up same in best small pica type to form a volume of about 320 p.p., machine on good antique paper, bind in red cloth with title in gold lettering, and put up in specially designed artistic wrapper, at cost to yourself of only £600 (Six Hundred Pounds) and to publish same at our own expense in the United Kingdom at a net price of 15/ (Fifteen Shillings). We believe it will form a most acceptable and popular volume which should command a wide sale.

We will further agree to send you on date of publication twelve presentation copies, and to send copies for review to all principal magazines and newspapers, and further to pay you a royalty of 25% (twenty-five per cent) on all copies sold of this Work.

The work can be put in hand immediately on receipt of your acceptance of these terms.

Trusting to hear from you at your earliest convenience,

We beg to remain, dear Sir, Faithfully yours, for
HERBERT G. PARSTONE & Co.
Herbert G. Parstone,
Managing Director

Simon folded the letter and handed it back with a sigh of relief.

"Okay, Peter," he said cheerfully. "I bought that one. What's the swindle, and can I come in on it?"

"I don't know of any swindle," said Peter puzzledly. "What do you mean?"

The Saint frowned. "D'you mean to tell me you sent your book to Parstone in all seriousness?"

"Of course I did. I saw an advertisement of his in some literary paper, and I don't know much about publishers—"

"You've never heard of him before?"

"No."

Simon picked up his glass and strengthened himself with a deep draught.

"Herbert G. Parstone," he said, "is England's premier exponent of the publishing racket. Since you don't seem to know it, Peter, let me tell you that no reputable publisher in this or any other country publishes books at the author's expense, except an occasional highly technical work which goes out for posterity rather than profit. I gather that your book is by no means technical. Therefore you don't pay the publisher: he pays you—and if he's any use he stands you expensive lunches as well."

"But Parstone offers to pay—"

"A twenty-five per cent royalty. I know. Well, if you were something like a best seller you might get that, but on a first novel no publisher would give you more than ten, and then he'd probably lose money. After six months Parstone would probably send you a statement showing a sale of two hundred copies, you'd get a cheque from him for thirty-seven pounds ten, and that's the last trace you'd see of your six hundred quid. He's simply trading on the fact that one out of every three people you meet thinks he could write a book if he tried, one out of every three of 'em try it, and one out of every three of those tries to get it published.

"The very fact that a manuscript is sent to him tells him that the author is a potential sucker, because anyone who goes into the writing business seriously takes the trouble to find out a bit about publishers before he starts slinging his stuff around. The rest of his game is just playing on the vanity of mugs. And the mugs—mugs like yourself, Peter—old gents with political theories, hideous women with ghastly poems, schoolgirls with nauseating love stories—rush up to pour their money into his lap for the joy of seeing their repulsive tripe in print. I've known about Herbert for many years, old lad, but I never thought you'd be the sap to fall for him."

"I don't believe you," said Peter glumly.

An elderly mouse-like man who was drinking at the bar beside him coughed apologetically and edged bashfully nearer.

"Excuse me, sir," he said diffidently, "but your friend's telling the truth."

"How do you know?" asked Peter suspiciously. "I can usually guess when he's telling the truth—he makes a face as if it hurt him."

"He isn't pulling your leg this time, sir," said the man. "I happen to be a proof-reader at Parstone's."

The surprising thing about coincidences is that they so often happen. The mouse-like man was one of those amazing accidents on which the fate of nations may hinge, but there was no logical reason why he should not have been drinking at that bar as probably as at any other hostel in the district. And yet there is no doubt that if Mr Herbert Parstone could have foreseen the accident he would have bought that particular public house for the simple pleasure of closing it down lest any such coincidence should happen, but unhappily for him Mr Herbert Parstone was not a clairvoyant.

This proof-reader—the term, by the way, refers to the occupation and not necessarily to the alcoholic content of the man—had been with Parstone for twelve years, and he was ready for a change.

"I was with Parstone when he was just a small jobbing printer," he said, "before he took up this publishing game. That's all he is now, really—a printer. But he's going to have to get along without me. In the last three years I've taken one cut after another, till I don't earn enough money to feed myself properly, and I can't stand it any longer. I've got four more months on my contract, but after that I'm going to take another job."

"Did you read my book?" asked Peter.

The man shook his head.

"Nobody read your book, sir—if you'll excuse my telling you. It was just put on a shelf for three weeks, and after that Parstone sent you his usual letter. That's what happens to everything that's sent in to him. If he gets his money, the book goes straight into the shop, and the proof-reader's the first man who has to wade through it. Parstone doesn't care whether it's written in Hindustani."

"But surely," protested Peter half-heartedly, "he couldn't carry on a racket like that in broad daylight and get away with it?"

The reader looked at him with a rather tired smile on his mouse-like features.

"It's perfectly legal, sir. Parstone publishes the book. He prints copies and sends them around. It isn't his fault if the reviewers won't review it and the booksellers won't buy it. He carries out his legal undertaking. But it's a dirty business."

After a considerably longer conversation, in the course of which a good deal more Scotch was consumed, Peter Quentin was convinced. He was so crestfallen on the way home that Simon took pity on him.

"Let me read this opus," he said, "if you've got a spare copy. Maybe it isn't so lousy, and if there's anything in it we'll send it along to some other place."

He had the book the next day, and after ploughing through the first dozen pages his worst fears were realized. Peter Quentin was not destined to take his place in the genealogy of literature with Dumas, Tolstoy, and Conan Doyle. The art of writing was not in him. His spelling had a grand simplicity that would have delighted the more progressive orthographists, his grammatical constructions followed in the footsteps of Gertrude Stein, and his punctuation marks seemed to have more connection with intervals for thought and opening beer-bottles than with the requirements of syntax. Moreover, like most first novels, it was embarrassingly personal.

It was this fact which made Simon follow it to the bitter end, for the hero of the story was one "Ivan Grail, the Robbin Hood of modern crime," who could without difficulty be identified with the Saint himself, his "beutiful wife," and "Frank Morris his acomplis whos hard-bitten featurs consealed a very clever brain and witt." Simon Templar swallowed all the flattering evidences of hero-worship that adorned the untidy pages, and actually blushed. But after he had reached the conclusion—inscribed "FINNIS" in triumphant capitals—he did some heavy thinking.

Later on he saw Peter again.

"What was it that bit your features so hard?" he asked. "Did you try to kiss an alligator?"

Peter turned pink. "I had to describe them somehow," he said defensively.

"You're too modest," said the Saint, after inspecting him again. "They were not merely bitten—they were thoroughly chewed."

"Well, what about the book?" said Peter hopefully. "Was it any good?"

"It was lousy," Simon informed him, with the privileged candour of friendship. "It would have made Dumas turn in his grave. All the same, it may be more readable after I've revised it for you. And perhaps we will let Comrade Parstone publish it after all."

Peter blinked. "But I thought—"

"I have an idea," said the Saint. "Parstone has published dud books too long. It's time he had a good one. Will you get your manuscript back from him, Peter—tell him you want to make a few corrections, and that you'll send him his money and let him print it. For anyone who so successfully conceals a very clever brain and wit," he added cruelly, "there are much more profitable ways of employing them than writing books, as you ought to know."

For two weeks after that the Saint sat at his typewriter for seven hours a day, hammering out page after page of neat manuscript at astonishing speed. He did not merely revise Peter Quentin's story—he re-wrote it from cover to cover, and the result would certainly not have been recognized by its original creator.

The book was sent in again from his own address, and consequently Peter did not see the proofs. Simon Templar read them himself, and his ribs were aching long before he had finished.

The Gay Adventurer, by Peter Quentin, was formally pushed out upon a callous world about two months later. *The Times* did not notice it, the library buyers did not refill their fountain pens to sign the order forms, the lynx-eyed scouts of Hollywood did not rush in with open contracts, but nevertheless it was possible for a man with vast patience and dogged determination to procure a copy, by which achievement Mr Parstone had fulfilled the letter of his contract.

Simon Templar did not need to exercise patience and determination to obtain his copy, because the author's presentation dozen came to his apartment, and it happened that Peter Quentin came there on the same morning.

Peter noticed the open parcel of books, and fell on them at once, whinnying like an eager stallion. But he had scarcely glanced over the first page when he turned to the Saint with wrathful eyes.

"This isn't my book at all," he shouted indignantly.

"We'll call it a collaboration if you like," said the Saint generously. "But I thought you might as well have the credit. My name is so famous already—"

Peter had been turning the pages frantically.

"But this . . . this is awful!" he expostulated. "It's . . . it's—"

"Of course it is," agreed the Saint. "And that's why you must never tell anyone that I had anything to do with it. When the case comes to court, I shall expect you to perjure yourself blue in the face on that subject."

After the revelations that have been made in the early stages of this story, no one will imagine that on the same morning Mr Herbert Parstone was pacing feverishly up and down his office, quivering with anxiety and parental pride, stopping every now and then to peer at the latest circulation figures rushed in by scurrying office-boys and bawling frantic orders to an excited staff of secretaries, salesmen, shippers, clerks, exporters, and truck drivers.

As a matter of fact, even the most important and reputable publishers do not behave like that. They are usually too busy concentrating on mastering that loose shoulder and smooth follow-through which carries the ball well over that nasty bunker on the way to the fourteenth.

Mr Herbert Parstone was not playing golf, because he had a bad cold, and he was in his office when the Saint called. The name on the card that was sent in to him was unfamiliar, but Mr Parstone never refused to see anyone who was kind enough to walk into his parlour.

He was a short ginger-haired man with the kind of stomach without which no morning coat and gold watch-chain can be seen to their best advantage, and the redness of his prominent nose was not entirely due to his temporary affliction.

"Mr Teblar?" he said, with great but obstructed geniality. "Please sit dowd. I dode thig I've had the pleasure of beetig you before, have I?"

"I don't think so," said the Saint pleasantly. "But any real pleasure is worth waiting for." He took the precious volume which he was carrying from under his arm, and held it up. "Did you publish this?"

Mr Parstone looked at it. "Yes," he said, "that is one of our publicashuds. A bost excelledd ad ibportad book, if I bay perbid byself to say so. A book, I bight say, which answers problebs which are dear to every wud of us today."

"It will certainly have some problems to answer," said the Saint, "and I expect they'll be dear enough. Do you know the name of the principal character in this book? Do you know who this biography is alleged to be about?"

"Biography?" stammered Mr Parstone, blinking at the cover. "The book is a dovel. A work of fickshud. It is clearly explaid—"

"The book is supposed to be a biography," said the Saint. "And do you know the name of the principal character?"

Mr Parstone's brow creased with thought.

"Pridcipal character?" he repeated. "Led be see, led be see. I ought to dough, oughtud I?" He blew his nose several times, sniffed, sighed, and spread out his hand uncertainly. "Iddn it abazing?" he said. "The dabe was od the tip of by tug, but dow I cadd rebember id."

"The name is Simon Templar," said the Saint grimly, and Mr Parstone sat up.

"What?" he ejaculated.

Simon opened the book and showed him the name in plain print. Then he took it away to a chair and lighted a cigarette.

"Rather rude of you, wasn't it?" he murmured.

"Well, by dear Bister Teblar," said Parstone winningly. "I trust you are dot thinkig that any uncomblibendary referedds was intended. Far frob id. These rebarkable coidcidedces will happud. Ad yet it is dot every yug bad of your age who fides his dabe preserved for posterity id such a work as that. The hero of that book, as I rebember him, was a fellow of outstaddig charb—"

"He was a low criminal," said the Saint virtuously. "Your memory is failing you, Herbert. Let me read you some of the best passages."

He turned to a page he had marked.

"Listen to this, Herbert," he said. "'Simon Templar was never particular about how he made money, so long as he made it. The drug traffic was only one of his many sources of income, and his conscience was never touched by the thought of the hundreds of lives he ruined by his insatiable avarice. Once, in a night club, he pointed out to me a fine and beautiful girl on whose lovely face the ravages of dope were already beginning to make their mark. "I've had two thousand pounds from her since I started her on the stuff," he said gloatingly, "and I'll have five thousand more before it kills her." I could multiply instances of that kind by the score, and refrain only from fear of nauseating my readers. Sufficient, at least, has already been said to show what an unspeakable ruffian was this man who called himself the Saint.'"

However hard it might have been for Mr Parstone to place the name of Simon Templar, he was by no means ignorant of the Saint. His watery eyes popped halfway out of their sockets, and his jaw hardened at the same time.

"So you're the Saind?" he said.

"Of course," murmured Simon.

"Id your own words, a low cribidal—"

Simon shook his head.

"Oh, no, Herbert," he said. "By no means as low as that. My reputation may be bad, but it's only rumour. You may whisper it to your friends, but the law doesn't allow you to put it in writing. That's libel. And you couldn't even get Chief Inspector Teal to testify that my record would justify anything like the language this book of yours has used about me.

"My sins were always fairly idealistic, and devoted to the squashing of beetles like yourself—not to trading in drugs and grinding the faces of the poor. But you haven't heard anything like the whole of it. Listen to some more."

He turned to another selected passage.

"'The Saint,'" he read, "'always seemed to derive a peculiar malicious pleasure from robbing and swindling those who could least afford to lose. To my dying day, I shall be haunted by the memory of the fiendish glee which distorted his face when he told me that he had stolen five pounds from a woman with seven children, who had scraped and saved for months to get the money together. He accepted the money from her as a fee for trying to trace the grave of her father, who had been reported "missing" in 1943. Of course he never made any attempt to carry out his share of the bargain. He played this cruel trick on several occasions, and always with the same sadistic pleasure, which I believe meant far more to him than the actual cash which he derived from it.'"

"Is that id the book too?" asked Parstone hoarsely.

"Naturally," said the Saint. "That's what I'm reading it from. And there are lots more interesting things. Look here. 'The bogus companies floated by Templar, in which thousands upon thousands of widows and orphans were deprived—'"

"Wait!" interrupted Parstone tremblingly. "This is terrible—a terrible coidcideds. The book will be withdrawd at wuds. Hardly eddywud will have had tibe to read it. Ad if eddy sball cobbensation I cad give—"

Simon closed his book with a smile and laid it on Mr Parstone's desk.

"Shall we say fifty thousand pounds?" he suggested affably.

Mr Parstone's face reddened to the verge of an apoplectic stroke, and he brought up his handkerchief with shaking hands.

"How buch?" he whispered.

"Fifty thousand pounds," repeated the Saint. "After all, that's a very small amount of damages to ask for a libel like this. If the case has to go to court, I think it will be admitted that never in the whole history of modern law has such a colossal libel been put on paper. If there is any crime under the sun of which I'm not accused in that book, I'll sit down right now and eat it. And there are three hundred and twenty pages of it—eighty thousand words of continuous and unbridled insult. For a thing like that, Herbert, I think fifty thousand pounds is pretty cheap."

"You could'n get it," said Parstone harshly. "It's the author's liability—"

"I know that clause," answered the Saint coolly, "and you may be interested to know that it has no legal value whatever. In a successful libel action, the author, printer, and publisher are joint tortfeasors, and none of them can indemnify the other. Ask your solicitor. As a matter of fact," he added prophetically, "I don't expect I shall be able to recover anything from the author, anyway. Authors are usually broke. But you are both the printer and the publisher, and I'm sure I can collect from you."

Mr Parstone stared at him with blanched lips.

"But fifty thousad pouds is ibpossible," he whined. "It would ruid be!"

"That's what I mean to do, dear old bird," said the Saint gently. "You've gone on swindling a lot of harmless idiots for too long already, and now I want you to see what it feels like when it happens to you."

He stood up, and collected his hat.

"I'll leave you the book," he said, "in case you want to entertain yourself some more. But I've got another copy, and if I don't receive your cheque by the first post on Friday morning it will go straight to my solicitors. And you can't kid yourself about what that will mean."

For a long time after he had gone Mr Herbert Parstone sat quivering in his chair. And then he reached out for the book and began to skim through its pages. And with every page his livid face went greyer. There was no doubt about it. Simon Templar had spoken the truth. The book was the most monumental libel that could ever have found its way into print. Parstone's brain reeled before the accumulation of calumnies which it unfolded.

His furious ringing of the bell brought his secretary running.

"Fide me that proof-reader!" he howled. "Fide be the dab fool who passed this book!" He flung the volume on to the floor at her feet. "Sed hib to be at wuds! I'll show hib. I'll bake hib suffer. By God, I'll—"

The other things that Mr Parstone said he would do cannot be recorded in such a respectable publication as this.

His secretary picked up the book and looked at the title.

"Mr Timmins left yesterday—he was the man you fired four months ago," she said, but even then Mr Parstone was no wiser.

THE NOBLE SPORTSMAN

It would be difficult to imagine two more ill-assorted guests at a country house party than Simon Templar and Chief Inspector Teal. The Saint, of course, was in his element. He roared up the drive in his big cream and red sports car and a huge camel-hair coat as if he had been doing that sort of thing for half his life, which he had. But Mr Teal, driving up in the ancient and rickety station taxi, and alighting cumbrously in his neat serge suit and bowler hat, fitted less successfully into the picture. He looked more like a builder's foreman who had called to take measurements for a new bathroom, which he was not.

But that they should have been members of the same house party at all was the most outstanding freak of circumstance, and it was only natural that one of them should take the first possible opportunity to inquire into the motives of the other.

Mr Teal came into the Saint's room while Simon was dressing for dinner, and the Saint looked him over with some awe.

"I see you've got a new tie," he murmured. "Did your old one come undone?"

The detective ran a finger round the inside of his collar, which fitted as if he had bought it when he was several years younger and measured less than eighteen inches around the neck.

"How long have you known Lord Yearleigh?" he asked bluntly.

"I've met him a few times," said the Saint casually.

He appeared to be speaking the truth, and Mr Teal was not greatly surprised—the Saint had a habit of being acquainted with the most unlikely people. But Teal's curiosity was not fully satisfied.

"I suppose you're here for the same reason as I am," he said.

"More or less, I take it," answered Simon. "Do you think Yearleigh will be murdered?"

"You've seen the anonymous letters he's been receiving?"

"Some of 'em. But lots of people get anonymous threatening letters without getting a Chief Inspector of Scotland Yard sent down as a private pet."

"They aren't all MPs, younger sons of dukes, and well-known influential men," said the detective rather cynically. "What do you think about it?"

"If he is murdered, I hope it's exciting," said the Saint callously. "Poison is so dull. A hail of machine-gun bullets through the library window would be rather diverting, though . . . What are you getting at, Claud—are you trying to steal my act or are you looking for an alliance?"

Mr Teal unwrapped a wafer of chewing gum and stuck it in his mouth, and watched the Saint fixing buttons in a white waistcoat with a stolid air of detachment that he was far from feeling. It was sometimes hard for him to remember that that debonair young brigand with the dangerous mouth and humorous blue eyes had personally murdered many men, beyond all practical doubt but equally beyond all possibility of legal proof, and he found it hard to remember then. But nevertheless he remembered it. And the fact that those men had never died without sound reason did not ease his mind—the Saint had a disconcerting habit of assassinating men whose pollution of the universe was invisible to anyone else until he unmasked it.

"I'd like to know why you were invited," said Mr Teal.

Simon Templar put on his waistcoat, brushed his tuxedo, and put that on also. He stood in front of the dressing-table, lighting a cigarette.

"If I suggested that Yearleigh may have thought that I'd be more use than a policeman, you wouldn't be flattered," he remarked. "So why worry about suspecting me until he really is dead? I suppose you've already locked up the silver and had the jewels removed to the bank, so I don't see how I can bother you any other way."

They went downstairs together, with Chief Inspector Teal macerating his spearmint in gloomy silence. If the Saint had not been a fellow-guest he would have taken his responsibilities less seriously, and yet he was unable to justify any suspicion that the Saint was against him. He knew nothing about his host which might have inspired the Saint to take an unlawful interest in his expectation of life.

The public, and what was generally known of the private, life of Lord Thornton Yearleigh was so far above reproach that it was sometimes held up as a model for others. He was a man of about sixty-five with a vigour that was envied by men who were twenty-five years his junior, a big-built natural athlete with snow-white hair that seemed absurdly premature as a crown for his clear ruddy complexion and erect carriage. At sixty-five, he was a scratch golfer, a first-class tennis player, a splendid horseman, and a polo player of considerable skill. In those other specialised pastimes which in England are particularly dignified with the name of "sport," hunting, shooting, and fishing, his name was a by-word. He swam in the sea throughout the winter, made occasional published comments on the decadence of modern youth, could always be depended on to quote "mens sana in corpore sano" at the right moment, and generally stood as the living personification of those robust and brainless spartan ideals of cold baths and cricket which have contributed so much to England's share in the cultural progress of the world. He was a jovial and widely popular figure, and although he was certainly a member of the House of Commons, the

Saint had not yet been known to murder a politician for that crime alone—even if he had often been known to express a desire to do so.

There was, of course, no reason at all why the prospective assassin should have been a member of the party, but his reflections on the Saint's character had started a train of thought in the detective's mind, and he found himself weighing up the other guests speculatively during dinner.

The discussion turned on the private bill which Yearleigh was to introduce, with the approval of the Government, when Parliament reassembled during the following week, and Teal, who would have no strong views on the subject until his daily newspaper told him what he ought to think, found that his role of obscure listener gave him an excellent chance to study the characters of the others who took part.

"I shouldn't be surprised if that bill of mine had something to do with these letters I've been getting," said Yearleigh. "Those damned Communists are capable of anything. If they only took some exercise and got some fresh air they'd work all that nonsense out of their systems. Young Maurice is a bit that way himself," he added slyly.

Maurice Vould flushed slightly. He was about thirty-five, thin and spectacled and somewhat untidy, with a curiously transparent ivory skin that was the exact antithesis of Yearleigh's weather-beaten complexion. He was, Teal had already ascertained, a cousin of Lady Yearleigh's; he had a private income of about 800 pounds a year, and devoted his time to writing poems and essays which a very limited public acclaimed as being of unusual worth.

"I admit that I believe in the divine right of mankind to earn a decent wage, to have enough food to eat and a decent house to live in, and to be free to live his life without interference," he said in a rather pleasant quiet voice. "If that is Communism, I suppose I'm a Communist."

"But presumably you wouldn't include armed attack by a foreign power under your heading of interference," said a man on the opposite side of the table.

He was a sleek well-nourished man with heavy sallow cheeks and a small diamond set in the ring on his third finger, and Teal knew that he was Sir Bruno Walmar, the chairman and presiding genius of the Walmar Oil Corporation and all its hundred subsidiaries. His voice was as harsh as his appearance was smooth, with an aggressive domineering quality to it which did not so much offer argument as defy it, but the voice did not silence Vould.

"That isn't the only concern of Yearleigh's bill," he said.

The Right Honourable Mark Ormer, War Minister in the reigning Government, scratched the centre of his grey moustache in the rather old-maidish gesture which the cartoonist had made familiar to everyone in England, and said, "The National Preparedness Bill merely requires a certain amount of military training to be included in the education of every British boy, so that if his services should be needed in the defence of his country in after life, he should be qualified to play his part without delay. No other eventuality has been envisaged."

"How can you say that no other eventuality has been envisaged?" asked Vould quietly. "You take a boy and teach him the rudiments of killing as if they were a desirable thing to know. You give him a uniform to wear and impress upon him the fact that he is a fighting man in the making. You make him shoot blank cartridges at other boys, and treat the whole pantomime as a good joke. You create a man who will instinctively answer a call to arms whenever the call is made, and how can you sit there tonight and say that you know exactly and only in what circumstances somebody will start to shout the call?"

"I think we can depend on the temperament of the English people to be sure of that," said Ormer indulgently.

"I think you can also depend on the hysteria of most mobs when their professional politicians wave a flag," answered Maurice Vould. "There probably was a time when people fought to defend their countries, but now they have to fight to save the faces of their politicians and the bank balances of their business men."

"Stuff and nonsense!" interjected Lord Yearleigh heartily. "Englishmen have got too much sense. A bit of military training is good for a boy. Teaches him discipline. Besides, you can't stop people fighting—healthy people—with that watery pacifist talk. It's human nature."

"Like killing your next-door neighbour because you want to steal his lawn mower," said Vould gently. "That's another primitive instinct which human nature hasn't been able to eradicate."

Yearleigh gave a snort of impatience, and Sir Bruno Walmar rubbed his smooth hands over each other and said in his rasping voice, "I suppose you were a conscientious objector during the last war, Mr Vould?"

"I'm sorry to disappoint you," said Vould, with a pale smile, "but I was enjoying the experience of inhaling poison gas when I was sixteen years old. While you, Ormer, were making patriotic speeches, and you, Walmar, were making money. That's the difference between us. I've seen a war, and so I know what it's like, and I've also lived long enough after it to know how much good it does."

"What's your opinion, Mr Templar?" asked Yearleigh. "Don't you think Maurice is talking like one of these damned street-corner Reds?" The Saint nodded.

"Yes, I do," he said. There was a moment's silence, and then he added thoughtfully, "I rather like these street-corner Reds—one or two of them are really sincere."

Chief Inspector Teal nibbled a crust of bread secure in his voluntary self-effacement, while Mrs Ormer made some twittering remark and the thread of conversation drifted off into a less dangerously controversial topic. He had, he admitted, failed dismally in his little solitaire game of spotting the prospective murderer. A Cabinet Minister, a multi-millionaire, and a poet did not seem to comprise a gathering amongst whom a practical detective could seek hopefully for felons. The only suspect left for him was still the Saint, and yet even when the meal was finished, after the ladies had retired and the port and cigars had been passed around, he had no reason, actual or intuitive, to believe that Simon Templar was meditating the murder of his host.

Yearleigh rose, and there was a general pushing back of chairs. The noble sportsman caught the detective's eye, and for the first time since Teal's arrival the object of his invitation was brought up again.

"I've had another of those damned letters," he said.

He produced it from his pocket, and held it out in a movement that was a general announcement that anyone who cared to might peruse it. Vould and the Saint, who were nearest, shared it with Mr Teal.

The message contained two lines in laboured script.

> *Since you have ignored my previous warnings,*
> *you will learn your lesson tonight.*

There was no signature—not even the skeleton haloed figure which Teal had half expected to see.

The detective folded the letter and put it away in his wallet. His faded sleepy eyes turned back to his host.

"I'd like to have a talk with you later on, sir," he said. "I have some men in the village, and with your permission I'd like to post special guards."

"Certainly," agreed Yearleigh at once. "Have your talk now. I'm sure the others will excuse us. . . . Wait a moment, though." He turned to Maurice Vould. "You wanted to have a talk with me as well, didn't you?"

Vould nodded.

"But it can wait a few minutes," he said, and both Teal and the Saint saw that his pale face was even paler, and the eyes behind his big glasses were bright with sudden strain.

"Why should it?" exclaimed Yearleigh good-humouredly. "You modern young intellectuals are always in a hurry, and I promised you this talk three or four days ago. You should have had it sooner if I hadn't had to go away. Inspector Teal won't mind waiting, and I don't expect to be murdered for another half-hour."

Simon fell in at Teal's side as they went down the hall, leaving the other two on their way to Yearleigh's study, and quite naturally the detective asked the question which was uppermost in his mind.

"Have you any more ideas?"

"I don't know," was the Saint's unsatisfactory response. "Who were you most interested in at dinner?"

"I was watching Vould," Teal confessed.

"You would be," said the Saint. "I don't suppose you even noticed Lady Yearleigh."

Teal did not answer, but he admitted to himself that the accusation was nearly true. As they went into the drawing-room his sleepy eyes looked for her at once, and saw her talking to Ormer on one side of her and Walmar on the other. He suddenly realised that she was young enough to be Yearleigh's daughter—she might have been thirty-five, but she scarcely looked thirty. She had the same pale and curiously transparent complexion as her cousin Vould, but in her it combined with blue eyes and flaxen hair to form an almost ethereal beauty. He could not help feeling the contrast between her and her husband—knowing Yearleigh only by reputation, and never having visited the house, he would have expected Lady Yearleigh to be a robust horsey woman, at her best in tweeds and given to brutal bluntness. Mr Teal had never read poetry, but if he had, Rossetti's "Blessed Damozel" would have perfectly expressed what he felt about this Lady Yearleigh whom Simon Templar had made him notice practically for the first time.

"She's very attractive," said Teal, which was a rhapsody from him.

"And intelligent," said the Saint. "Did you notice that?"

The detective nodded vaguely.

"She has a wonderful husband."

Simon put down his cigar-butt in an ashtray and took out his cigarette-case. Teal knew subconsciously that his hesitation over those commonplace movements was merely a piece of that theatrical timing in which the Saint delighted to indulge; he knew that the Saint was about to say something illuminating, but even as Simon Templar opened his mouth the sound of the shot boomed through the house.

There was an instant's terrible stillness, while the echoes of the reverberation seemed to vibrate tenuously through the tense air like the vibrations of a cello-string humming below the pitch of hearing, and then Lady Yearleigh came to her feet like a ghost rising, with her ivory skin and flaxen hair making her a blanched apparition in the dimly lighted room.

"My God," she breathed, "he's killed him!"

Teal, who was nearest the door, awoke from his momentary stupor and rushed towards it, but the Saint reached it first. He ran at the Saint's shoulder to the study, and as they came to it the door was flung open and Lord Yearleigh stood there, a straight steady figure with a revolver in his hand.

"You're too late," he said, with a note of triumph in his voice. "I got him myself."

"Who?" snapped Teal, and burst past him into the room, to see the answer to his question lying still and sprawled out in the middle of the rich carpet.

It was Maurice Vould.

Teal went over to him. He could barely distinguish the puncture of the bullet in the back of Vould's dinner jacket, but the scar in his shirt-front was larger, with a spreading red stain under it. Teal opened the dead man's fingers and detached an old Italian dagger, holding it carefully in his handkerchief.

"What happened?" he asked.

"He started raving," said Yearleigh, "about that bill of mine. He said it would be better for me to die than to take that bill into the House. I said, 'Don't be silly,' and he grabbed that dagger—I use it as a paper-knife—off the desk, and attacked me. I threw him off, but he'd become a maniac. I got a drawer open and pulled out this revolver, meaning to frighten him. He turned to the window and yelled, 'Come in, comrades! Come in and kill!' I saw another man at the window with a scarf round his face, and fired at him. Maurice must have moved, or I must have been shaken up, or something, because I hit Maurice. The other man ran away."

Still holding the knife, Teal turned and lumbered towards the open french windows. Ormer and Walmar, who had arrived while Yearleigh was talking, went after him more slowly, but the Saint was beside him when he stood outside, listening to the murmurs of the night.

In Teal's mind was a queer amazement and relief, that for once Simon Templar was proved innocent and he had not that possibility to contend with, and he looked at the Saint with half a mind to apologise for his suspicions. And then he saw that the Saint's face was deeply lined in the dim starlight, and he heard the Saint muttering in a terrible whisper, "Oh, hell! It was my fault. It was my fault!"

"What do you mean?" asked the startled detective. Simon gripped him by the arm, and looked over his shoulder. Ormer and Walmar were behind them, venturing more cautiously into the dangerous dark. The Saint spoke louder.

"You've got your job to do," he said rather wildly. "Photographers—finger-prints—"

"It's a dear case," protested Teal, as he felt himself being urged away.

"You'll want a doctor—coroners—your men from the village. I'll take you in my car . . ."

Feeling that the universe had suddenly sprung a high fever, Teal found himself hustled helplessly around the broad terrace to the front of the house. They had reached the drive before he managed to collect his wits and stop.

"Have you gone mad?" he demanded, planting his feet solidly in the gravel and refusing to move further. "What do you mean—it was your fault?"

"I killed him," said the Saint savagely. "I killed Maurice Vould!"

"You?" Teal ejaculated, with an uncanny start. "You're crazy," he said.

"I killed him," said the Saint, "by culpable negligence. Because I could have saved his life. I was mad. I was crazy. But I'm not now. All right. Go back to the house. You have somebody to arrest."

A flash of memory went across Teal's mind—the memory of a pale ghostly woman rising from her chair, her voice saying, "My God, he's killed him!"—the hint of a frightful foreknowledge. A cold shiver touched his spine.

"You don't mean—Lady Yearleigh?" he said incredulously. "It's impossible. With a husband like hers—"

"You think he was a good husband, don't you?" said the Saint. "Because he was a noble sportsman. Cold baths and cricket. Hunting, shooting, and fishing. I suppose it's too much to expect you to put yourself in the place of a woman—a woman like her—who was married to that?"

"You think she was in love with Vould?"

"Of course she was in love with Vould. That's why I asked you if you'd looked at her at all during dinner—when Vould was talking. If you had, even you might have seen it. But you're so full of conventions. You think that any woman ought to adore a great fat-headed blustering athlete—because a number of equally fat-headed men adore him. You think she oughtn't to think much of a pale poet who wears glasses, because the fat-headed athletes don't understand him, as if the ability to hit a ball with a bat were the only criterion of value in the world. But I tried to tell you that she was intelligent. Of course she was in love with Vould, and Vould with her. They were made for each other. I'll also bet you that Vould didn't want an interview with Yearleigh to make more protests about that bill, but to tell him that he was going to run away with his wife."

Teal said helplessly, "You mean—when Yearleigh objected—Vould had made up his mind to kill him. Lady Yearleigh knew, and that's what she meant by—"

"She didn't mean that at all," said the Saint. "Vould believed in peace. You heard him at dinner. Have you forgotten that remark of his? He pointed out that men had learned not to kill their neighbours so that they could steal their lawn mowers. Why should he believe that they ought to kill their neighbours so that they could steal their wives?"

"You can't always believe what a man says—"

"You can believe him when he's sincere."

"Sincere enough," Teal mentioned sceptically, "to try to kill his host."

Simon was quiet for a moment, kicking the toe of his shoe into the gravel.

"Did you notice that Vould was shot in the back?" he said.

"You heard Yearleigh's explanation."

"You can't always believe what a man says—can you?"

Suddenly the Saint reached out and took the dagger which Teal was still holding. He unwrapped the handkerchief from it, and Teal let out an exclamation. "You damn fool!"

"Because I'm destroying your precious finger-prints?" murmured the Saint coolly. "You immortal ass! If you can hold a knife in your handkerchief to keep from marking it, couldn't anybody else?"

The detective was silent. His stillness after that instinctive outburst was so impassive that he might have gone to sleep on his feet. But he was very much awake. And presently the Saint went on, in that gentle, somewhat mocking voice which Teal was listening for.

"I wonder where you get the idea that a 'sportsman' is a sort of hero," he said. "It doesn't require courage to take a cold bath—it's simply a matter of whether your constitution likes it. It doesn't require courage to play cricket—haven't you ever heard the howls of protest that shake the British Empire if a batsman happens to get hit with a ball? Perhaps it requires a little more courage to watch a pack of hounds pull down a savage fox, or to loose off a shot-gun at a ferocious grouse, or to catch a great man-eating trout with a little rod and line. But there are certain things you've been brought up to believe, and your mind isn't capable of reasoning them out for itself. You believe that a 'sportsman' is a kind of peculiarly god-like gladiator, without fear and without reproach. You believe that no gentleman would shoot a sitting partridge, and therefore you believe that he wouldn't shoot a sitting poet."

A light wind blew through the shrubbery, and the detective felt queerly cold.

"You're only talking," he said. "You haven't any evidence."

"I know I haven't," said the Saint, with a sudden weariness. "I've only got what I think. I think that Yearleigh planned this days ago—when Vould first asked for the interview, as Yearleigh mentioned. I think he guessed what it would be about. I think his only reason for putting it off was to give himself time to send those anonymous threats to himself—to build up the melodrama he had invented. I think you'll find that those anonymous threats started on the day when Vould asked for a talk with him, and that Yearleigh had no sound reason for going away except that of putting Vould off. I think that when they were in the study tonight, Yearleigh pointed to the window and made some excuse to get Vould to turn round, and then shot him in the back in cold blood, and put this paper-knife in his hand afterwards. I think that that is what Lady Yearleigh, who must have known Yearleigh so much better than any of us, was afraid of, and I think that when she said 'He's killed him,' she meant that Yearleigh had killed Vould, and not that Vould had killed Yearleigh."

The Saint's lighter flared, like a bomb bursting in the dark, and Teal looked up and saw his lean brown face, grim and curiously bitter in the light of the flame as he put it to his cigarette. And then the light went out again, and there was only Simon Templar's quiet voice speaking out of the dark.

"I think that I killed Maurice Vould as surely as if I'd shot him myself, because I couldn't see all those things until now, when it's too late. If I had seen them, I might have saved him."

"But in the back," said Teal harshly. "That's the part I can't swallow."

The tip of the Saint's cigarette glowed and died.

"Yearleigh was afraid of him," he said. "He couldn't risk any mistake—any cry or struggle that might have spoilt his scheme. He was afraid of Vould because, in his heart, he knew that Vould was so much cleverer and more desirable, so much more right and honest than he would ever be. He was fighting the old hopeless battle of age against youth. He knew that Vould had seen through the iniquity of his bill. The bill could never touch Yearleigh. He was too old for the last war, when I seem to remember that he made a great reputation by organising cricket matches behind the lines. He would be too old for the next. He had no children. But it's part of the psychology of life, whether you like it or not, that war is the time when the old men come back into their own, and the young men who are pressing on their heels are miraculously removed. Yearleigh knew that Vould despised him for it, and he was afraid . . . Those are only the things I think, and I can't prove any of them," he said, and Teal turned abruptly on his heel and walked back towards the house.

THE DAMSEL IN DISTRESS

"You need brains in this life of crime," Simon Templar would say sometimes, "but I often think you need luck even more."

He might have added that the luck had to be consistent.

Mr Giuseppe Rolfieri was lucky up to a point, for he happened to be in Switzerland when the astounding Liverpool Municipal Bond forgery was discovered. It was a simple matter for him to slip over the border into his own native country, and when his four partners in the swindle stumbled down the narrow stairway that leads from the dock of the Old Bailey to the terrible blind years of penal servitude, he was comfortably installed in his villa at San Remo with no vengeance to fear from the Law. For it is a principle of international law that no man can be extradited from his own country, and Mr Rolfieri was lucky to have retained his Italian citizenship even though he had made himself a power in the City of London.

Simon Templar read about the case—he could hardly have helped it, for it was one of those sensational scandals which rock the financial world once in a lifetime—but it did not strike him as a matter for his intervention. Four out of the five conspirators, including the ringleader, had been convicted and sentenced, and although it is true that there was a certain amount of public indignation at the immunity of Mr Rolfieri, it was inevitable that the Saint, in his career of shameless lawlessness, sometimes had to pass up one inviting prospect in favour of another nearer to hand. He couldn't be everywhere at once—it was one of the very few human limitations which he was ready to admit.

A certain Domenick Naccaro, however, had other ideas.

He called at the Saint's apartment in Piccadilly one morning—a stout bald-headed man in a dark blue suit and a light blue waistcoat, with an unfashionable stiff collar and a stringy black tie and a luxuriant scroll of black moustache ornamenting his face—and for the first moment of alarm Simon wondered if he had been mistaken for somebody else of the same name but less respectable morals, for Signor Naccaro was accompanied by a pale pretty girl who carried a small infant swathed in a shawl.

"Is this-a Mr Templar I have-a da honour to spik to?" asked Naccaro, doffing his bowler elaborately.

"This is one Mr Templar," admitted the Saint cautiously.

"Ha!" said Mr Naccaro. "It is-a da Saint himself?"

"So I'm told," Simon answered.

"Then you are da man we look-a for," stated Mr Naccaro, with profound conviction.

As if taking it for granted that all the necessary formalities had therewith been observed, he bowed the girl in, bowed himself in after her, and stalked into the living-room. Simon closed the door and followed the deputation with a certain curious amusement.

"Well, brother," he murmured, taking a cigarette from the box on the table. "Who are you, and what can I do for you?"

The flourishing bowler hat bowed the girl into one chair, bowed its owner into another, and came to rest on its owner's knees.

"Ha!" said the Italian, rather like an acrobat announcing the conclusion of a trick. "I am Domenick Naccaro!"

"That must be rather nice for you," murmured the Saint amiably. He waved his cigarette towards the girl and her bundle. "Did you come here to breed?"

"That," said Mr Naccaro, "is-a my daughter Maria. And in her arms she hold-as a leedle baby. A baby," he said, with his black eyes suddenly swimming, "wis-a no father."

"Careless of her," Simon remarked. "What does the baby think about it?"

"Da father," said Mr Naccaro, contradicting himself dramatically, "is-a Giuseppe Rolfieri."

Simon's brows came down in a straight line, and some of the bantering amusement fell back below the surface of his blue eyes. He hitched one hip on to the edge of the table and swung his foot thoughtfully.

"How did this happen?" he asked.

"I keep-a da small-a restaurant in-a Soho," explained Mr Naccaro. "Rolfieri, he come-a there often to eat-a da spaghetti. Maria, she sit at-a da desk and take-a da money. You, signor, you see-a how-a she is beautiful. Rolfieri, he notice her. When-a he pay his bill, he stop-a to talk-a wis her. One day he ask-a her to go out wis him."

Mr Naccaro took out a large chequered handkerchief and dabbed his eyes. He went on, waving his hands in broken eloquence.

"I do not stop her. I think-a Rolfieri is-a da fine gentleman, and it is nice-a for my Maria to go out wis him. Often, they go out. I tink-a that Maria perhaps she makes-a presently da good-a marriage, and I am glad for her. Then, one day, I see she is going to have-a da baby."

"It must have been a big moment," said the Saint gravely.

"I say to her, 'Maria, what have-a you done?'" recounted Mr Naccaro, flinging out his arms. "She will-a not tell-a me." Mr Naccaro shut his mouth firmly. "But presently she confess it is-a Rolfieri. I beat-a my breast." Mr Naccaro beat his breast. "I say, I will keell-a heem, but first-a he shall marry you.'"

Mr Naccaro jumped up with native theatrical effect.

"Rolfieri does-a not come any more to eat-a da spaghetti. I go to his office, and they tell me he is-a not there. I go to his house, and they tell me he is-a not there. I write-a letters, and he does-a not answer. Da time is going so quick. Presently I write-a da letter and say, 'If you do not-a see me soon I go to da police.' He answer that one. He say he come soon. But he does-a not come. Then he is-a go abroad. He write again, and he say he come-a to see me when he get back. But he does not-a come back. One day I read in da paper that he is-a da criminal, and da police are already look-a for him. So Maria she have-a da baby—and Rolfieri will-a never come back!"

Simon nodded.

"That's very sad," he said sympathetically. "But what can I do about it?"

Mr Naccaro mopped his brow, put away his large chequered handkerchief, and sat down again.

"You are-a da man who help-a da poor people, no?" he said pleadingly. "You are-a da Saint who always work-a to make justice?"

"Yes, but—"

"Then it is settled. You help-a me. Listen, signor, everything, everything is-a arrange. I have-a da good friends in England and in-a San Remo, and we put-a da money together to make-a this right. We kidnap-a Rolfieri. We bring him here in da aeroplane. But we do not-a know anyone who can fly. You, *signor*, you can fly-a da aeroplane." Mr Naccaro suddenly fell on his knees and flung out his arms. "See, *signor*—I humble myself. I kiss-a your feet. I beg-a you to help us and not let Maria have-a da baby wis-a no father!"

Simon allowed the operatic atmosphere to play itself out, and thereafter listened with a seriousness from which his natural superficial amusement did not detract at all. It was an appeal of the kind which he heard sometimes, for the name of the Saint was known to people who dreamed of his assistance as well as to those who lived in terror of his attentions, and he was never entirely deaf to the pleadings of those troubled souls who came to his home with a pathetic faith in miracles.

Mr Naccaro's proposition was more practical than most.

He and his friends, apparently, had gone into the problem of avenging the wickedness of Giuseppe Rolfieri with the conspiratorial instinct of professional vendettists. One of them had become Mr Rolfieri's butler in the villa at San Remo. Others, outside, had arranged the abduction down to a precise time-table. Mr Naccaro himself had acquired an old farmhouse in Kent at which Rolfieri was to be held prisoner, with a large field adjoining it at which an aeroplane could land. The aeroplane itself had been bought, and was ready for use at Brooklands Aerodrome. The only unit lacking was a man qualified to fly it.

Once Rolfieri had been taken to the farmhouse, how would they force him through the necessary marriage?

"We make-a him," was all that Naccaro would say, but he said it with grim conviction.

When the Saint finally agreed to take the job, there was another scene of operatic gratitude which surpassed all previous demonstrations. Money was offered, but Simon had already decided that in this case the entertainment was its own reward. He felt pardonably exhausted when at last Domenick Naccaro, bowing and scraping and yammering incoherently, shepherded his daughter, his illegitimate grandchild, and his own curling whiskers out of the apartment.

The preparations for his share in the abduction occupied Simon Templar's time for most of the following week. He drove down to Brooklands and tested the plane which the syndicate had purchased—it was an ancient Avro which must have secured its certificate of airworthiness by the skin of its ailerons, but he thought it would complete the double journey, given luck and good weather. Then there was a half-way refuelling base to be established somewhere in France—a practical necessity which had not occurred to the elemental Mr Naccaro. Friday had arrived before he was able to report that he was ready to make the trip, and there was another scene of embarrassing gratitude.

"I send-a da telegram to take Rolfieri on Sunday night," was the essence of Mr Naccaro's share in the conversation, but his blessings upon the Saint, the bones of his ancestors, and the heads of his unborn descendants for generations, took up much more time.

Simon had to admit, however, that the practical contribution of the Naccaro clan was performed with an efficiency which he himself could scarcely have improved upon. He stood beside the museum Avro on the aerodrome of San Remo at dusk on the Sunday evening, and watched the kidnapping cortège coming towards him across the field with genuine admiration. The principal character was an apparently mummified figure rolled in blankets, which occupied an invalid chair wheeled by the unfortunate Maria in the uniform of a nurse. Her pale lovely face was set in an expression of beatific solicitude at which Simon, having some idea of the fate which awaited Signor Rolfieri in England, could have hooted aloud. Beside the invalid chair stalked a sedate spectacled man whose role was obviously that of the devoted physician. The airport officials, who had already checked the papers of pilot and passengers, lounged boredly in the far background, without a single disturbing suspicion of the classic getaway that was being pulled off under their noses.

Between them, Simon and the "doctor" tenderly lifted the mummified figure into the machine.

"He will not wake before you arrive, signor," whispered the man confidently, stooping to arrange the blankets affectionately round the body of his patient.

The Saint grinned gently, and stepped back to help the "nurse" into her place. He had no idea how the first stage of the abduction had been carried out, and he was not moved to inquire. He had performed similar feats himself, no less slickly, without losing the power to stand back and impersonally admire the technique of others in the same field. With a sigh of satisfaction he swung himself up into his own cockpit, signalled to the mechanic who stood waiting by the propeller of the warmed-up engine, and sent the ship roaring into the wind through the deepening dusk.

The flight north was consistently uneventful. With a south wind following to help him on, he sighted the three red lights which marked his fuelling station at about half past two, and landed by the three flares that were kindled for him when he blinked his navigating lights. The two men procured from somewhere by Mr Naccaro replenished his tank while he smoked a cigarette and stretched his legs, and in twenty minutes he was off again. He passed over Folkestone in the early daylight, and hedge-hopped for some miles before he reached his destination so that no inquisitive yokel should see exactly where he landed.

"You have him?" asked Mr Naccaro, dancing about deliriously as Simon climbed stiffly down.

"I have," said the Saint. "You'd better get him inside quickly—I'm afraid your pals didn't dope him up as well as they thought they had, and from the way he was behaving just now I shouldn't be surprised if he was going to have-a da baby, too."

He stripped off his helmet and goggles, and watched the unloading of his cargo with interest. Signor Giuseppe Rolfieri had recovered considerably from the effects of the drug under whose influence he had been embarked, but the hangover, combined with some bumpy weather on the last part of the journey, restrained him hardly less effectively from much resistance. Simon had never known before that the human skin could really turn green, but the epidermis of Signor Rolfieri had literally achieved that remarkable tint.

The Saint stayed behind to help the other half of the reception committee—introduced as Mr Naccaro's brother—wheel the faithful Avro into the shelter of a barn, and then he strolled back to the farmhouse. As he reached it the door opened, and Naccaro appeared.

"Ha!" he cried, clasping the Saint's shoulders. "Meester Templar—you have already been-a so kind—I cannot ask it—but you have-a da car—will you go out again?"

Simon raised his eyebrows.

"Can't I watch the wedding?" he protested. "I might be able to help."

"Afterwards, yes," said Nacarro. "But we are not-a ready. *Ecco*, we are so hurry, so excited, when we come here we forget-a da mos' important tings. We forget-a da soap!"

Simon blinked.

"Soap?" he repeated. "Can't you marry him off without washing him?"

"No, no, no!" spluttered Naccaro. "You don't understand. Da soap, she is not-a to wash. She is to persuade. I show you myself, afterwards. It is my own idea. But-a da soap we mus' have. You will go, please, please, *signor*, in your car?"

The Saint frowned at him blankly for a moment, and then he shrugged.

"Okay, brother," he murmured. "I'd do more than that to find out how you persuade a bloke to get married with a cake of soap."

He stuffed his helmet and goggles into the pocket of his flying coat, and went around to the barn where he had parked his car before he took off for San Remo. He had heard of several strange instruments of persuasion in his time, but it was the first time he had ever met common or household soap in the guise of an implement of torture or moral coercion. He wondered whether the clan Naccaro had such a prejudiced opinion of Rolfieri's personal cleanliness that they thought the mere threat of washing him would terrify him into meeting his just obligations, or whether the victim was first smeared with ink and then bribed with the soap, or whether he was made to eat it, and he was so fascinated by these provocative speculations that he had driven nearly half a mile before he remembered that he was not provided with the wherewithal to buy it.

Simon Templar was not stingy. He would have bought any necessitous person a cake of soap, any day. In return for a solution of the mystery which was perplexing him at that moment, he would cheerfully have stood Mr Naccaro a whole truckload of it. But the money was not in his pocket. In a moment of absent-mindedness he had set out on his trip with a very small allowance of ready cash, and all he had left of it then was two Italian lire, the change out of the last meal he had enjoyed in San Remo.

He stopped the car and scowled thoughtfully for a second. There was no place visible ahead where he could turn it, and he had no natural desire to back half a mile down that narrow lane, but the road had led him consistently to the left since he set out, and he stood up to survey the landscape in the hope that the farmhouse might only be a short distance across the fields as the crow flies or he could walk. And it was by doing this that he saw a curious sight.

Another car, of whose existence nobody had said anything, stood in front of the farmhouse, and into it Mr Naccaro and his brother were hastily loading the body of the unfortunate Signor Rolfieri, now trussed with several fathoms of rope like an escape artist before demonstrating his art. The girl Maria stood by, and as soon as Rolfieri was in the car she followed him in, covered him with a rug, and settled herself comfortably on the seat. Naccaro and his brother jumped into the front, and the car drove rapidly away in the opposite direction to that which the Saint had been told to take.

Simon Templar sank slowly back behind the wheel and took out his cigarette-case. He deliberately paused to tap out a cigarette, light it, and draw the first two puffs as if he had an hour to spare, and then he pushed the gear lever into reverse and sent the great cream and red Hirondel racing back up the lane at a speed which gave no indication that he had ever hesitated to perform the manoeuvre.

He turned the car round in the farmhouse gates and went on with the cut-out closed and his keen eyes vigilantly scanning the panorama ahead. The other car was a sedan, and half the time he was able to keep the roof in sight over the low hedges which hid the open Hirondel from its quarry. But it is doubtful whether the possibility of pursuit ever entered the heads of the party in front, who must have been firm in their belief that the Saint was at that moment speeding innocently towards the village to which they had directed him. Once, at a fork, he lost them, and then he spotted a tiny curl of smoke rising from the grass bank a little way up one turning, and drove slowly up to it. It was the lighted stub of a cigar which could not have been thrown out at any place more convenient for a landmark, and the Saint smiled and went on.

In a few seconds he had picked up the sedan again, and very shortly afterwards he jammed on his brakes and brought the Hirondel to a sudden halt.

The car in front had stopped before a lonely cottage whose thatched roof was clearly visible. In a flash the Saint was out of his own seat and walking silently up the lane towards it. When the next turn would have brought him within sight of the car, he slipped through a gap in the hedge and sprinted for the back of the house. In broad daylight, there was no chance of further concealment, and it was neck or nothing at that point. But his luck held, and so far as he could tell he gained the lee of his objective unobserved. And once there, an invitingly open kitchen window was merely another link in the chain of chance which had stayed with him so benevolently throughout that adventure.

Rolfieri and the Naccaro team were already inside. He could hear the muffled mutter of their voices as he tiptoed down the dark passage towards the front of the house, and presently he stood outside the door of the room where they were. Through the keyhole he was able to take in the scene.

Rolfieri, still safely trussed, was sitting in a chair, and the Naccaro brothers were standing over him. The girl Maria was curled up on the settee, smoking a cigarette and displaying a remarkable length of stocking for a betrayed virgin whose honour was at stake. The conversation was in Italian, which was only one language out of the Saint's comprehensive repertoire, and it was illuminating.

"You cannot make me pay," Rolfieri was saying, but his stubbornness could have been more convincing.

"That is true," Naccaro agreed. "I can only point out the disadvantages of not paying. You are in England, where the police would be very glad to see you. Your confederates have already been tried and sentenced, and it would be a mere formality for you to join them. The lightest sentence that any of them received was five years, and they could hardly give you less. If we left you here, and informed the police where to find you, it would not be long before you were in prison yourself. Surely twenty-five thousand pounds is a very small price to pay to avoid that."

Rolfieri stared sullenly at the floor for a while, and then he said, "I will give you ten thousand."

"It will be twenty-five thousand or nothing," said Naccaro. "Come, now—I see you are prepared to be reasonable. Let us have what we ask, and you will be able to leave England again before dark. We will tell that fool Templar that you agreed to our terms without the persuasion of the soap, and that we hurried you to the church before you changed your mind. He will fly you back to San Remo and you will have nothing more to fear."

"I have nothing to fear now," said Rolfieri, as if he was trying to hearten himself. "It would do you no good to hand me over to the police."

"It would punish you for wasting so much of our time and some of our money," put in the girl, in a tone which left no room for doubt that that revenge would be taken in the last resort.

Rolfieri licked his lips and squirmed in the tight ropes which bound him—he was a fat man, and they had a lot to bind. Perhaps the glimpse of his well-fed corporation which that movement gave him made him realize some of the inescapable discomforts of penal servitude to the amateur of good living, for his voice was even more half-hearted when he spoke again.

"I have not so much money in England," he said.

"You have a lot more than that in England," answered the other Naccaro harshly. "It is deposited in the City and Continental Bank under the name of Pierre Fontanne, and we have a cheque on that bank made out ready for you. All we require is your signature and a letter in your own hand instructing the bank to pay cash. Be quick and make up your mind, now—we are losing patience."

It was inevitable that there should be further argument on the subject, but the outcome was a foregone conclusion.

The cheque was signed and the letter was written, and Domenick Naccaro handed them over to his brother.

"Now you will let me go," said Rolfieri.

"We will let you go when Alessandro returns with the money," said Domenick Naccaro. "Until then, you stay here. Maria will look after you while I go back to the farm and detain Templar."

The Saint did not need to hear any more. He went back to the kitchen with soundless speed, and let himself out of the window by which he had entered. But before he left he picked up a trophy from a shelf over the sink.

Domenick Naccaro reached the farmhouse shortly after him and found the Saint reading a newspaper.

"Rolfieri has-a marry Maria," he announced triumphantly, and kissed the Saint on both cheeks. "So after all I keep-a da secret of my leedle trick wis-a da soap. But everyting we owe to you, my friend!"

"I guess you do," Simon admitted. "Where are the happy couple?"

"Ha! That is-a da romance. It seems that Signer Rolfieri was always fond of Maria, and when he hear that she have-a da baby, and he see her again—*presto!*—he is in love wis her. So now they go to London to get-a da clothes, queeck, so she can go wis him for da honeymoon. So I tink we drink-a da Antinori wine till they come back."

They spent a convivial morning, which Simon Templar would have enjoyed more if caution had not compelled him to tip most of his drinks down the back of his chair.

It was half past one when a car drew up outside, and a somewhat haggard Rolfieri, a jubilant Alessandro Naccaro, and a quietly smiling Maria came in. Domenick jumped up.

"Everything is all right?" he asked.

"Pairfect," beamed Alessandro.

That was as much as the Saint was waiting to hear. He uncoiled himself from his chair and smiled at them all.

"In that case, boys and girls," he drawled, "would you all put up your hands and keep very quiet?"

There was an automatic in his hand, and six eyes stared at it mutely. And then Domenick Naccaro smiled a wavering and watery smile.

"I tink you make-a da joke, no?" he said.

"Sure," murmured the Saint amiably. "I make-a da joke. Just try to get obstreperous, and watch me laugh."

He brought the glowering Alessandro towards him and searched his pockets. There was no real question of anybody getting obstreperous, but the temptation to do so must have been very near when he brought out a sheaf of new banknotes and transferred them one-handed to his own wallet.

"This must seem rather hard-hearted of me," Simon remarked, "but I have to do it. You're a very talented family—if you really are a family—and you must console yourselves with the thought that you fooled me for a whole ten days. When I think how easily you might have fooled me for the rest of the way, it sends cold shivers up and down my spine. Really boys, it was a rather brilliant scheme, and I wish I'd thought of it myself."

"You wait till I see you da next time, you pig," said Domenick churlishly.

"I'll wait," Simon promised him.

He backed discreetly out of the room and out of the house to his car, and they clustered in the doorway to watch him. It was not until he pressed the starter that the fullest realization dawned upon Signor Rolfieri.

"But what happens to me?" he screamed. "How do I go back to San Remo?"

"I really don't know, Comrade," answered the Saint callously. "Perhaps Domenick will help you again if you give him some more money. Twenty-five thousand quid instead of five years' penal servitude was rather a bargain price, anyway."

He let in the clutch gently, and the big car moved forward. But in a yard or two he stopped it again, and felt in one of his pockets. He brought out his souvenir of a certain fortunate kitchen, and tossed it to the empurpled Domenick.

"Sorry, brother," he called back over his shoulder. "I forget-a da soap!"

THE LOVING BROTHERS

"You never saw a couple of brothers like 'em," said the garrulous Mr Penwick. "They get enough pleasure out of doing anybody down, but if one of 'em can cheat the other out of anything it's a red-letter day."

Dissension between brothers is unhappily nothing new in the world's history. Jacob and Esau, Cain and Abel, disagreed in a modest way, according to the limitations of their time. Walter and Willie Kinsall, living in days when a mess of pottage has no great bargaining value, disagreed on a much more lavish scale.

Naturally this lavishness of discord was a thing which grew up through the years. It was not achieved at one stroke. When Walter, aged four, realized that Willie, aged two months, was commanding the larger share of his parents' time and attention, and endeavoured to brain him with a toy tomahawk, their mutual jealousy was merely embryonic.

When Willie, aged seven, discovered that by lying awake at night until after Walter, aged eleven, had gone to sleep, he was able to rifle Walter's pockets of a judicious share of their current collection of sweets, pennies, pieces of string, and paper clips, his ideas of retaliation were only passing through the experimental stage.

But when Walter, aged twenty, found that he was able to imitate the handwriting of Willie, aged sixteen, so well that he succeeded in drawing out of Willie's savings bank account a quantity of money whose disappearance was ever afterwards a mystery, it might be said that their feud was at least within sight of the peaks to which it was destined later to rise.

The crude deceptions of youth, of course, gave place to subtler and less overtly illegal stratagems as the passing years gave experience and greater guile. Even their personal relationship was glossed over with a veneer of specious affability which deceived neither.

"How about running down to my place for the weekend?" suggested Willie, aged twenty-seven.

Walter ran down, and at dead of night descended to the study and perused all of Willie's private correspondence that he could find, obtaining an insight into his brother's affairs which enabled him to snap up the bankrupt shoe repairing business which Willie was preparing to take over at a give-away price.

"Come and have lunch one day," invited Walter, aged thirty-five.

Willie came at a time when Walter was out, and beguiled a misguided secretary into letting him wait in Walter's private office. From letters which were lying on the desk he gained the information through which he subsequently sneaked a mining concession in Portuguese East Africa from under Walter's very nose.

The garrulous Mr Penwick had several other anecdotes on the same lines to tell, the point of which was to establish beyond dispute the fraternal affection of the Brothers Kinsall.

"Even their father got fed up with them," said Mr Penwick. "And he wasn't a paragon, by any means. You must have heard of Sir Joseph Kinsall, the South African millionaire? Well, he's their father. Lives in Malaga now, from what I hear. I used to be his solicitor, before I was struck off the rolls. Why, I've still got his last will and testament at home. Living abroad, he doesn't know about my misfortune, and I've kept the will because I'm going to be reinstated. I had an awful time with him when he was over here. First he made a will leaving everything to 'em equally. Then he tore it up and left everything to Walter. Then he tore that one up and left everything to Willie. Then he tore that up and made another. He just couldn't make up his mind which of 'em was the worst. I remember once . . ."

What Mr Penwick remembered once he could be counted on to remember again. His garrulousness was due only in part to a natural loquacity of temperament: the rest of it could without injustice be credited to the endless supplies of pink gin which Simon Templar was ready to pay for.

The Saint had met Mr Penwick for the first time in a West End bar, and thereafter had met him a number of times in other bars. He had never had the heart to shatter Mr Penwick's fond dream that reinstatement was just round the corner, but it is doubtful whether Mr Penwick really believed it himself.

Gin was Mr Penwick's fatal weakness, and after several encounters with his watery eyes, his shaky hands, and his reddened and bulbous nose, it was hard to imagine that he could ever occupy his former place in the legal profession again. Nevertheless, Simon Templar had sought his company on many occasions, for the Saint was not snobbish, and he had his own vocation to consider.

The uninitiated may sometimes be tempted to think that the career of a twentieth-century brigand is nothing but a series of dramatically satisfying high spots interluded with periods of ill-gotten ease, but nothing could be farther from the truth. The Saint's work was never done. He knew better than anyone that golden-fleeced sheep rarely fall miraculously out of Heaven for the shearing, and while he certainly enjoyed a liberal allowance of high spots, many of the intervals between them were taken up with the dull practical business of picking up clues, sifting stray fragments of gossip from all quarters that came his way, and planning the paths by which future high spots were to be attained.

He followed a score of false scents for every one that led him to profit, and there was none which he could pass by, for he never knew until the moment of coincidence and inspiration which would lead him to big game and which would lead to nothing more than a stray mouse.

The garrulousness of Mr Penwick was a case in point. Lawyers hear many secrets, and when they have been struck off the rolls and nurse a grievance, and their downward path is lubricated by a craving for juniper juice which they are not financially equipped to indulge as deeply as they would wish, there is always the chance that a modern buccaneer with an attentive mind, who will provide gin in limitless quantities, may sooner or later hear some item of reminiscence that will come in useful one day.

Some weeks passed before Mr Penwick came in useful, and Simon was not thinking of him at all when Patricia Holm looked up from the newspaper one morning and said, "I see your friend Sir Joseph Kinsall is dead."

The Saint, who was smoking a cigarette on the window-sill and looking down into the sunlit glades of the Green Park, was not immediately impressed.

"He's not my pal—he's the bibulous Penwick's," he said, and in his mind ran over the stories which Mr Penwick had told him. "May I see?"

He read through the news item, and learned that Sir Joseph had succumbed to an attack of pneumonia at ten o'clock the previous morning. A well-known firm of London solicitors was said to be in possession of his will, and the disposition of his vast fortune would probably be disclosed later that day.

"Well, that'll give Walter and Willie something new to squabble over," Simon remarked, and thought nothing more about it until that evening when a late edition told him that the Kinsall millions, according to a will made in 1927, would be divided equally between his two sons.

That appeared to close the incident, and Simon decided that the late Sir Joseph had found the only possible answer to the choice between two such charming heirs as the gods had blessed him with. He dismissed the affair with a characteristic shrug as only one of the false scents which had crossed his path in his twelve years of illicit hunting.

He was turning to the back page for the result of the 4:30 when a wobbly hand clutched his sleeve, and he looked round to behold a vision of the garrulous Mr Penwick arrayed in a very creased and moth-eaten frock coat and a top hat which had turned green in the years of idleness.

"Hullo," Simon murmured, and automatically ordered a double pink gin. "Whose funeral have you been to?"

Mr Penwick clutched at the glass which was provided, downed half the contents, and wiped his mouth on his sleeve.

"Ole boy," he said earnestly, "I'm going to be reinshtated. Congrashiilate me."

Indubitably he was very drunk, and the Saint relaxed into perfunctory attention.

"Splendid," he said politely. "When did you hear the news?"

"They got to reinshtate me now," said Mr Penwick, "because I'm only schap hoosh got Kinshallsh will." He dabbed astigmatically at the Saint's evening paper. "Jew read newsh? They shay moneysh divided between Wallern Willie 'cording to will he made in nineen-twenny-sheven. Pish!" said Mr Penwick, snapping his fingers. "Bosh! That will wash revoked ycarsh ago. I got the will he made in nineneen-thirry-two. Sho they got to reinshtate me. Can't have sholishitor shtruck off rollsh hoosh got will worth millionsh."

Simon's relaxation had vanished in an instant—it might never have overcome him. He glanced round the bar in sudden alarm, but fortunately the room was empty and the barmaid was giggling with her colleague at the far end of her quarters.

"Wait a minute," he said firmly, and steered the unsteady Mr Penwick to a table as far removed as possible from potential eavesdroppers. "Tell me this again, will you?"

"Sh-shirnple," said Mr Penwick, emptying his glass and looking pathetically around for more. "I got Kinshallsh lasht willan teshtamen. Revoking all othersh. I wash going to Law Society to tellum, shoonsh I read the newsh, but I shtopped to have drink an' shellybrate. Now I shpose Law siety all gone home." He flung out his arms, to illustrate the theme of the Law Society scattering to the four corners of the globe. "Have to wait till tomorrer. Have 'nother drink inshtead. Thishish on me."

He fumbled in his pockets, and produced two halfpennies and a sixpence. He put them on the table and blinked at them hazily for a moment, and then, as if finally grasping the irrefutable total, he covered his face with his hands and burst into tears.

"All gone," he sobbed. "All gone. Moneysh all gone. Len' me a pound, ole boy, an' I'll pay for drinksh."

"Mr Penwick," said the Saint slowly, "have you got that will on you?"

"'Coursh I got will on me. I tole you, ole boy—I wash goin' Lawshiety an' show 'em, so they could reinshtate me. Pleash pay for drinksh."

Simon lifted his Peter Dawson and drank unhurriedly. "Mr Penwick, will you sell me that will?"

The solicitor raised shocked but twitching eyebrows. "Shell it, old boy? Thash imposhible. Professhnal etiquette. Norrallowed to sell willsh. Len' me ten bob—"

"Mr Penwick," said the Saint, "what would you do if you had five hundred a year for life?"

The solicitor swallowed noisily, and an ecstatic light gleamed through his tears like sunshine through an April shower.

"I'd buy gin," he said. "Bols an' bols an' bols of gin. Barrelsh of gin. Lloyd's gin. I'd have a bath full of gin, an' shwim myshelf to shleep every Sarrerdy night."

"I'll give you five hundred a year for life for that will," said the Saint. "Signed, settled, and sealed—in writing—this minute. You needn't worry too much about your professional etiquette. I'll give you my word not to destroy or conceal the will, but I would like to borrow it for a day or two."

Less than an hour later he was chivalrously ferrying the limp body of Mr Penwick home to the ex-solicitor's lodgings, for it is a regrettable fact that Mr Penwick collapsed rather rapidly under the zeal with which he insisted on celebrating the sale of his potential reinstatement. Simon went on to his own apartment, and told Patricia of his purchase.

"But aren't you running a tremendous risk?" she said anxiously. "Penwick won't be able to keep it secret—and what use is it to you anyway?"

"I'm afraid nothing short of chloroform would stop Penwick talking," Simon admitted. "But it'll take a little time for his story to get dangerous, and I'll have had all I want out of the will before then. And the capital which is going to pay his five hundred a year will only be half of it."

Patricia lighted a cigarette. "Do I help?"

"You are a discontented secretary with worldly ambitions and no moral sense," he said. "The part should be easy for you."

Mr Willie Kinsall had never heard of Patricia Holm.

"What's she like?" he asked the typist who brought in her name.

"She's pretty," said the girl cynically.

Mr Willie Kinsall appeared to deliberate for a while, and then he said, "I'll see her."

When he did see her, he admitted that the description was correct. At her best, Patricia was beautiful, but for the benefit of Mr Willie she had adopted a vivid red lipstick, an extra quantity of rouge, and a generous use of mascara to reduce herself to something close to the Saint's estimate of Mr Willie's taste.

"How do you do, my dear?" he said. "I don't think we've . . . er—"

"We haven't," said the girl coolly. "But we should have. I'm your brother Walter's secretary—or I was."

Mr Willie frowned questioningly. "Did he send you to see me?"

Patricia threw back her head and gave a hard laugh.

"Did he send me to see you! If he knew I was here he'd probably murder me."

"Why?" asked Willie Kinsall cautiously.

She sat on the corner of his desk, helped herself to a cigarette from his box, and swung a shapely leg.

"See here, beautiful," she said. "I'm here for all I can get. Your brother threw me out of a good job just because I made a little mistake, and I'd love to see somebody do him a bad turn. From what he's said about you sometimes, you two aren't exactly devoted to each other. Well, I think I can put you in the way of something that'll make Walter sick, and the news is yours if you pay for it."

Mr Kinsall drummed his fingertips on the desk and narrowed his eyes thoughtfully. By no stretch of imagination could he have been truthfully described as beautiful, but he had a natural sympathy for pretty girls of her type who called him by such endearing names. The rat-faced youth of sixteen had by no means mellowed in the Willie Kinsall of thirty-eight; he was just as scraggy and no less ratlike, and when he narrowed his beady eyes they almost disappeared into their deep-set sockets.

"I'm sorry to hear you've lost your job, my dear," he said insincerely. "What was this mistake you made?"

"I opened a letter, that's all. I open all his letters at the office, of course, but this one was marked 'private and confidential.' I came in rather late that morning, and I was in such a hurry I didn't notice what it said on the envelope. I'd just finished reading it when Walter came in, and he was furious. He threw me out then and there—it was only yesterday."

"What was this letter about?" asked Mr Kinsall.

"It was about your father's will," she told him, and suddenly Mr Kinsall sat up. "It was from a man who's been to see him once or twice before—I've listened at the keyhole when they were talking," said the girl shamelessly, "and I gather that the will which was reported in the papers wasn't the last one your father made. This fellow—he's a solicitor—had got a later one, and Walter was trying to buy it from him. The letter I read was from the solicitor, and it said that he had decided to accept Walter's offer of ten thousand pounds for it."

Mr Willie's eyes had recovered from their temporary shrinkage. During the latter part of her speech they had gone on beyond normal, and at the end of it they genuinely bulged. For a few seconds he was voiceless, and then he exploded.

"The dirty swine!" he gasped.

That was his immediate and inevitable reaction, but the rest of the news took him longer to grasp. If Walter was willing to pay ten thousand pounds for the will . . . Ten thousand pounds! It was an astounding, a staggering figure. To be worth that, it could only mean that huge sums were at stake—and Willie could only see one way in which that could have come about. The second will had disinherited Walter. It had left all the Kinsall millions to him, Willie.

And Walter was trying to buy it and destroy it—to cheat him out of his just inheritance.

"What is this solicitor's name?" demanded Willie hoarsely.

Patricia smiled. "I thought you'd want that," she said. "Well, I know his name and address, but they'll cost you money."

Willie looked at the clock, gulped, and reached into a drawer for his cheque-book.

"How much?" he asked. "If it's within reason, I'll pay it."

She blew out a wreath of smoke and studied him calculatingly for a moment.

"Five hundred," she said at length.

Willie stared, choked, and shuddered. Then, with an expression of frightful agony on his predatory face, he took up his pen and wrote.

Patricia examined the cheque and put it away in her hand-bag. Then she picked up a pencil and drew the note-block towards her.

Willie snatched up the sheet and gazed at it tremblingly for a second. Then he heaved himself panting out of his chair and dashed for the hatstand in the corner.

"Excuse me," he got out. "Must do something about it. Come and see me again. Good-bye."

Riding in a taxi to the address she had given him, he barely escaped a succession of nervous breakdowns every time a traffic light or a slow-moving dray obstructed their passage. He bounced up and down on the seat, pulled off his hat, pulled out his watch, looked at his hat, tried to put on his watch, mopped his brow, craned his head out of the window, bounced, sputtered, gasped, and sweated in an anguish of impatience that brought him to the verge of delirium.

When at last they arrived at the lodging-house in Bayswater which was his destination, he fairly hurled himself out of the cab, hauled out a handful of silver with clumsy hands, spilt some of it into the driver's palm and most of it into the street, stumbled cursing up the steps, and plunged into the bell with a violence which almost drove it solidly through the wall.

While he waited, fuming, he dragged out his watch again, dropped it, tried to grab it, missed, and kicked it savagely into the middle of the street with a shrill squeal of sheer insanity, and then the door opened and a maid was inspecting him curiously.

"Is Mr Penwick in?" he blurted.

"I think so," said the maid. "Will you come in?"

The invitation was unnecessary. Breathing like a man who had just run a mile without training, Mr Willie Kinsall ploughed past her, and kicked his heels in a torment of suspense until the door of the room into which he had been ushered opened, and a tall man came in.

It seems superfluous to explain that this man's name was not really Penwick, and Willie Kinsall did not even stop to consider the point. He did look something like a solicitor of about forty, which is some indication of what Simon Templar could achieve with a black suit, a wing collar and a bow tie, a pair of gold-rimmed pince-nez, and some powder brushed into his hair.

Willie Kinsall did not even pause to frame a diplomatic line of approach.

"Where," he demanded shakily, "is this will, you crook?"

Mr Penwick raised his grey eyebrows.

"I don't think I have—ah—had the pleasure—"

"My name's Kinsall," said Willie, skipping about like a grasshopper on a hot plate. "And I want that will—the will you're trying to sell to my dirty swindling brother. And if I don't get it, I'm going straight to the police!"

The solicitor put his fingertips together.

"What proof have you, Mr—ah—Kinsall," he inquired gently, "of the existence of this will?"

Willie stopped skipping for a moment. And then, with a painful wrench, he flung bluff to the winds. He had no proof, and he knew it.

"All right," he said. "I won't go to the police. I'll buy it. What do you want?"

Simon pursed his lips.

"I doubt," he said, "whether the will is any longer for sale. Mr Walter's cheque is already in my bank, and I am only waiting for it to be cleared before handing the document over to him."

"Nonsense!" yelped Willie, but he used a much coarser word for it. "Walter hasn't got it yet. I'll give you as much as he gave—and you won't have to return his money. He wouldn't dare go into court and say what he gave it to you for."

The Saint shook his head.

"I don't think," he said virtuously, "that I would break my bargain for less than twenty thousand pounds."

"You're a thief and a crook!" howled Willie.

"So are you," answered the temporary Mr Penwick mildly. "By the way, this payment had better be in cash. You can go around to your bank and get it right away. I don't like to have to insist on this, but Mr Walter said he was coming here in about an hour's time, and if you're going to make your offer in an acceptable form—"

It is only a matter of record that Willie went. It is also on record that he took his departure in a speed and ferment that eclipsed even his arrival, and Simon Templar went to the telephone and called Patricia.

"You must have done a great job, darling," he said. "What did you get out of it?"

"Five hundred pounds," she told him cheerfully. "I got an open cheque and took it straight over to his bank—I'm just pushing out to buy some clothes, as soon as I've washed this paint off my face."

"Buy a puce sweater," said the Saint, "and christen it Willie. I want to keep it for a pet."

Rather less than an hour had passed when the front door bell pealed again, and Simon looked out of the window and beheld the form of Walter Kinsall standing outside. He went to let the caller in himself.

Mr Walter Kinsall was a little taller and heavier than his brother, but the rat-like mould of his features and his small beady eyes were almost the twins of his brother's. At that point their external resemblance temporarily ended, for Walter's bearing was not hysterical.

"Well, Mr Penwick," he said gloatingly, "has my cheque been cleared?"

"It ought to be through by now," said the Saint. "If you'll wait a moment, I'll just call the bank and make sure."

He did so, while the elder Kinsall rubbed his hands. He paused to reflect, with benevolent satisfaction, what a happy chance it was that his first name, while bearing the same initial as his brother's, still came first in index sequence, so that this decayed solicitor, searching the telephone directory for putative kin of the late Sir Joseph, had phoned him first. What might have happened had their alphabetical order been different, Walter at that moment hated to think.

"Your cheque has been cleared," said the Saint, returning from the telephone, and Walter beamed.

"Then, Mr Penwick, you have only to hand me the will—"

Simon knit his brows.

"The situation is rather difficult," he began, and suddenly Walter's face blackened.

"What the devil do you mean . . . difficult?" he rasped. "You've had your money. Are you trying—"

"You see," Simon explained, "your brother has been in to see me."

Walter gaped at him apoplectically for a space, and then he took a threatening step forward.

"You filthy double-crossing—"

"Wait a minute," said the Saint. "I think this is Willie coming back."

He pushed past the momentarily paralyzed Walter, and went to open the front door again.

Willie stood on the step, puffing out his lean rat-like cheeks and quivering as if he had just escaped from the paws of a hungry cat. He scrabbled in his pockets, tugged out a thick sheaf of banknotes, and crushed them into the Saint's hands as they went down the hall.

"It's all there, Mr Penwick," he gasped. "I haven't been long, have I? Now will you give me—"

It was at that instant that he entered the room which Simon Templar had rented for the occasion, and saw his brother; and his failure to complete the sentence was understandable.

For a time there was absolute silence, while the two devoted brothers glared at each other with hideous rigidity. Simon Templar took out his cigarette-case and selected a smoke at luxurious leisure, while Willie stared at Walter with red-hot eyes, and Walter glowered at Willie with specks of foam on his lips.

Then the Saint stroked the cog of his lighter, and at the slight sound, as if invisible strait-jackets which held them immobile had been conjured away, the two men started towards each other with simultaneous detonations of speech.

"You slimy twister!" snarled Walter.

"You greasy shark!" yapped Willie.

And then, as if this scorching interchange of fraternal compliments made them realize that there was a third party present who had not been included, and who might have felt miserably neglected, they checked their murderous advance towards one another and swung round on him together.

Epithets seared through their minds and slavered on their jaws—ruder, unkinder, more malignant words than they had ever shaped into connected order in their lives. And then with one accord, they realized that those words could not be spoken yet, and deprived of that outlet, they simmered in a second torrid silence.

Walter was the first to come out of it. He opened his aching throat and brought forth trembling speech.

"Penwick," he said, "whatever that snivelling squirt has given you, I'll pay twice as much."

"I'll pay three times that," said Willie feverishly. "Four times—five times—I'll give you twenty per cent of anything I get out of the estate—"

"Twenty-five per cent," Walter shrieked wildly. "Twenty-seven and a half—"

The Saint raised his hand. "One minute, boys," he murmured. "Hadn't you better hear the terms of the will first?"

"I know them," barked Walter.

"So do I," bellowed Willie. "Thirty per cent—"

The Saint smiled. He took a large sealed envelope from his breast pocket, and opened it.

"I may have misled you," he said, and held up the document for them to read.

They crowded closer, breathing stertorously, and read:

> *I, Joseph Kinsall, hereby give and bequeath everything of which I die possessed, without exception, to the Royal London Hospital, believing that it will be better spent than it would have been by my two worthless sons.*

It was in the late Sir Joseph Kinsall's own hand, and it was properly signed, sealed, and witnessed.

Simon folded it up and put it carefully away again, and Willie looked at Walter, and Walter looked at Willie. For the first time in their lives they found themselves absolutely and unanimously in tune. Their two minds had but a single thought. They drew deep breaths, and turned . . .

It was unfortunate that neither of them was very athletic. Simon Templar was, and he had promised Mr Penwick that the will should come to no harm.

THE TALL TIMBER

The queer things that have led Simon Templar into the paths of boodle would in themselves form a sizeable volume of curiosities, but in the Saint's own opinion none of these strange starting-points could ever compare, in sheer intrinsic uniqueness, with the moustache of Mr Sumner Journ.

Simon Templar's relations with Chief Inspector Teal were not always unpleasant. On that morning he had met Mr Teal in Old Compton Street and insisted on standing him lunch, and both of them had enjoyed the meal.

"And yet you'll probably be trying to arrest me again next week," said the Saint.

"I shouldn't be surprised," said Mr Teal heavily.

They stood in the doorway of Wheeler's, preparing to separate, and Simon was idly scanning the street when the moustache of Mr Sumner Journ hove into view.

Let it be said at once that it was no ordinarily overgrown moustache, attracting attention by nothing but its mere vulgar size. It was, in fact, the reverse. From a slight distance no moustache was visible at all, and the Saint was looking at Mr Journ simply by accident, as a man standing in the street will sometimes absent-mindedly follow the movements of another. As Mr Journ drew nearer, the moustache was still imperceptible, but there appeared to be a slight shadow on his upper lip, as if it were disfigured by a small mole. And it was not until he was passing a yard away that the really exquisite singularity of the growth dawned upon Simon Templar's mind.

On Mr Sumner Journ's upper lip, approximately fourteen hairs had been allowed to grow, so close together that the area they occupied could scarcely have been larger than a shirt button. These fourteen hairs had been carefully parted in the middle, and each little clique of seven had been carefully waxed and twisted together so that they stuck out about half an inch from their patron's face like the horns of a snail. In the whole of Simon Templar's life, which had encountered a perhaps unusual variety of developments of facial hair, ranging from the handlebar protuberances of the Southshire Insurance Company's private detective to the fine walrus effect sported by a Miss Gertrude Tinwiddle who contributed the nature notes in *The Daily Gazette*, he had never seen any example of hair culture in which such passionate devotion to detail, such a concentrated ecstasy or miniaturism, such an unostentatious climax of originality, had simultaneously arrived at concrete consummation.

Thus did the moustache of Mr Journ enter the Saint's horizon and pass on, accompanied by Mr Journ, who looked at them rather closely as he went by, and lest any suspicious reader should be starting to get ideas into his head, the historian desires to explain at once that this moustache has nothing more to do with the story, and has been described at such length solely on account of its own remarkable features qua face-hair. But, as we claimed at the beginning, it is an immutable fact that if it had not been for this phenomenal decoration the Saint would hardly have noticed Mr Journ at all, and would thereby have been many thousands of pounds poorer. For, shorn of that incomparable appendage, Mr Journ was quite an ordinary-looking business man, thin, dark, hatchet-faced, well and quietly dressed, and although he was noticeably hard about the eyes and mouth, there was really nothing else about him which would have caused the Saint to stare fascinatedly after him and ejaculate in a hushed voice, "Well, I am a piebald pelican balancing rubber balls on my beak!"

Wherefore Mr Teal would have had no reason to turn his somnolent gaze back to the Saint with a certain dour and puzzled humour, and to say, "I should have thought he was a fellow you'd be sure to know."

"Never set eyes on him in my life," said the Saint. "Do you know who he is?"

"His name's Sumner Journ," Mr Teal said reluctantly, after a slight pause.

Simon shook his head.

"Even that doesn't ring a bell," he said. "What does he do? No bloke who cultivated a nose-tickler like that could do anything ordinary."

"Sumner Journ doesn't," stated the detective flatly.

He seemed to have realized that he had said too much already, and it was impossible to draw any further information from him. He took his leave rather abruptly, and Simon gazed after his plump departing back with a tiny frown. The only plausible explanation of Teal's sudden taciturnity was that Mr Journ was engaged in some unlawful or nearly unlawful activities—Teal had had enough trouble with the victims whom the Saint found for himself, without conceiving any ambition to press fresh material into his hands. But if Chief Inspector Teal did not want the Saint to know more about Mr Sumner Journ, that was sufficient reason for the Saint to become abnormally inquisitive, and as a matter of fact, his investigations had not proceeded very far when a minor coincidence brought them up to date without further effort.

"This might interest you," said Monty Hayward one evening.

"This" was a very tastefully prepared booklet, on the cover of which was printed: "Brazilian Timber Bonds: *A Gold Mine for the Small Investor*." Simon took it and glanced at it casually, and then he saw something on the first page of the pamphlet which brought him to attention with a delighted start:

Managing Director

SUMNER JOURN, Esq., Associate of the Institute of Timber Planters, Fellow of the International Association of Wood Pulp Producers; formerly Chairman of South American Mineralogical Investments, Ltd., etc., etc.

"How did you get hold of this, Monty?" he asked.

"A young fellow in the office gave it to me," said Monty. "Apparently he was trying to make a bit of money on the side by selling these bonds, but lots of people seem to have heard about 'em. I pinched the book, and told him not to be an ass because he'd probably find himself in clink with the organizers when it blew up, but I thought you might like to have a look at it."

"I would," said the Saint thoughtfully and poured another whisky.

He read the booklet through at his leisure, later, and felt tempted to send Monty Hayward a complimentary case of Old Curio on the strength of it, for the glow of contentment and goodwill towards men which spreads over the rabid entomologist who digs a new kind of beetle out of a log is as the frosts of Siberia to the glow which warms the heart of the professional buccaneer who uncovers a new swindle.

For the stock-in-trade of Mr Sumner Journ was Trees.

It may be true, as the poet bleats, that Only God Can Make a Tree, but it is also true that only a man capable of growing such a moustache as lurked coyly beneath the sheltering schnozzola of Mr Sumner Journ could have invented such an enticing method of making God's creation pay gigantic dividends.

The exposition started off with a picture of some small particles of matter collected in a tea-cup, and it was explained that these were the seeds of *pinus palustris*, or the long-leaved pine. "Obviously," said the writer, "even a child must know that these can only be worth a matter of pennies." There followed an artistic photograph of some full-grown pines rearing towards the sky. "Just as obviously," said the writer, "everyone must see that these trees must have some value worth mentioning; probably a value that would run into pounds." The actual value, it was explained, did indeed run into pounds; in fact, the value of the trees illustrated would be three pounds or more. Furthermore, declared the writer, whereas in Florida these trees took forty-five years to reach maturity, In the exceptional climate of the Brazilian mountains they attained their full growth in about ten years. The one great drain on timber profits hitherto had been the cost of transport, but this the Brazilian Timber Company had triumphantly eliminated by purchasing their ground along the banks of the Parana River (inset photograph of large river) which by the force of its current would convey all logs thrown into it to the coast at *no cost at all.*

Investors were accordingly implored, in their own interests, to gather together at least thirty pounds and purchase with it a Brazilian Timber Bond—which could be arranged, if necessary, by instalments. On buying this bond, they would become the virtual owners of an acre of ground in this territory, and the seeds of trees would be planted in it without further charge. It was asserted that twenty-five trees could easily grow on this acre, which when cut down at maturity would provide one hundred cords of wood. Taking the price of wood at three pounds a cord, it was therefore obvious that in about ten years' time this acre would be worth three hundred pounds—"truly," said the prospectus, "a golden return on such a modest investment." The theme was developed at great length with no little literary skill, even going so far as to suggest that on the figures quoted, the investor who bought one thirty-pound bond every year for ten years would in the eleventh year commence to draw an annuity of three hundred pounds per annum *for ever*, since as soon as the trees had been felled in the first acre *it could be planted out again.*

"Well, have you bought your Brazilian Timber Bond?" asked Monty Hayward a day or two later.

Simon grinned and looked out of the window—he was down at the country house in Surrey which he had recently bought for a week-end retreat.

"I've got two acres here," he murmured. "We might look around for somebody to give us sixty quid to plant some more trees in it."

"The really brilliant part of it," said Monty, filling his pipe, "is that this bloke proposes to pay out all the profit in a lump in ten years' time, but until then he doesn't undertake to pay anything. So if he's been working this stunt for four years now, as it says in the book, he's still got another five years clear to go on selling his bonds before any of the bondholders has a right to come around and say, 'Oi, what about my three hundred quid?' Unless some nosey parker makes a special trip into the middle of Brazil and comes back and says there aren't any pine trees growing in those parts, or he's seen the concession and it's just a large swamp with a few blades of grass and a lot of mosquitoes buzzing about, I don't see how he can help getting away with a fortune if he finds enough mugs."

The Saint lighted a cigarette.

"There's nothing to stop him taking it in," he remarked gently, "but he's still got to get away with it."

Mr Sumner Journ would have seen nothing novel in the qualification. Since the first day when he began those practical surveys of the sucker birth-rate, the problem of finally getting away with it, accompanied by his moustache and his plunder, had never been entirely absent from his thoughts, although he had taken considerable pains to steer a course which would keep him outside the reach of the Law. But the collapse of South American Mineralogical Investments, Ltd., had brought him within unpleasantly close range of danger, and about the ultimate fate of Brazilian Timber Bonds he had no illusions.

Simon Templar would have found nothing psychologically contradictory in the fact that a man who, cultivating the world's most original moustache with microscopic perfection of detail, had overlooked the fundamental point that a moustache should be visible, should, when creating a Timber Company, have overlooked the prime essential that the one thing which a Timber Company must possess, its *sine qua non*, so to speak, is timber. Mr Journ had compiled his inducements with unlimited care from encyclopaedias and the information supplied by genuine timber-producing firms, calculating the investors' potential profits according to a mathematical system of his own; the only thing he had omitted to do was to provide himself with the requisite land for afforestation. He had selected his site from an atlas, and had immediately forgotten all the other necessary steps towards securing a title to it.

In the circumstances, it was only natural that Mr Sumner Journ, telling tall stories about timber, should remember that the day was coming when he himself would have to set out, metaphorically at least, in the direction of the tall timber which is the fugitive's traditional refuge, but he reckoned that the profit would be worth it. The only point on which he was a trifle hazy, as other such schemers have been before him, was the precise moment at which the getaway ought to be made, and it was with a sudden sinking of heart that he heard the name of the man who called to see him at his office on a certain afternoon.

"Inspector Tombs?" he said with a rather pallid heartiness. "I think I have met you somewhere before."

"I'm the CID Inspector in this division," said the visitor blandly.

Mr Journ nodded. He knew now where he had seen his caller before—it was the man who had been talking to Chief Inspector Teal in Swallow Street, and who had stared at him so intently.

Mr Journ opened a drawer and took out a box of cigars with unsteady hands.

"What can I do for you, Inspector?" he asked.

Somewhat to his surprise, Inspector Tombs willingly helped himself to a handful, and sat down in an armchair.

"You can give me money," said Inspector Tombs brazenly, and the wild leaping of Sumner Journ's heart died down to a painful throbbing.

"For one of your charities, perhaps? Well, I have never been miserly—"

The Saint shook his head.

"For me," he said flatly. "The Yard has asked us to keep an eye on you, and I think you need a friend in this manor. Chuck the bluffing, Journ—I'm here for business."

Sumner Journ was silent for a moment, but he was not thinking of resuming the bluff. That wouldn't help. He had to thank his stars that his first police visitor was a man who so clearly and straightforwardly understood the value of hard cash.

"How much do you want?"

"Two hundred pounds," was the calm reply.

Mr Journ put up a hand and twirled one of the tiny horns of his wee moustache with the tip of his finger and thumb. His hard brown eyes studied Inspector Tombs unwinkingly.

"That's a lot of money," he said with an effort.

"What I can tell you is worth it," Simon told him grimly.

Mr Journ hesitated for a short time longer, and then he took out a cheque-book and dipped his pen in the inkwell.

"Make it out to Bearer," said the Saint, who in spite of his morbid affection for the cognomen of "Tombs" had not yet thought it worthwhile opening a bank account in that name.

Journ completed the cheque, blotted it, and passed it across the desk. In his mind he was wondering if it was the fee for Destiny's warning; if Scotland Yard had asked the local division to "keep an eye on him," it was a sufficient hint that his activities had not passed unnoticed, and a suggestion that further inquiries might be expected to follow. He had not thought that it would happen so soon, but since it had happened, he felt a leaden heaviness at the pit of his stomach and a restless anxiety that arose from something more than a mere natural resentment at being forced to pay petty blackmail to a dishonest detective. And yet, so great was his seasoning of confidence that even then he was not anticipating any urgent danger.

"Well, what can you tell me?" he said.

Simon put the cheque away.

"The tip is to get out," he said bluntly, and Mr Journ went white.

"Wha . . . what?" he stammered.

"You shouldn't complain," said the Saint callously. "You've been going for four years, and you must have made a packet. Now we're on to you. When I tell you to get out, I mean it. The Yard didn't ask us to keep an eye on you. What they did was to send an order through for a raid this afternoon. Chief Inspector Teal is coming down himself at four o'clock to take charge of it. That's worth two hundred pounds to know, isn't it?"

He stood up.

"You've got about an hour to clear out—you'd better make the most of it," he said.

For several minutes after the detective had gone Mr Journ was in a daze. It was the first time that the consequences of his actions had loomed up in his vision as glaring realities. Arrest—police court—remand—the Old Bailey—penal servitude—the whole gamut of a crash, he had known about in the abstract like everyone else, but his self-confident imagination had never paused to put himself in the leading role. The sudden realisation of what had crept up upon him struck him like a blow in the solar plexus. He sat trembling in his chair, gasping like a stranded fish, feeling his knee-joints melting like butter in a frightful paralysis of panic. Whenever he had visualized the end before, it had never been like this: it had been on a date of his own choosing, after he had made all his plans in unhurried comfort, when he could pack up and beat his trail for the tall timber as calmly as if he had been going off on a legitimate business trip, without fear of interference. This catastrophe pouncing on him out of a clear sky scattered his thoughts like dry leaves in a gale.

And then he got a grip on himself. The getaway still had to be made. He still had an hour—and the banks were open. If he could keep his head, think quickly, act and plan as he had never had to do before, he might still make the grade.

"I'm feeling a bit washed out," he told his secretary, and certainly he looked it. "I think I'll go home."

He went out and hailed a taxi, half expecting to feel a heavy hand drop on his shoulder even as he climbed in.

It was getting late, and he had several things to do. He had been so sure that his Brazilian Timber Bonds had a long lease of life ahead of them that he had not yet given any urgent thought to the business of shifting his profits out of the country. At the first bank where he called he presented a cheque whose size pushed up the cashier's eyebrows.

"This will practically close your account, Mr Journ," he said.

"It won't be out for long," Journ told him, with all the nonchalance he could muster. "I'm putting through a rather big deal this afternoon, and I've got to work in cash."

He stopped at two other banks, where he had accounts in different names, and also at a safe-deposit, where his box yielded him a thick wad of various European currencies. When he had finished, his briefcase was bulging with more than sixty thousand pounds in negotiable cash.

He climbed back into his taxi and drove to his apartment near Baker Street. There would not be much time for packing, he reflected, studying his watch feverishly, but he must pick up his passport, and as many everyday necessities as he could cram into a valise in five minutes would be a help. The taxi stopped, and Mr Journ opened the door and prepared to jump out, but before he could do so a man appeared at the opening and plunged in on top of him, practically throwing him back on to the seat. Sumner Journ's heart leaped sickeningly into his mouth, and then he recognized the dark piratical features of "Inspector Tombs."

"Whasser matter?" Journ got out hoarsely.

"You can't go in there," rapped the Saint. "Teal's on his way. Put the raid forward half an hour. They're looking for you." He opened the driver's partition, "South Kensington Station," he ordered. "And step on it!"

The taxi moved on again, and Mr Journ stared wildly out of the windows. A uniformed constable chanced to cross the street behind them towards his door. He sank back in terror, and Simon closed the partition and settled into the other corner.

"But what am I going to do?" quavered Journ. "My passport's in there!"

"It wouldn't be any use to you," said the Saint tersely. "We know you've got one, and we know what name it's in. They'll be watching for you at all the ports. You'd never get through."

"But where can I go?" Journ almost sobbed.

Simon lighted a cigarette and looked at him.

"Have you any more money?"

"Yes." Sumner Journ saw his companion's keen blue eyes fixed on the swollen briefcase which he was clutching on his knees, and added belatedly, "A little."

"You'll need a lot," said the Saint. "I've risked my job standing outside your apartment to catch you when you arrived, if you got there before Teal, and I didn't do it for nothing. Now listen. I've got a friend who does a bit of smuggling from the Continent with a private plane. He's got his own landing-grounds, here and in France. I've done him a few favours, the same as I've done for you already, and I can get him to take you to France—or farther, if you want to go. It's your only chance, and it'll cost you two thousand pounds."

Mr Journ swallowed.

"All right," he gulped. "All right. I'll pay it."

"It's cheap at the price," said Inspector Tombs, and leaned forward to give further instructions to the driver.

Presently they turned into a mews off Queen's Gate. Simon paid off the cab, and asked the garage proprietor for the use of a telephone. He spoke a few cryptic words to his connection, and returned smiling.

"It's all fixed," he said. "Let's go."

There was a car waiting—a big cream and red speedster that looked as if it could pass anything else on the road and cost its owner a small fortune for the privilege. In a few moments Mr Journ, still clutching his precious bag, found himself being whirled recklessly through the outskirts of London.

He released one hand from his bag to hold on to his hat, and submitted to the hurricane speed of the getaway in a kind of trance. The brilliant driving of his guide made no impression on his numbed brain, and even the route they took registered itself on his mind only subconsciously. His whole existence had passed into a sort of cyclonic nightmare which took away his breath and left a ghastly gnawing emptiness in his chest. The passage of time was merely a change in the positions of the hands of his watch, without any other significance.

And then, in the same deadened way, he became aware that the car had stopped, and the driver was getting out. They were in a narrow lane far from the main road, somewhere between Tring and Aylesbury.

"This is as far as we go, brother," said the Saint.

Mr Journ levered himself stiffly out. There were open fields all around, partly hidden by the hedges which lined the lane.

Inspector Tombs was lighting another cigarette. "And now, dear old bird," he murmured, "you must pay your fare."

Sumner Journ nodded, and fumbled with the fastening of his case.

"But I don't mind taking it in the bag," Simon said quietly.

Mr Journ looked up. There was a subtle implication in the way the words were said which struck a supernatural chill into his blood. And in the next second he knew why, for his lifting eyes looked straight into the muzzle of an automatic.

Slowly Mr Journ's eyes dilated. He stopped breathing. A cold intangible hand closed round his heart in a vice-like grip, and the muscles of his face twitched spasmodically.

"But you can't do that!" he screamed suddenly. "You can't take it all!"

"That is a matter of opinion," said the Saint equably, and then, before Mr Journ really knew what was happening, a strong brown hand had shot out and grasped the briefcase and twitched it out of Mr Journ's desperate grip with a deft twist that was too quick for the eye to follow.

With a guttural gasp Sumner Journ lurched forward to tear it back, and found himself pushed away like a child.

"Now don't be silly," said the Saint. "I don't want to hurt you—much. You've lived like a prince for four years on the sucker crop, and a bloke like you can always think up a new racket. Don't take it so much to heart. Disguise yourself and make a fresh start. Shave off your moustache, and no one will recognize you."

"But what am I going to do?" Sumner Journ shrieked at him as he seated himself again in the car. "How am I going to get away?"

Simon stopped with his foot on the clutch.

"Bless my soul!" he said. "I almost forgot."

He dipped a long arm under the seat and brought up a small article which he pushed into Mr Journ's trembling hands. Then the great car leapt away with a sudden roar from the exhaust, and Mr Journ was left staring at his consolation prize with a face that had gone ashen grey.

It was a little toy aeroplane, and tied to it was a tag label on which was written:

With the compliments of the Saint.

THE ART PHOTOGRAPHER

"It becomes increasingly obvious," said the Saint, "that the time has arrived when we shall have to squash Mr Gilbert Tanfold."

He did not utter this prophecy within the hearing of Mr Tanfold, for that would have been a gesture of a kind in which Simon Templar indulged more rarely now than he had once been wont to do. If the time had arrived when the squashing of Mr Tanfold became a public service which no altruistic freebooter could refuse to perform, the time had also passed when the squashing could be carried out with full theatrical honours, with a haloed drawing on a plain card left pinned to the resultant blob of grease to tell the world that Simon Templar had been there. There was too much interest in his activities at Scotland Yard for anything like that to be entered upon without an elaborate preparation of alibis, which was rather more trouble than he thought Mr Tanfold was worth. But the ripeness for squashing, the *zerquetschenreiflichkeit*, if we may borrow a word which the English language so unhappily lacks, of Mr Gilbert Tanfold, even if it could not be made a public ceremony, could not be overlooked altogether for any such trivial reason.

The advertisements of Mr Tanfold appeared in the back pages of several appropriate journals, and were distinguished by their prodigality of exclamation marks and their unusual vagueness of content. The specimen which was answered by a certain Mr Tombs was fairly typical.

It was an advertisement which regularly brought in a remarkable amount of business, considering that it left so much to the imagination, but certain imaginations are like that.

PARISIAN ART PHOTOS!
RARE! EXTRAORDINARY!!

Special Offer! (Cannot be repeated!) 100 unique poses,

3/6 post free. Exceptional rarities, 10/-, 15/-, £1, £5 each!
Also BOOKS!!!!
all editions, curiosities, erotica, etc.! "Garden of Love" (very rare) 10/6.
Send for illustrated catalogue and samples!!!

G. TANFOLD & CO.,
Gaul St., Birmingham.

The imagination of Mr Gilbert Tanfold, however, soared far above the ordinary financial possibilities of this commonplace catering to pornography. If ever there was a man who did not believe in Art for Art's sake, this man walked the earth with his ankles enveloped in the spats of Mr Gilbert Tanfold. Where any other man trading in these artistic lines would have been content with the generous profit from the sale of his "exceptional rarities," Mr Tanfold had made them merely stepping-stones to bigger things, which was one of the reasons for his tempting *zerquetschenreiflichkeit* aforesaid.

Every letter which came to his cheap two-roomed office in Birmingham was examined with an interest that would have astonished the unsuspecting writer. Those which, by inferior notepaper, cheaply printed letterheads, and/or clumsy handwriting, branded their authors as persons of no great substance, merely had their orders filled by return, as specified; and that, so far as Mr Tanfold was concerned, was the end of them. But those letters which, by expensive paper, die-stamped letterheads, and/or an educated hand, hinted at a client who really had no business to be collecting rude pictures or "curiosities," came under the close scrutiny of Mr Tanfold himself, and their orders were merely the beginning of many other things.

Mr Tombs wrote on the notepaper of the Palace Royal Hotel, London, which was so expensive that only millionaires, film stars, and buccaneers could afford to live there, and it is a curious fact that Mr Tanfold entirely forgot that third category of possible guests when he saw the letter. It must be admitted, in extenuation, that Simon Templar misled him. For as his profession (which all customers were asked to state with their order) he gave "*Businessman (Australian).*"

Mr Gilbert Tanfold, like others of his ilk, had a sound working knowledge of the peculiar psychology of wealthy Colonials at large in London—of that openhearted, almost pathetically guileless eagerness to be good fellows which leads them to buy gold bricks in the Strand, or to hand thousands of pounds in small change to two perfect strangers as evidence of their good faith—and he was so impressed with the potentialities of Mr Tombs that he ordered the very choicest pictures in his stock to be included in the filling of the order, and made a personal trip to London the next day to find out more about this Heaven-sent bird from the bush.

The problem of making stealthy inquiries about a guest in a place like the Palace Royal Hotel might have troubled anyone less apt in the art of investigating prospective victims, but to Mr Tanfold it was little more than a matter of routine, a case for Method C4 (*g*). He knew that lonely men in a big city will always talk to a barman, and simply followed the same procedure himself. To a man as practised as he was in the technique of drawing gossip out of unwitting informants, results came quickly. Yes, the barman at the Palace Royal knew Mr Tombs.

"A tall dark gentleman with glasses—is that him?"

"That's him," agreed Mr Tanfold glibly, and learned, as he had hoped, that Mr Tombs was a regular and solitary patron of the bar.

It did not take him much longer to discover that Mr Tombs's father was an exceedingly rich and exceedingly pious citizen of Melbourne, a loud noise in the Chamber of Commerce, an only slightly smaller noise in the local government, and an indefatigable guardian of public morality. He also gathered that Mr Tombs, besides carrying on his father's business, was expected to carry on his moralizing activities also, and that this latter inheritance was much less acceptable to Mr Tombs, Jr., than it should have been to a thoroughly well-brought-up young man. The soul of Sebastian Tombs II, it appeared, yearned for naughtier things: the panting of the psalmist's heart after the water-brooks, seemingly, was positively as no pant at all compared with the panting of the heart of Tombs *fils* after those spicy improprieties on which it was the devoted hobby of Tombs *père* to bring down all the weight of public indignation. The barman knew this because the younger Tombs had sought his advice on the subject of wild-oat sowing in London, and had confessed himself sadly disappointed with the limited range of fields available to the casual sower. He was, in fact, living only for the day when the business which had brought him to England would be over, and he would be free to continue his search for sin in Paris.

Mr Tanfold did not rub his hands gloatingly, but he ordered another drink, and when it had been served he laid a five-pound note on the bar.

"You needn't bother about the change," he said, "if you'd like to do me a small favour."

The barman looked at the money, and picked it up. The only other customers at the bar at that moment were two men at the other end of the room, who were out of earshot.

"What can I do, sir?" he asked.

Mr Tanfold put a card on the counter—it bore the name of a firm of private inquiry agents who existed only in his imagination.

"I've been engaged to make some inquiries about this fellow," he said. "Will you point him out to me when he comes in? I'd like you to introduce us. Tell him I'm another lonely Australian, and ask if he'd like to meet me—that's all I want."

The barman hesitated for a second, and then folded the note and put it in his pocket with a cynical nod. Mr Tombs meant nothing to him, and five pounds was five pounds.

"That ought to be easy enough, sir," he said. "He usually gets here about this time. What name do I say?"

It was, as a matter of fact, almost ridiculously simple—so simple that it never occurred to Mr Tanfold to wonder why. To him, it was only an ordinary tribute to the perfection of his routine—it is an illuminating sidelight on the vanity of "clever" criminals that none of Simon Templar's multitudinous victims had ever paused to wonder whether perhaps someone else might not be able to duplicate their brilliantly applied psychology, and do it just a little better than they did.

Mr Tombs came in at half past six. After he had had a drink and glanced at an evening paper, the barman whispered to him. He looked at Mr Tanfold. He left his stool and walked over. Mr Tanfold beamed. The barman performed the requisite ceremony. "What'll you have?" said Mr Tombs. "This is with me," said Mr Tanfold.

It was as easy as that.

"Cheerio," said Mr Tombs.

"Here's luck," said Mr Tanfold.

"Lousy weather," said Mr Tombs, finishing his drink at the second gulp.

"Well," said Mr Tanfold, "London isn't much of a place to be in at any time."

The blue eyes of Mr Tombs, behind their horn-rimmed spectacles, focused on him with a sudden dawn of interest. Actually, Simon was assuring himself that any man born of woman could really look as unsavoury as Mr Tanfold and still remain immune to beetle-paste. In this he had some justification, for Mr Gilbert Tanfold was a small and somewhat fleshy man with a loose lower lip and a tendency to pimples, and his natty clothes and the mauve shirts which he affected did not improve his appearance, though no doubt he believed they did. But the only expression which Mr Tanfold discerned was that which might have stirred the features of a weeping Israelite by the waters of Babylon who perceived a fellow exile drawing nigh to hang his harp on an adjacent tree.

"You've found that too, have you?" said Mr Tombs, with the morbid satisfaction of a hospital patient discovering an equally serious case in the next bed.

"I've found it for the last six months," said Mr Tanfold firmly. "And I'm still finding it. No fun to be had anywhere. Everything's too damn respectable. I hope I'm not shocking you—"

"Not a bit," said Mr Tombs. "Let's have another drink."

"This is with me," said Mr Tanfold.

The drinks were set up, raised, and swallowed.

"I'm not respectable," said Mr Tanfold candidly. "I like a bit of fun. You know what I mean," Mr Tanfold winked—a contortion of his face which left no indecency unsuggested. "Like you can get in Paris, if you know where to look for it."

"I know," said Mr Tombs hungrily. "Have you been there?"

"Have I been there!" said Mr Tanfold.

Considering the point later, the Saint was inclined to doubt whether Mr Tanfold had been there, for the stories he was able to tell of his adventures in the Gay City were far more lurid than anything else of its kind which the Saint had ever heard—and Simon Templar reckoned that he knew Paris from the Champs-Élysées to the fortifs. Nevertheless, they served to pass the time very congenially until half past seven, when Mr Tanfold suggested that they might have dinner together and afterwards pool their resources in The quest for "a bit of fun."

"I've been here a bit longer than you," said Mr Tanfold generously, "so perhaps I've found a few places you haven't come across."

It was a very good dinner washed down with liberal quantities of liquid, for Mr Tanfold was rather proud of the hardness of his head. As the wine flowed, his guest's tongue loosened—but there, again, it had never occurred to Mr Tanfold that a tongue might be loosened simply because its owner was anxious that no effort should be spared to give its host all the information which he wanted to hear.

"If my father knew I'd been to Paris, I'm perfectly certain he'd disinherit me," Mr Tombs revealed. "But he won't know. He thinks I'm sailing from Tilbury, but I'm going to have a week in Paris and catch the boat at Marseilles. He thinks Paris is a sort of waiting-room for hell. But he's like that about any place where you can have a good time. And five years ago he disowned a younger brother of mine just because he'd been seen at a night club with a girl who was considered a bit fast. Wouldn't listen to any excuses—just threw him out of the house and out of the business, and hasn't even mentioned his name since. That's the sort of puritan he is."

Mr Tanfold made sympathetic noises with his tongue, while the area of flesh under the front of his mauve shirt which might by some stretch of imagination have been described as his bosom warmed with the glowing ecstasy of a dog sighting a new and hitherto undreamed-of lamp-post.

"When are you making this trip to Paris, old man?" he asked enviously.

"At the end of next week, I hope," said the unregenerate scion of the house of Tombs. "It all depends on how soon I can get my business finished. I've got to go to Birmingham on Friday to see some manufacturers, worse luck—and that'll probably be even deadlier than London."

Mr Tanfold's head hooked forward on his neck, and his eyes expanded.

"Birmingham?" he ejaculated. "Well, I'm damned! What a coincidence!"

"What is?"

"Why, your going to Birmingham. And you think it's a deadly place! Haven't you ever heard of Gilbert Tanfold?"

Mr Tombs nodded.

"Sells pictures, doesn't he? Yes, I've had some of 'em. I didn't think they were so hot."

Mr Tanfold was so happy that this aspersion on his Art glanced off him like a pea off a tortoise.

"You can't have had any of his good ones," he said. "He keeps those for people he knows personally. I met him last week, and he showed me pictures . . ." Mr Tanfold went into details which eclipsed even his adventures in Paris. "The coincidence is," he wound up, "that I've got an invitation to go to Birmingham on Friday myself and visit his studio."

Mr Tombs swallowed so that his Adam's apple jiggered up and down.

"Gosh," he said jealously, "that ought to be interesting. I wish I had your luck."

Tanfold's face lengthened commiseratingly, as if the thought that his new-found friend would be unable to share his good fortune had taken away all his enthusiasm for the project. And then, as if the solution had only just struck him, he brightened again.

"But why shouldn't you?" he demanded. "I said we'd pool our resources, and I ought to be able to arrange it. Now, suppose we go to Birmingham together—that is, if you don't think I'm thrusting myself on you too much—"

And that part also was absurdly easy, so that Mr Gilbert Tanfold returned to his more modest hotel much later that night with his heart singing the happy song of a vulture diving on a particularly fruity morsel of carrion. He had not even had to devise any pretext to induce the simple Tombs to travel to Birmingham—Mr Tombs had already planned the trip in his itinerary with a thoughtfulness which almost suggested that he had foreseen Mr Tanfold's need. And yet, once again, this obvious explanation never occurred seriously to Gilbert Tanfold. He preferred to believe in miracles wrought for his benefit by a kindly Providence, which was a disastrous error for him to make.

The rest of his preparations proceeded with the same smoothness of routine. They went to Birmingham together on the Friday, and kept the steward busy on the Pullman throughout the journey. In Birmingham they had lunch together, diluted with more liquor. By the time they were ready for their visit to the studios of G. Tanfold & Co., Mr Tanfold estimated that his companion was in an ideal condition to enjoy his experience. On arrival they were informed, most unveraciously, that urgent business had called Mr Tanfold himself to London, but he had arranged that they should have the free run of the premises. The entertainment offered, it is sufficient to record, was one in which Mr Tanfold believed he had surpassed himself as an impresario of impropriety.

Mr Tombs, with remarkable fortune, was able to conclude his business on the Saturday morning, and returned to London on the Sunday. He announced his intention of leaving for Paris on the Tuesday, and they parted with mutual expressions of goodwill. Mr Tanfold said that he himself would return to London on Monday, and they arranged to lunch together on that day and go on to paint the town red.

When Mr Tanfold arrived at the Palace Royal Hotel a little before one o'clock on Monday, however, he did not have the air of a man who was getting set to experiment with what could be done with a pot of red paint and the metropolitan skyline. Laying his hat and stick on the table and pulling off his lavender-tinted gloves in Mr Tombs's suite, he was laconically unresponsive to the younger Tombs's effusive cries of welcome.

"Look here, Tombs," he said bluntly, when he had straightened his heliotrope tie, "there's something you'd better know."

"Tell me all, dear old wombat," said Mr Tombs, who appeared to have acquired some of the frothier mannerisms of the city during his visit. "What have you done?"

"I haven't introduced myself properly," said his guest brazenly. "I am Gilbert Tanfold."

For a moment the antipodean Tomblet seemed taken aback, and then he grinned good-humouredly.

"Well, you certainly spruced me, Gilbert," he said. "What a joke! So it was really your own studio we went to!"

"Yes," said Mr Tanfold grimly, "it was my own studio."

Mr Tombs grinned again. He made remarks about Mr Tanfold's unparalleled sense of humour in terms which were clearly designed to be flattering, but which were too biological in trend to be acceptable in mixed company. Mr Tanfold, however, was not there to be flattered. He cut his host short with a flick of one well-manicured hand.

"Let's talk business," he said shortly. "I've got a photograph that was taken of you while you were at the studio."

Mr Tombs's expression wavered uncertainly, and it may be mentioned that that waver was not the least difficult of the facial exercises which the Saint had had to go through during his acquaintance with Mr Tanfold. For the expression which was at that moment spreading itself across Simon Templar's inside was a wholly different affair, which would have made the traditional Cheshire cat look like a mask of melancholy: even then, he had not outgrown the urchin glee of watching the feet of the ungodly planting themselves firmly on the banana-skin of doom.

Nevertheless, outwardly he wavered.

"Photograph?" he repeated.

Mr Tanfold drew out his wallet, extracted a photograph therefrom, and handed it over. The Saint stared at it, and beheld his own unmistakable likeness, except for the horn-rimmed spectacles which were not a normal part of his attire, wrapped in a most undignified grapple with a damsel whose clothing set up its own standard of the irreducible minimum of diaphanous underwear.

"Good Lord!" he gasped. "When was this taken?"

"You ought to remember," said Mr Tanfold, polishing his fingernails on his coat lapel.

"But . . . but . . ." The first dim inkling of the perils of the picture which he held seemed to dawn on Mr Tombs, and he choked. "But this was an accident! You remember, Tanfold. They wanted her to sit on top of a step-ladder—they asked me to help her up—and I only caught her when she slipped—"

"I know," said Mr Tanfold. "But nobody else does. You're the mug, Tombs. That photograph wouldn't look so good in a Melbourne paper, would it? With a caption saying, 'Son of prominent Melbourne businessman "holding the baby" at artists' revel in Paris'—or something like that."

Mr Tombs swallowed.

"But I can explain it all," he protested. "It was—"

"Your father wouldn't listen to any explanations when your younger brother made a mistake, would he?" said Tanfold. "Besides, what were you doing in that studio at all? Take a look at where you are, Tombs, and get down to business. I'm here to sell you the negative of that picture—at a price."

The Saint's mouth opened.

"But that . . . that's blackmail!" he gasped.

"It doesn't bother me what you call it," Tanfold said smugly. "There's the position, and I want five thousand pounds to let you out of it."

Simon's eyes narrowed.

"Well, perhaps this'll bother you," he said, and a fist like a chunk of stone shot over and sent Tanfold sprawling into the opposite corner of the room. Mr Tombs unbuttoned his coat. "Get up and come back for some more, you lousy crook," he invited.

Tanfold wiped his smashed lip with his handkerchief, and spat out a tooth. His small eyes went black and evil, but he did not get up.

"Just for that, it'll cost you ten thousand," he said viciously. "That stuff won't help you, you damn fool. Whatever you do, you won't get the negative back that way."

"It gives me a lot of fun, anyhow," said the Saint coldly. "And I only wish your miserable body could stand up to more of it."

He picked Mr Tanfold up by the front of his mauve shirt with one hand, and slammed him back into the corner again with the other, and then he dropped into a chair by the table, pushed Mr Tanfold's hat and stick on to the floor, and took out a cheque-book and a fountain pen.

He made out the cheque with some care, and dropped that also on the floor.

"There's your money," he said, and watched the trembling Mr Tanfold pick it up. "Now you can get out."

Mr Tanfold had more things to say, but caught a glimpse of the unholy light in Mr Tombs's mild blue eyes, and changed his mind in the nick of time. He gathered up his hat and stick and got out.

In one of the washrooms of the hotel he repaired some of the damage that had been done to his natty appearance, and reflected malevolently that Mr Tombs was somewhat optimistic if he thought he was going to secure his negative for a paltry ten thousand pounds after what had happened. In a day or two he would make a further demand—but this time he would take the precaution of doing it by telephone. With a photograph like that in his possession, Mr Tanfold could see nothing to stop him bleeding his victim to the verge of suicide, and he was venomously prepared to do it.

He looked at the cheque again. It was made payable to Bearer, and was drawn on a bank in Berkeley Street. Ten minutes later he was passing it through the grille.

"Do you mind waiting a few moments, sir?" said the cashier. "I don't know whether we have enough currency to meet this without sending out."

Mr Tanfold took a chair and waited, continuing his spiteful thoughts.

He waited five minutes. He waited ten minutes. Then he went to the counter again.

"We're a bit short on cash, sir," explained the cashier, "and it turns out that the bank we usually borrow from is a bit short too. We've sent a man to another branch, and he ought to be back any minute now."

A few moments later the clerk beckoned him.

"Would you step into the manager's office, sir?" he asked. "We don't like passing such a large sum as ten thousand pounds over the counter. I'll give it to you in there, if you don't mind."

Still unsuspecting, Mr Tanfold stepped in the direction indicated. And the first person he saw in the office was the younger Tombs.

Mr Tanfold stopped dead, and his heart missed several beats. A wild instinct urged him to turn and flee, but the strength seemed to have ebbed out of his legs. It would have availed him nothing, anyway, for the courteous clerk had slipped from behind the counter and followed him—and he was a healthy young heavyweight who looked as if he would have been more at home on a football field than behind the grille of a cashier's desk.

"Come in, Tanfold," said the manager sternly.

Mr Tanfold forced himself to come in. Even then he did not see what could possibly have gone wrong—certainly he was unable to envisage any complication in which the photograph he held would not be a deciding factor.

"Are you the gentleman who just presented this cheque?" asked the manager, holding it up.

Tanfold moistened his lips.

"That's right," he said boldly.

"You were asked to wait," said the manager, "because Mr Tombs rang us up a short while ago and said that this cheque had been stolen from his book, and he asked us to detain anyone who presented it until he got here."

"That's an absurd mistake," Tanfold retorted loudly. "The cheque's made out to me—Mr Tombs wrote it out himself only a few minutes ago."

The manager put his finger-tips together.

"I am familiar with Mr Tombs's handwriting," he said dryly, "and this isn't a bit like it. It looks like a very amateurish forgery to me."

Mr Tanfold's eyes goggled, and his stomach flopped down past the waistband of his trousers and left a sick void in its place. His tongue clove to the roof of his mouth. Whatever else he might have feared, he had never thought of anything like that, and for some seconds the sheer shock held him speechless.

In the silence, Simon Templar smiled—he had only recently decided that his *alter ego* had earned a bank account in its own name, and he did not know how he could have christened it better. He turned to the manager.

"Of course it's a forgery," he said. "But I don't want to be too hard on the man—that's why I asked you over the phone not to send for the police at once. I really believe there's some good in him. You can see from the clumsy way he tried to forge my signature that it's a first attempt."

"That's as you wish, of course, Mr Tombs," said the manager doubtfully. "But—"

"Yes, yes," said the Saint, with a paralysing oleaginousness that would have served to lubricate the bearings of a high-speed engine, "but I've spent a lot of time trying to make this fellow go straight and you can't deny me a last attempt. Let me take him home and talk to him for a while. I'll be responsible for him, and you and the cashier can still be witnesses to what he did if I can't make him see the error of his ways."

Mr Tanfold's bouncing larynx almost throttled him. Never in all his days had he so much as dreamed of being the victim of such a staggering unblushing impudence. In a kind of daze, he felt himself being gripped by the arm, and a brief panorama of London streets swam dizzily through his vision and dissolved deliriously into the facade of the Palace Royal Hotel. Even the power of speech did not return to him until he found himself once more in the painfully reminiscent surroundings of Mr Tombs's suite.

"Well," he demanded hoarsely, "what's the game?"

"The game," answered Simon Templar genially, "is the royal and ancient sport of hoisting engineers with their own petards, dear old wallaby. Take a look at where you are, Gilbert. I'm here to let you out of the mess—at a price."

Mr Tanfold's mouth opened.

"But that . . . that's blackmail!" he gasped.

"It doesn't bother me what you call it," Simon said calmly. "I want twenty-five thousand pounds to forget that you forged my signature. How about it?"

"You can't get it," Tanfold spat out. "If I published that photograph—"

"I should laugh myself sick," said the Saint. "I'm afraid there's something you'd better get wise to, brother. My father isn't a prominent Melbourne business man and social reformer at all, except for your benefit, and you can paste enlargements of that picture all over Melbourne Town Hall for all I care. Make some inquiries outside the bar downstairs, gorgeous, and get up to date. Come along, now—which is it to be? Twenty-five thousand smackers or the hoosegow? Take your choice."

Mr Tanfold's face was turning green.

"I haven't got so much money in cash," he squawked.

"I'll give you a week to find it," said the Saint mercilessly, "and I don't really care much if you do go bankrupt in the process. I find you neither ornamental nor useful. But just in case you think forgery is the only charge you have to answer, you might like to listen to this."

He went through the communicating door to the bedroom, and was back in a moment. Suddenly, through the door, Mr Tanfold heard the sounds of his own voice.

"Let's talk business . . . I've got a photograph that was taken of you while you were at the studio . . ."

With his face going paler and paler, Mr Tanfold listened. He made no sound until the record was finished, and then he let out an abrupt squeal.

"But that isn't all of it!" he yelled. "It leaves off before the place where you gave me the cheque!"

"Of course it does," said the Saint shamelessly. "That would spike the forgery charge, wouldn't it? But as it stands, you've got two things to answer. First you tried to blackmail me, and then, when you found that wouldn't work, you forged my signature to a cheque for ten thousand quid. It was all very rash and naughty of you, Gilbert, and I'm sure the police would take a very serious view of the case—particularly after they'd investigated your business a bit more. Well, well, well, brother—we all make mistakes, and I'm afraid I shall have to send that Dictaphone record along to Chief Inspector Teal, as well as charging you with forgery, if you haven't come through with the spondulix inside seven days."

Once again words rose to Mr Tanfold's lips, and once again, glimpsing the unholy gleam in the Saint's eye and remembering his previous experience in that room, they stuck in his throat. And once again Simon went to the door and opened it.

"This is the way out," said the Saint.

Mr Gilbert Tanfold moved hazily towards the portal. As he passed through it, a pair of hands fell on his shoulders and steadied him with a light but masterful grip. Some premonition of his fate must have reached him, for his shrill cry disturbed the regal quietude of the Palace Royal Hotel even before the toe of a painfully powerful shoe impacted on his tender posterior had lifted him enthusiastically on his way.

THE MAN WHO LIKED TOYS

Chief Inspector Claud Eustace Teal rested his pudgy elbows on the table and unfolded the pink wrappings from a fresh wafer of chewing gum.

"That's all there was to it," he said. "And that's the way it always is. You get an idea, you spread a net out among the stool pigeons, and you catch a man. Then you do a lot of dull routine work to build up the evidence. That's how a real detective does his job, and that's the way Sherlock Holmes would have had to do it if he'd worked at Scotland Yard."

Simon Templar grinned amiably, and beckoned a waiter for the bill. The orchestra yawned and went into another dance number, but the floor show had been over for half an hour, and the room was emptying rapidly. It was two o'clock in the morning, and a fair proportion of the patrons of the Palace Royal had some work to think of before the next midnight.

"Maybe you're right, Claud," said the Saint mildly.

"I know I'm right," said Mr Teal, in his drowsy voice. And then, as Simon pushed a fiver on to the plate, he chuckled. "But I know you like pulling our legs about it, too."

They steered their way around the tables and up the stairs to the hotel lobby. It was another of those rare occasions when Mr Teal had been able to enjoy the Saint's company without any lurking uneasiness about the outcome. For some weeks his life had been comparatively peaceful. No hints of further Saintly lawlessness had come to his ears.

At such times he admitted to himself, with a trace of genuine surprise, that there were few things which entertained him more than a social evening with the gay buccaneer who had set Scotland Yard more mysteries than they would ever solve.

"Drop in and see me next time I'm working on a case, Saint," Teal said in the lobby, with a truly staggering generosity for which the wine must have been partly responsible. "You'll see for yourself how we really do it."

"I'd like to," said the Saint, and if there was the trace of a smile in his eyes when he said it, it was entirely without malice.

He settled his soft hat on his smooth dark head and glanced around the lobby with the vague aimlessness which ordinarily precedes a parting at that hour. A little group of three men had discharged themselves from a nearby lift and were moving boisterously and a trifle unsteadily towards the main entrance. Two of them were hatted and overcoated—a tallish man with a thin line of black moustache, and a tubby red-faced man with rimless spectacles. The third member of the party, who appeared to be the host, was a flabby flat-footed man of about fifty-five with a round bald head and a rather bulbous nose that would have persuaded any observant onlooker to expect that he would have drunk more than the others, which in fact he obviously had. All of them had the dishevelled and rather tragically ridiculous air of Captains of Industry who have gone off duty for the evening.

"That's Lewis Enstone—the chap with the nose," said Teal, who knew everyone. "He might have been one of the biggest men in the City if he could have kept off the bottle."

"And the other two?" asked the Saint incuriously, because he already knew.

"Just a couple of smaller men in the same game. Albert Costello—that's the tall one—and John Hammel." Mr Teal chewed meditatively on his spearmint. "If anything happens to them, I shall want to know where you were at the time," he added warningly.

"I shan't know anything about it," said the Saint piously.

He lighted a cigarette and watched the trio of celebrators disinterestedly. Hammel and Costello he knew something about, but the more sozzled member of the party was new to him.

"You do unnerstan', boys, don't you?" Enstone was articulating pathetically, with his arms spread around the shoulders of his guests in an affectionate manner which contributed helpfully towards his support. "It's jus' business. I'm not hard-hearted. I'm kind to my wife and children an' everything, God bless 'em. An' anytime I can do anything for either of you—why, you jus' lemme know."

"That's awfully good of you, old man," said Hammel, with the blurry-eyed solemnity of his condition.

"Le's have lunch together on Tuesday," suggested Costello. "We might be able to talk about something that'd interest you."

"Right," said Enstone dimly. "Lush Tooshday. Hic."

"An' don't forget the kids," said Hammel confidentially.

Enstone giggled.

"I shouldn't forget that." In obscurely elaborate pantomime, he closed his fist with his forefinger extended and his thumb cocked vertically upwards, and aimed the forefinger between Hammel's eyes. "Shtick 'em up," he commanded gravely, and at once relapsed into further merriment, in which his guests joined somewhat hysterically.

The group separated at the entrance amid much handshaking and back-slapping and alcoholic laughter, and Lewis Enstone wended his way back with cautious and preoccupied steps toward the lift. Mr Teal took a fresh bite on his gum and tightened his mouth disgustedly.

"Is he staying here?" asked the Saint.

"He lives here," said the detective. "He's lived here even when we knew for a fact that he hadn't got a penny to his name. Why I remember once—"

He launched into a lengthy anecdote which had all the vitality of personal bitterness in the telling. Simon Templar, listening with the half of one well-trained ear that would prick up into instant attention if the story took any twist that might provide the germ of an adventure, but would remain intently passive if it didn't, smoked his cigarette and gazed abstractedly into space. His mind had that gift of complete division, and he had another job on hand to think about. Somewhere in the course of the story he gathered that Mr Teal had once lost some money on the Stock Exchange over some shares in which Enstone was speculating, but there was nothing much about that misfortune to attract his interest, and the detective's mood of disparaging reminiscence was as good an opportunity as any other for him to plot out a few details of the campaign against his latest quarry.

". . . So I lost my money, and I've kept the rest of it in gilt-edged stuff ever since," concluded Mr Teal rancorously, and Simon took the last inhalation from his cigarette and dropped the stub into an ashtray.

"Thanks for the tip, Claud," he said lightly. "I gather that next time I murder somebody you'd like me to make it a financier."

Teal grunted, and hitched his coat around. "I shouldn't like you to murder anybody," he said from his heart. "Now I've got to go home—I have to get up in the morning."

They walked towards the street doors. On their left they passed the information desk, and beside the desk had been standing a couple of bored and sleepy page-boys. Simon had observed them and their sleepiness as casually as he had observed the colour of the carpet, but all at once he realized that their sleepiness had vanished. He had a sudden queer sensitiveness of suppressed excitement, and then one of the boys said something loud enough to be overheard which stopped Teal in his tracks and turned him abruptly.

"What's that?" he demanded.

"It's Mr Enstone, sir. He just shot himself."

Mr Teal scowled. To the newspapers it would be a surprise and a front-page sensation; to him it was a surprise and a potential menace to his night's rest if he butted into any responsibility. Then he shrugged.

"I'd better have a look," he said, and introduced himself.

There was a scurry to lead him towards the lifts. Mr Teal ambled bulkily into the nearest car, and quite brazenly the Saint followed him. He had, after all, been kindly invited to "drop in" the next time the plump detective was handling a case. Teal put his hands in his pocket and stared in mountainous drowsiness at the downward-flying shaft. Simon studiously avoided his eye, and had a pleasant shock when the detective addressed him almost genially.

"I always thought there was something fishy about that fellow. Did he look as if he'd anything to shoot himself about, except the head that was waiting for him when he woke up?"

It was as if the decease of any financier, however caused, was a benison upon the earth for which Mr Teal could not help being secretly and quite immorally grateful. That was the subtle impression he gave of his private feelings, but the rest of him was impenetrable stolidity and aloofness. He dismissed the escort of page-boys and strode to the door of the millionaire's suite. It was closed and silent. Teal knocked on it authoritatively, and after a moment it opened six inches and disclosed a pale agitated face. Teal introduced himself again and the door opened wider, enlarging the agitated face into the unmistakable full-length portrait of an assistant manager. Simon followed the detective in, and endeavoured to look equally official.

"This will be a terrible scandal, Inspector," said the assistant manager.

Teal looked at him woodenly.

"Were you here when it happened?"

"No. I was downstairs, in my office—"

Teal collected the information, and ploughed past him. On the right, another door opened off the generous lobby, and through it could be seen another elderly man whose equally pale face and air of suppressed agitation bore a certain general similarity and also a self-contained superiority to the first. Even without his sombre black coat and striped trousers, grey side-whiskers and passive hands, he would have stamped himself as something more cosmic than the assistant manager of a hotel—the assistant manager of a man.

"Who are you?" asked Teal.

"I am Fowler, sir. Mr Enstone's valet."

"Were you here?"

"Yes, sir."

"Where is Mr Enstone?"

"In the bedroom, sir."

They moved back across the lobby, with the assistant manager assuming the lead. Teal stopped.

"Will you be in your office if I want you?" he asked with great politeness, and the assistant manager seemed to disappear from the scene even before the door of the suite closed behind him.

Lewis Enstone was dead. He lay on his back beside the bed, with his head half-rolled over to one side, in such a way that both the entrance and the exit of the bullet which had killed him could be seen. It had been fired squarely into his right eye, leaving the ugly trail which only a heavy-calibre bullet fired at close range can leave . . . The gun lay under the fingers of his right hand.

"Thumb on the trigger," Teal noted aloud.

He sat on the edge of the bed, pulling on a pair of gloves, pink-faced and unemotional. Simon observed the room. An ordinary, very tidy bedroom, barren of anything unusual except the subdued costliness of furnishing. Two windows, both shut and fastened. On a table in one corner, the only sign of disorder, the remains of a carelessly-opened parcel. Brown paper, ends of string, a plain cardboard box—empty. The millionaire had gone no further towards undressing than loosening his tie and undoing his collar.

"What happened?" asked Mr Teal.

"Mr Enstone had friends to dinner, sir," explained Fowler, "A Mr Costello—"

"I know that. What happened when he came back from seeing them off?"

"He went straight to bed, sir."

"Was this door open?"

"At first, sir. I asked Mr Enstone about the morning, and he told me to call him at eight. I then asked him whether he wished me to assist him to undress, and he gave me to understand that he did not. He closed the door, and I went back to the sitting-room."

"Did you leave the door open?"

"Yes, sir. I was doing a little clearing up. Then I heard the shot, sir."

"Do you know any reason why Mr Enstone should have shot himself?"

"On the contrary, sir—I understand that his recent speculations had been highly successful."

"Where is his wife?"

"Mrs Enstone and the children have been in Madeira, sir. We are expecting them home tomorrow."

"What was in that parcel, Fowler?" ventured the Saint.

The valet glanced at the table. "I don't know, sir. I believe it must have been left by one of Mr Enstone's guests. I noticed it on the dining-table when I brought in their coats and Mr Enstone came back for it on his return and took it into the bedroom with him."

"You didn't hear anything said about it?" Simon asked.

"No, sir. I was not present after the coffee had been served—I understand that the gentlemen had private business to discuss."

"What are you getting at?" Mr Teal asked seriously.

The Saint smiled apologetically, and being nearest the door, went out to open it as a second knocking disturbed the silence, and let in a grey-haired man with a black bag. While the police surgeon was making his preliminary examination, he drifted into the living-room. The relics of a convivial dinner were all there—cigar-butts in the coffee cups, stains of spilt wine on the cloth, crumbs and ash everywhere, the stale smell of food and smoke hanging in the air—but those things did not interest him. He was not quite sure what would have interested him, but he wandered rather vacantly around the room, gazing introspectively at the prints of character which a long tenancy leaves even on anything so characterless as a hotel apartment. There were pictures on the walls and the side tables, mostly enlarged snapshots revealing Lewis Enstone relaxing in the bosom of his family, which amused Simon for some time. On one of the side tables he found a curious object. It was a small wooden plate on which half a dozen wooden fowls stood in a circle. Their necks were pivoted at the base, and underneath the plate were six short strings joined to the necks and knotted together some distance further down where they were all attached at the same point to a wooden ball. It was these strings, and the weight of the ball at their lower ends, which kept the birds' heads raised, and Simon discovered that when he moved the plate so that the ball swung in a circle underneath, thus tightening and slackening each string in turn, the fowls mounted on the plate pecked vigorously in rotation at an invisible and apparently inexhaustible supply of corn, in a most ingenious mechanical display of gluttony.

He was still playing thoughtfully with the toy when he discovered Mr Teal standing beside him. The detective's round pink face wore a look of almost comical incredulity.

"Is that how you spend your spare time?" he demanded.

"I think it's rather clever," said the Saint soberly. He put the toy down, and blinked at Fowler. "Does it belong to one of the children?"

"Mr Enstone brought it home with him this evening, sir, to give Miss Annabel tomorrow," said the valet. "He was always picking up things like that. He was a very devoted father, sir."

Mr Teal chewed for a moment, and then he said, "Have you finished? I'm going home."

Simon nodded pacifically, and accompanied him to the lift. As they went down he asked, "Did you find anything?"

"What did you expect me to find?"

Teal blinked.

"I thought the police were always believed to have a clue," murmured the Saint innocently.

"Enstone committed suicide," said Teal flatly. "What sort of clues do you want?"

"Why did he commit suicide?" asked the Saint, almost childishly.

Teal ruminated meditatively for a while, without answering. If anyone else had started such a discussion he would have been openly derisive. The same impulse was stirring in him then, but he restrained himself. He knew Simon Templar's wicked sense of humour, but he also knew that sometimes the Saint was most worth listening to when he sounded most absurd.

"Call me in the morning," said Mr Teal at length, "and I may be able to tell you."

Simon Templar went home and slept fitfully. Lewis Enstone had shot himself—it seemed an obvious fact. The windows had been closed and fastened, and any complicated trick of fastening them from the outside and escaping up or down a rope-ladder was ruled out by the bare two or three seconds that could have elapsed between the sound of the shot and the valet rushing in. But Fowler himself might . . . Why not suicide, anyway? But the Saint could run over every word and gesture and expression of leave-taking which he himself had witnessed in the hotel lobby, and none of it had carried even a hint of suicide. The only oddity about it had been the queer inexplicable piece of pantomime—the fist clenched, with the forefinger extended and the thumb cocked up in crude symbolism of a gun—the abstruse joke which had dissolved Enstone into a fit of inanely delighted giggling, with the hearty approval of his guests . . . The psychological problem fascinated him. It muddled itself up with a litter of brown paper and a cardboard box, a wooden plate of pecking chickens, photographs . . . and the tangle kaleidoscoped through his dreams in a thousand different convolutions until morning.

At half past twelve he found himself turning on to the embankment with every expectation of being told that Mr Teal was too busy to see him, but he was shown up a couple of minutes after he had sent in his name.

"Have you found out why Enstone committed suicide?" he asked.

"I haven't," said Teal, somewhat shortly. "His brokers say it's true that he'd been speculating successfully. Perhaps he had another account with a different firm which wasn't so lucky. We'll find out."

"Have you seen Costello or Hammel?"

"I've asked them to come and see me. They're due here about now."

Teal picked up a typewritten memorandum and studied it absorbedly. He would have liked to ask questions in his turn, but he didn't. He had failed lamentably, so far, to establish any reason whatsoever why Enstone should have committed suicide, and he was annoyed. He felt a personal grievance against the Saint for raising the question without also taking steps to answer it, but pride forbade him to ask for enlightenment. Simon lighted a cigarette and smoked imperturbably until in a few minutes Costello and Hammel were announced. Teal stared at the Saint thoughtfully while the witnesses were seating themselves, but strangely enough he said nothing to intimate that police interviews were not open to outside audiences.

Presently he turned to the tall man with the thin black moustache.

"We're trying to find a reason for Enstone's suicide, Mr Costello," he said. "How long have you known him?"

"About eight or nine years."

"Have you any idea why he should have shot himself?"

"None at all, Inspector. It was a great shock. He had been making more money than most of us. When we were with him last night, he was in very high spirits—his family was on the way home, and he was always happy when he was looking forward to seeing them again."

"Did you ever lose money in any of his companies?"

"No."

"You know we can investigate that?"

Costello smiled slightly.

"I don't know why you should take that attitude, Inspector, but my affairs are open to any examination."

"Have you been making money yourself lately?"

"No. As a matter of fact, I've lost a bit," said Costello frankly. "I'm interested in International Cotton, you know."

He took out a cigarette and a lighter, and Simon found his eyes riveted on the device. It was of an uncommon shape, and by some reason or other it produced a glowing heat instead of a flame. Quite unconscious of his own temerity, the Saint said, "That's something new, isn't it? I've never seen a lighter like that before."

Mr Teal sat back blankly and gave the Saint a look which would have shrivelled any other interrupter to a cinder, and Costello turned the lighter over and said, "It's an invention of my own—I made it myself."

"I wish I could do things like that," said the Saint admiringly. "I suppose you must have had a technical training."

Costello hesitated for a second. Then:

"I started in an electrical engineering workshop when I was a boy," he explained briefly, and turned back to Teal's desk.

After a considerable pause the detective turned to the tubby man with the glasses, who had been sitting without any signs of life except the ceaseless switching of his eyes from one speaker to another.

"Are you in partnership with Mr Costello, Mr Hammel?" he asked.

"A working partnership—yes."

"Do you know any more about Enstone's affairs than Mr Costello has been able to tell us?"

"I'm afraid not."

"What were you talking about at dinner last night?"

"It was about a merger. I'm in International Cotton, too. One of Enstone's concerns was Cosmopolitan Textiles. His shares were standing high and ours aren't doing too well, and we thought that if we could induce him to amalgamate it would help us."

"What did Enstone think about that?"

"He didn't think there was enough in it for him. We had certain things to offer, but he decided they weren't sufficient."

"There wasn't any bad feeling about it?"

"Why, no. If all the business men who have refused to combine with each other at different times became enemies, there'd hardly be two men in the City on speaking terms."

Simon cleared his throat. "What was your first important job, Mr Hammel?" he queried.

Hammel turned his eyes without moving his head. "I was chief salesman for an appliance manufacturer in the Midlands."

Teal concluded the interview soon afterwards without securing any further revelations, shook hands perfunctorily with the two men, and ushered them out. When he came back he looked down at the Saint like a cannibal inspecting the latest missionary.

"Why don't you join the force yourself?" he inquired heavily. "The new Police College is open now, and the Commissioner's supposed to be looking for men like you."

Simon took the sally like an armoured car taking a snowball. He was sitting up on the edge of his chair with his blue eyes glinting with excitement.

"You big sap," he retorted, "do you look as if the Police College could teach anyone to solve a murder?"

Teal gulped as if he couldn't believe his ears. He took hold of the arms of his chair and spoke with an apoplectic restraint, as if he were conscientiously determined to give the Saint every chance to recover his sanity before he rang down for the bugs wagon.

"What murder are you talking about?" he demanded. "Enstone shot himself."

"Yes, Enstone shot himself," said the Saint. "But it was murder just the same."

"Have you been drinking something?"

"No. But Enstone had."

Teal swallowed, and almost choked himself in the process.

"Are you trying to tell me," he exploded, "that any man ever got drunk enough to shoot himself while he was making money?"

"They made him shoot himself."

"What do you mean—blackmail?"

"No."

The Saint pushed a hand through his hair. He had thought of things like that. He knew Enstone had shot himself, because no one else could have done it. Except Fowler, the valet—but that was the man whom Teal would have suspected at once if he had suspected anyone, and it was too obvious, too insane. No man in his senses could have planned a murder with himself as the most obvious suspect.

Blackmail, then? But the Lewis Enstone he had seen in the lobby had never looked like a man bidding farewell to blackmailers.

And how could a man so openly devoted to his family have been led to provide the commoner materials of blackmail?

"No, Claud," said the Saint. "It wasn't that. They just made him do it."

Mr Teal's spine tingled with the involuntary reflex chill that has its roots in man's immemorial fear of the supernatural. The Saint's conviction was so wild and yet real that for one fantastic moment the detective had a vision of Costello's intense black eyes fixed and dilating in a hypnotic stare, his slender sensitive hands moving in weird passes, his lips under the thin black moustache mouthing necromantic commands.

. . . It changed into another equally fantastic vision of two courteous but inflexible gentlemen handing a weapon to a third, bowing and going away, like a deputation to an officer who has been found to be a traitor, offering the graceful alternative to a court-martial—for the Honour of High Finance.

. . . Then it went sheer to derision.

"They just said, 'Lew, why don't you shoot yourself?' and he thought it was a great idea—is that it?" he gibed.

"It was something like that," Simon answered soberly. "You see, Enstone would do almost anything to amuse his children."

Teal's mouth opened, but no sounds came from it. His expression implied that a whole volcano of devastating sarcasm was boiling on the tip of his tongue, but that the Saint's lunacy had soared into realms of waffiness beyond the reach of repartee.

"Costello and Hammel had to do something," said the Saint. "International Cottons have been very bad for a long time—as you'd have known if you hadn't packed all the pennies away in a gilt-edged sock. On the other hand, Enstone's interest—Cosmopolitan Textiles—was good. Costello and Hammel could have pulled out in two ways: either by a merger, or else by having Enstone commit suicide so that Cosmopolitans would tumble down in the scare and they could buy them in—you'll probably find they've sold a bear in them all through the month, trying to break the price.

"And if you look at the papers this afternoon you'll see that all Enstone's securities have dropped through the bottom of the market—a bloke in his position can't commit suicide without starting a panic. Costello and Hammel went to dinner to try for the merger, but if Enstone turned it down they were ready for the other thing."

"Well?" said Teal obstinately, but for the first time there seemed to be a tremor in the foundations of his disbelief.

"They only made one big mistake. They didn't arrange for Lew to leave a letter."

"People have shot themselves without leaving letters."

"I know. But not often. That's what started me thinking."

"Well?" said the detective again.

Simon rumpled his hair into more profound disorder, and said, "You see, Claud, in my disreputable line of business you're always thinking, 'Now, what would A do?—and what would B do?—and what would C do?' You have to be able to get inside people's minds and know what they're going to do and how they're going to do it, so you can always be one jump ahead of 'em. You have to be a practical psychologist—just like the head salesman of an appliance manufacturer in the Midlands."

Teal's mouth opened, but for some reason which was beyond his conscious comprehension he said nothing. And Simon Templar went on, in the disjointed way that he sometimes fell into when he was trying to express something which he himself had not yet grasped in bare words: "Sales psychology is just a study of human weaknesses. And that's a funny thing, you know. I remember the manager of one of the biggest novelty manufacturers in the world telling me that the soundest test of any idea for a new toy was whether it would appeal to a middle-aged business man. It's true, of course. It's so true that it's almost stopped being a joke—the father who plays with his little boy's birthday presents so energetically that the little boy has to shove off and smoke papa's pipe. Every middle-aged business man has that strain of childishness in him somewhere, because without it he would never want to spend his life gathering more paper millions than he can ever spend, and building up rickety castles of golden cards that are always ready to topple over and be built up again. It's just a glorified kid's game with a box of bricks."

Simon raised his eyes suddenly—they were very bright and in some queer fashion sightless, as if his mind was separated from every physical awareness of his surroundings.

"Lewis Enstone was just that kind of a man," he said.

"Are you still thinking of that toy you were playing with?" Teal asked restlessly.

"That—and other things we heard. And the photographs. Did you notice them?"

"No."

"One of them was Enstone playing with an electric train. In another of them he was under a rug, being a bear. In another he was working a big model merry-go-round. Most of the pictures were like that. The children came into them, of course, but you could see that Enstone was having the swellest time."

Teal, who had been fidgeting with a pencil, shrugged brusquely and sent it clattering across the desk.

"You still haven't shown me a murder," he stated.

"I had to find it myself," said the Saint gently. "You see, it was a kind of professional problem. Enstone was happily married, happy with his family, no more crooked than any other big-time financier, nothing on his conscience, rich and getting richer—how were they to make him commit suicide? If I'd been writing a story with him in it, for instance, how could I have made him commit suicide?"

"You'd have told him he had cancer," said Teal caustically, "and he'd have fallen for it."

Simon shook his head. "No. If I'd been a doctor—perhaps. But if Costello or Hammel had suggested it, he'd have wanted confirmation. And did he look like a man who'd just been told that he might have cancer?"

"It's your murder," said Mr Teal, with the beginnings of a drowsy tolerance that was transparently rooted in sheer resignation. "I'll let you solve it."

"There were lots of pieces missing at first," said the Saint. "I only had Enstone's character and weaknesses. And then it came out—Hammel was a psychologist. That was good, because I'm a bit of a psychologist myself, and his mind would work something like mine. And then Costello could invent mechanical gadgets and make them himself. He shouldn't have fetched out that lighter, Claud—it gave me another of the missing pieces. And then there was the box."

"Which box?"

"The cardboard box—on his table, with the brown paper. You know Fowler said that he thought either Hammel or Costello left it. Have you got it here?"

"I expect it's somewhere in the building."

"Could we have it up?"

With the gesture of a blasé hangman reaching for the noose, Teal took hold of the telephone on his desk.

"You can have the gun, too, if you like," he said.

"Thanks," said the Saint. "I wanted the gun."

Teal gave the order, and they sat and looked at each other in silence until the exhibits arrived. Teal's silence explained in fifty different ways that the Saint would be refused no facilities for nailing down his coffin in a manner that he would never be allowed to forget, but for some reason his facial register was not wholly convincing. When they were alone again, Simon went to the desk, picked up the gun, and put it in the box. It fitted very well.

"That's what happened, Claud," he said with quiet triumph. "They gave him the gun in the box."

"And he shot himself without knowing what he was doing," Teal said witheringly.

"That's just it," said the Saint, with a blue devil of mockery in his gaze. "He didn't know what he was doing."

Mr Teal's molars clamped down cruelly on the inoffensive merchandise of the Wrigley Corporation.

"Well, what did he think he was doing—sitting under a rug pretending to be a bear?"

Simon sighed. "That's what I'm trying to work out."

Teal's chair creaked as his full weight slumped back in it in hopeless exasperation.

"Is that what you've been taking up so much of my time about?" he asked wearily.

"But I've got an idea, Claud," said the Saint, getting up and stretching himself. "Come out and lunch with me, and let's give it a rest. You've been thinking for nearly an hour, and I don't want your brain to overheat. I know a new place—wait, I'll look up the address."

He looked it up in the telephone directory, and Mr Teal got up and took down his bowler hat from its peg. His baby blue eyes were inscrutably thoughtful, but he followed the Saint without thought.

Whatever else the Saint wanted to say, however crazy he felt it must be, it was something he had to hear or else fret over for the rest of his days.

They drove in a taxi to Knightsbridge, with Mr Teal chewing phlegmatically, in a superb affectation of bored unconcern. Presently the taxi stopped, and Simon climbed out. He led the way into an apartment building and into a lift, saying something to the operator which Teal did not catch.

"What is this?" he asked, as they shot upwards. "A new restaurant?"

"It's a new place," said the Saint vaguely.

The elevator stopped, and they got out. They went along the corridor, and Simon rang the bell at one of the doors. It was opened by a good-looking maid who might have been other things in her spare time.

"Scotland Yard," said the Saint brazenly, and squeezed past her. He found his way into the sitting-room before anyone could stop him. Chief Inspector Teal, recovering from the momentary paralysis of the shock, followed him; then came the maid.

"I'm sorry, sir—Mr Costello is out."

Teal's bulk obscured her. All the boredom had smudged itself off his face, giving place to blank amazement and anger.

"What the devil's this joke?"

"It isn't a joke, Claud," said the Saint recklessly. "I just wanted to see if I could find something—you know what we were talking about—"

His keen gaze was quartering the room, and then it alighted on a big cheap kneehole desk whose well-worn shabbiness looked strangely out of keeping with the other furniture. On it was a litter of coils and wire and ebonite and dials—all the junk out of which amateur radio sets are created.

Simon reached the desk in his next stride, and began pulling open the drawers. Tools of all kinds, various sizes of wire and screws, odd wheels and sleeves and bolts and scraps of aluminium and brass, the completely typical hoard of any amateur mechanic's workshop. Then he came to a drawer that was locked. Without hesitation he caught up a large screwdriver and rammed it in above the lock; before anyone could grasp his intentions he had splintered the drawer open with a skilful twist.

Teal let out a shout and started across the room. Simon's hand dived into the drawer, came out with a nickel-plated revolver—it was exactly the same as the one with which Lewis Enstone had shot himself, but Teal wasn't noticing things like that. His impression was that the Saint really had gone raving mad after all, and the sight of the gun in the hands of any other raving maniac would have pulled him up.

"Put that down, you fool!" he yelled, and then he let out another shout as he saw the Saint turn the muzzle of the gun close up to his right eye, with his thumb on the trigger, exactly as Enstone must have held it. Teal lurched forward and knocked the weapon aside with a sweep of his arm; then he grabbed Simon by the wrist.

"That's enough of that," he said, without realizing what a futile thing it was to say.

Simon looked at him and smiled. "Thanks for saving my life old beetroot," he murmured kindly. "But it really wasn't necessary. You see, Claud, that's the gun Enstone thought he was playing with!"

The maid was under the table letting out the opening note of a magnificent fit of hysterics. Teal let go the Saint, hauled her out, and shook her till she was quiet. There were more events cascading on him in those few seconds than he knew how to cope with, and he was not gentle.

"It's all right, miss," he growled. "I am from Scotland Yard. Just sit down somewhere, will you?" He turned to Simon. "Now, what's all this about?"

"The gun. Enstone's toy."

The Saint raised it again—his smile was quite sane, and with the feeling that he himself was the madman, Teal let him do what he wanted. Simon put the gun to his eye and pulled the trigger—pulled it, released it, pulled it again, keeping up the rhythmic movement. Something inside the gun whirred smoothly, as if wheels were whizzing around under the working of the lever. Then he pointed the gun straight into Teal's face and did the same thing.

Teal stared frozenly down the barrel and saw the black hole leap into a circle of light. He was looking at a flickering movie film of a boy shooting a masked burglar. It was tiny, puerile in subject, but perfect. It lasted about ten seconds, and then the barrel went dark again.

"Costello's present for Enstone's little boy," explained the Saint quietly. "He invented it and made it himself, of course—he always had a talent that way. Haven't you ever seen those electric flashlights that work without a battery? You keep on squeezing a lever, and it turns a miniature dynamo. Costello made a very small one, and fitted it into the hollow casting of a gun. Then he geared a tiny strip of film to it. It was a damn good new toy, Claud Eustace, and he must have been proud of it.

"They took it along to Enstone's, and when he'd turned down their merger and there was nothing else for them to do, they let him play with it just enough to tickle his palate, at just the right hour of the evening. Then they took it away from him and put it back in its box and gave it to him. They had a real gun in another box ready to switch."

Chief Inspector Teal stood like a rock, his jaws clamping a wad of spearmint that he had at last forgotten to chew. Then he said, "How did they know he wouldn't shoot his own son?"

"That was Hammel. He knew that Enstone wasn't capable of keeping his hands off a toy like that, and just to make certain he reminded Enstone of it the last thing before they left. He was a practical psychologist—I suppose we can begin to speak of him in the past tense now."

Simon Templar smiled again, and fished a cigarette out of his pocket. "But why I should bother to tell you all this when you could have got it out of a stool pigeon," he murmured, "is more than I can understand. I must be getting soft-hearted in my old age, Claud. After all, when you're so far ahead of Holmes."

Mr Teal gulped pinkly, and picked up the telephone.

THE MIXTURE AS BEFORE

"Crime," explained Simon Templar, squeezing a lemon-juice meditatively over a liberal slice of smoked salmon, "is a kind of Fourth Dimension. The sucker moves and has his being completely enclosed in a sphere of limitations which he assumes to be the natural laws of the universe. When he is offered an egg, he expects to be given an egg—not a sewing machine. The lad who takes the money off him is the lad who breaks the rules—the lad who hops outside the sucker's dimension, skids invisibly round ahead of him, and pops in again exactly at the point where the sucker would never dream of looking for him.

"But the lad who takes money off the lad who takes money off the sucker—the real aristocrat of the profession—is something even brighter. He duly delivers the egg; only it's also an aubergine. It's a plant."

The Saint could have continued in the same strain for some time, and not infrequently did.

Those moods of contemplative contentment were an integral part of Simon Templar's enjoyment of life, the restful twilights between buccaneering days and adventurous nights. They usually came upon him when the second glass of dry sherry had been tasted and found good, when the initial delicacy of a chain of fastidiously chosen dishes had been set before him, and the surroundings of white linen and gleaming silver and glass had sunk into their proper place as the background of that epicurean luxuriousness which to him was the goal of all worthwhile piracy. Those were the occasions on which the corsair put off his harness and discoursed on the philosophy of filibustering. It was a subject of which Simon Templar never tired, in the course of a flamboyant career which had been largely devoted to equalizing what he had always considered to be a fundamentally unjust distribution of wealth he had developed many theories about his own chosen field of art, and these he was always ready to expound. It was at such times as this that the Saint's keen dark head took on its most challenging alertness of line, the mocking blue eyes danced with their gayest humour . . . when everything about him matched the irresponsible spirit of his nickname except the technical morality of his discourse.

"Successful crime," said the Saint, "is simply the Art of the Unexpected."

Louie Fallon had similar ideas, although he was no philosopher. The finer abstractions of lawlessness left Louie not only cold but in a condition to make ice cream shiver merely by breathing on it. Neither were Louie's interpretations of those essential ideas particularly novel, but he was a very sound practitioner.

"It's a waste of time tryin' to think up new stunts, Olli," Louie declared, "while there's all the suckers you want still fallin' for the old ones. Anyone with a good uncut diamond can draw a dividend from it every day."

"Anyone who can put down two thousand pounds can have a good uncut diamond, Louie," replied Mr Olomo, sympathetic but cautious.

"Anyone who could put down two thousand quid could float a company and swindle people like a gentleman," said Louie.

Mr Olomo shook his head sadly. His business was patronized by a small and exclusive clientele which was rarely in a position to bargain with him.

"That's a pity, Louie. I like to see a good man get on."

"Now listen to me, you old shark," said Louie amiably. "I want a diamond, a real high-class bit of ice, and all I can afford is three hundred pounds. Look over your stock and see what you can find. And make it snappy. I want to get started this week."

"Three hundred pounds is for a cheap bit of paste," said Mr Olomo pathetically. "You know I haven't got anything like that in my shop, Louie."

Half an hour later he parted grudgingly with an excellent stone, for which Louie Fallen was persuaded to pay two hundred pounds, and the business-like tension of the interview relaxed in an exchange of cheap cigars. In the estimation of Mr Olomo, who had given seventy pounds for the stone, it was a highly satisfactory afternoon's work.

"You got a gift there, Louie," he said gloomily.

"I've got a gold-mine," said Louie confidently. "All I need beside this is psychology, and I don't have to pay for that. I'm just naturally psychological. You got to pick out the right kind of sucker. Then it goes like this."

The germ of that elusive quality which turns an otherwise normal and rational human being into a sucker has yet to be isolated. Louie Fallon, the man of action, had never bothered to probe into it.

He recognized one when he saw one, without analysing whys and wherefores, exactly as he was accustomed to recognizing a piece of cheese without a thought of the momentous dawn of life which it enshrines. Simon Templar himself had various theories.

Probably the species Sucker is the same as the common cold—there is no single virus to account for it. Nor is there likely to be any rigid definition of that precise shade of covetous innocence, that peculiarly grasping guilelessness, which stamps the hard-boiled West Country farmer, accustomed to prying into the pedigrees of individual oats before disgorging a penny on them, as a potential purchaser of the Tower of London for five hundred pounds down and the balance by instalments.

But whatever these symptoms may be, Simon Templar possessed them in their richest beauty. He had only to saunter in his most natural manner down the highways of the world, immaculate and debonair, with his soft hat slanted blithely over one eye, and the passing pageant of humanity crystallized into men who had had their pockets picked and only needed five shillings to get home, men with gold bricks, men with oil wells in Texas, men needing assistance in the execution of eccentric wills, men with charts showing the authenticated cemetery of Captain Kidd's treasure, men with horses that could romp home on one leg and a crutch, and men who just thought he might like a game of cards.

It was one of the Saint's most treasured assets, and he never ordered strawberries in December without a toast to the benign Providence that had endowed him with the gift of having all that he asked of life poured into his lap.

As a matter of fact he was sauntering down the Strand when he met Louie Fallon. He didn't actually run into him, but he did walk into him. There was nothing particularly remarkable about that, for the Strand is a street which contains more crooks to the square yard than any other area of ground outside a prison wall—which may be partly accounted for by the fact that it also has the reputation of being the favourite promenading ground of more potential suckers than any other thoroughfare in London.

Louie Fallon had a theory that he couldn't walk down the Strand on any day in the week without bumping into a perambulating gold-mine which only required skilful scratching to yield him its gilded harvest.

He walked towards the Saint, fumbling in his pockets with a preoccupied air and the kind of flurried abstraction of a man who has forgotten where he put his railway ticket on his way down the platform, with his eyes fluttering over every item of the perspective except those which were included in the direction in which he was going.

At any rate, the last person in the panorama whom he appeared to see was the Saint himself. Simon saw him, and swerved politely. But with the quick-witted agility of long practice, Louie Fallon blundered off to the same side. They collided with a slight bump, at the very moment when Louie had apparently discovered the article for which he had been searching.

It fell on to the pavement between them and rolled away between the Saint's feet, sparkling enticingly in the sunlight. Muttering profuse apologies, Louie scuffled round to retrieve it. The movement was so adroitly devised to entangle them that Simon would have had no chance to pass on and make his escape, even if he had wanted to.

But it is dawning—slowly and reluctantly, perhaps, but dawning, nevertheless—upon the chronicler that there can be very few students of these episodes who can still be cherishing any delusion that the Saint would ever want to escape from such a situation.

Simon stood by with a slight smile coming to his lips, while Louie wriggled round his legs and recovered his precious possession with a faint squeak of delight, and straightened up with the object clutched solidly in his hand.

"Phew!" said Mr Fallon, fanning himself with his hat. "That was near enough. Did you see where it went? Right to the edge of that grating. If it had rolled down . . ." He blew out his cheeks and rolled up his eyes in an eloquent register of horror at the dreadful thought. "For a moment I thought I'd lost it," he said, clarifying his point conclusively.

Simon nodded. It did not require any peculiar keenness of vision to see that the object of so much concern was a very nice-looking diamond, for Louie was making no attempt to hide it—he was, on the contrary, blowing on it and rubbing it affectionately on his sleeve to remove the invisible specks of grime and dust which it had collected on its travels.

"You must be lucky."

Louie's face fell abruptly. The transition between his almost childish delight and the shadow of awful gloom which suddenly passed across his countenance was quite startling. Mr Fallon's artistry had never been disputed even by his rivals in the profession.

"Lucky?" he practically yelped in a rising crescendo of mournful indignation. "Why, I'm the unluckiest man that ever lived!"

"Too bad," said the Saint, with profound sympathy.

"Lucky!" repeated Mr Fallon, with all the pained disgust of a hypochondriac who has been accused of looking well. "Why, I'm the sort of fellow if I saw a five-pound note lying in the street and tried to pick it up, I'd fall down and break my neck!"

It was becoming clear to Simon Templar that Mr Fallon felt that he was unlucky.

"There are people like that," the Saint said, reminiscently. "I remember an aunt of mine—"

"Lucky?" reiterated Mr Fallon, who did not appear to be interested in anyone else's aunt. "Why, right at this moment I'm the unluckiest man in London. Look here"—he clasped the Saint by the arm with the pathetically appealing movement of a drowning man clutching at a straw—"do you think you could help me? If you haven't got anything particular to do? I feel sort of—well—you look the sort of fellow who might have some ideas. Have you got time for a drink?"

Simon Templar could never have been called a toper, but on such occasions as this he invariably had time for a drink.

"I don't mind if I do," he said obligingly.

As a matter of fact, they were standing outside a miraculously convenient hostel at that moment, for Louie Fallon had always believed in bringing the mellowing influence of alcohol to bear as soon as he had scraped his acquaintance, and he staged his encounters with that idea in view.

With practised dexterity he steered the Saint towards the door of the saloon bar, cutting short the protest which Simon Templar had no intention whatsoever of making. In hardly any more time than it takes to record, he had got the Saint inside the bar, parked him at a table, invited him to name his poison, procured a double ration of the said poison from the barmaid, and settled himself in the adjoining chair to improve the shining hour.

To the discerning critic it might seem that he rushed at the process rather like an unleashed investor plunging after an absconding company promoter. But Louie Fallon's conception of improving shining hours had never included any unnecessary waste of time, and he had learnt by experience that the willingness of a Pigeon to listen is usually limited only by the ability of the prospective Plucker to talk.

"Yes," said Mr Fallon, reverting to his subject. "I am the unluckiest man you are ever likely to meet. Did you see that diamond I dropped just now?"

"Well," admitted the Saint truthfully, "I couldn't help seeing it."

Mr Fallon nodded. He fumbled in his waistcoat pocket, brought out the jewel again, and laid it on the table.

"I made that myself," he said.

Simon eyed the stone and Mr Fallon with the puzzled expression which was expected of him.

"What do you mean—you made it?"

"I made it myself," said Mr Fallon. "It's what you would call synthetic. It took about half an hour, and it cost me exactly threepence. But there isn't a diamond merchant in London who could prove that it wasn't dug up out of the ground in South Africa. Take it to anyone you like, and see if he doesn't swear that it's a perfectly genuine stone."

"You mean it's a fake?" said the Saint.

"Fake my eye!" said Mr Fallon, with emphatic if inelegant expressiveness. "It's a perfectly genuine diamond, the same as any other stone you'll ever see. The only difference is that I made it. You know how diamonds are made?"

The Saint had as good an idea of how diamonds are made as Louie Fallon was ever likely to have. But it seemed as if Louie liked talking, and in such circumstances as that Simon Templar was the last man on earth to interfere with anyone's enjoyment. He shook his head blankly.

"I thought they sort of grew," he said vaguely.

"I don't know that I should put it exactly like that," said Louie. "I'll tell you how diamonds happen. Diamonds are just carbon—like coal, or soot, or—or—"

"Paper?" suggested the Saint helpfully.

Louie frowned. "They're carbon," he said, "which is crystallized under pressure. When the earth was all sort of hot, like you read about in your history books—before it sort of cooled down and people started to live in it and things grew on it—there was a lot of carbon. Being hot, it burnt things, and when you burn things you usually get carbon. Well, after a time, when the earth started to cool down, it sort of shrunk, like—like—"

"A shirt when it goes to the wash?" said the Saint.

"Anyway it shrunk," said Louie, yielding the point and passing on. "And what happened then?"

"It got smaller," hazarded the Saint.

"It caused terrific pressure," said Mr Fallon firmly. "Just imagine it. Thousands of millions of tons of rock—and—"

"And rock."

"And rock, cooling down, and shrinking up, and getting hard. Well, naturally, any bits of carbon that were floating around in the rock got squeezed. So what happened?" demanded Louie, triumphantly reaching the climax of his lucid description.

He paused dramatically, and the Saint wondered whether he was expected to offer any serious solution to the riddle. Before he had really made up his mind, Mr Fallon was solving the problem for him.

"I'll tell you what happened," said Mr Fallon impressively, leaning over into a strategic position in which he could tap the Saint on the shoulder. Once again he paused, but there was no doubt that this hiatus at least was motivated solely by the requirements of theatrical suspense. *"Diamonds!"* said Mr Fallon, with an air of patronizing pride, which almost suggested that he personally had been responsible for the event.

The Saint took a draught from his glass, and gazed at him with that air of slightly perplexed awe which was one of the most precious assets in his infinitely varied stock of facial expressions. It was a gaze pregnant with so much ingenuous interest, such naïve wonder and curiosity, that Mr Fallon felt the cockles of his heart warming to a temperature at which, on a cold day, he would be tempted to dispense with his overcoat. Since he was not wearing an overcoat, he gave rein to his emotions by insisting that he should stand another round of drinks.

"Yes," he resumed, when he had refilled their glasses. "Diamonds. And that's how I make them—not," he admitted modestly, "that I mean I make the earth go hot and then cool down again. But I do the same thing on a smaller scale."

The Saint knitted his brows. It was the most ostentatious sign of a functioning brain that he could permit himself in the part he was playing.

"Now you tell me, I think I have heard something like that before," he said. "Hasn't somebody else done the same thing—I mean made synthetic diamonds by cooling chunks of iron under pressure?"

"I did hear of something on those lines," confessed Mr Fallon magnanimously. "But the process wasn't very good. They could only make very small diamonds that weren't worth anything in the market and cost ten times as much as real ones. I make 'em with things that you can buy in any chemist's shop for a few pennies. I don't even need a proper laboratory. I could make 'em in your bathroom."

He drank, wiped his lips, and looked at the Saint suddenly with bright plaintive eyes. "You don't believe me," he said accusingly.

"Why—yes, of course I do," protested the Saint, changing his expression with a guilty start.

Mr Fallon continued to shake his head. "No, you don't," he insisted morbidly, "and I can't blame you. I know it sounds like a tall story. But I'm not a liar."

"Of course not," agreed the Saint hastily.

"I'm not a liar," insisted Mr Fallon lingeringly, as if he was simply aching to be called one. "Anyone who calls me a liar is goin' to have to eat his words."

He was silent for a moment, while the idea appeared to develop in his mind, and then he slewed around in his seat abruptly, and tapped the Saint on the shoulder again.

"Look here—I'll prove it to you. You're a friendly sort—we ran into each other just now as perfect strangers, and now here you are havin' a drink with me. I don't know whether you believe in coincidences," said Louie, waxing metaphysical, "but you might be the very fellow I'm lookin' for. I like a chap who isn't too damned standoffish to have a drink with another chap without being introduced, and when I like a chap there isn't a limit to what I wouldn't mind doin' for him. Why, you might be the very chap. Well, what d'you say?"

"I didn't say anything," said the Saint innocently.

"What d'you say I prove to you that I can make diamonds? If you can spare half an hour—it wouldn't take much more than that and you might find it interesting. Are you game?"

Simon Templar was game. To put it perhaps a trifle crudely, such occasions as this found him so game that a two-year-old pheasant would have had to rise exceedingly high to catch him. Life, he felt, was still very much worth living while blokes like Louie Fallon were almost falling over themselves with eagerness to call you a Chap. To follow up the metaphor with which he was allowed to open this episode, he considered that Mr Fallon was certainly doing an impressive line of clucking, and he was profoundly interested to find out exactly what brand of egg would be the fruit thereof.

Mr Fallon, it appeared, was the proud tenant of an apartment in one of those streets running down between the Tivoli and the River which fall roughly within the postal address known as "Adelphi" because it sounds so much better than WC. The rooms were expensively and tastefully furnished, and the Saint surmised that Louie had not furnished them. Somewhere in London there would be an outraged landlord looking for his rent—and perhaps also the more valuable of his rented chattels—when Mr Fallon had finished with the premises, but this was not immediately Simon Templar's concern.

He followed Louie into the living-room, where a bottle of whisky and two glasses were produced and suitably dealt with, and cheerfully prepared to continue with the role of open-mouthed listener which the situation demanded of him. This called for no very fatiguing effort, for the role of open-mouthed listener was one in which the Saint had perfected himself more years ago than he could easily remember.

"I told you I could make my diamonds in a bathroom," said Louie, "and that's exactly what I am doin' at the moment."

He led the way onwards, glass in hand, and Simon followed him good-humouredly. It was quite a swanky bathroom, with a green marble bath and generous windows looking out over rows of smoke-stained housetops towards the Thames.

The materials that Louie Fallon used in making his chemical experiments were the only incongruous note in it. These consisted of an ancient and shabby marble-topped washstand, which had obviously started its new lease of life in a second-hand sale room, a fireproof crucible on a metal tripod, and a litter of test-tubes, burners, bottles, and other paraphernalia which Simon did not deny were most artistically arranged.

"Just to show you," said Mr Fallon generously, "I'll make a diamond for you now."

He went over to the washstand and picked up one of the bottles. "Magnesium," he said. He picked up another bottle. "Iron filings," he said. He picked up a third bottle and tipped a larger quantity of greyish powder on top of what he had taken from the first two, stirring the mixture on the marble table-top with a commonplace Woolworth teaspoon. "And the last thing," he said, "is the actual stuff that I make my diamonds with."

He picked up the crucible and held it below the level of the table, scraped his little mound of assorted powders into it, and turned around with a didactic air.

"Now I'll tell you what happens," he said. "When you burn magnesium with iron filings you produce a temperature of thousands of degrees Fahrenheit. It isn't quite as hot as the earth was when it was all molten, but it's nearly as hot. That melts the iron filings, and it also fuses the other mixture I put in which is exactly the same chemically as the stuff that diamonds are made of."

He struck a match and applied it to the crucible. There was a sudden spurt of eye-achingly brilliant flame, accompanied by a faint hissing sound. Simon could feel the intense heat of the flare on his cheeks, even though he was standing several feet away, and he watched the crucible becoming incandescent before his eyes, turning from a dull red through blazing pink to a blinding white glow.

"So there," said Mr Fallon, gazing at his fireworks with almost equally incandescent pride, "you have the heat. Right now that diamond powder is wrappin' itself up inside the melted iron filings. The mixture isn't quite as hot as it ought to be, because nobody has discovered how to produce as much heat as there was in the world back in those times when it was molten.

"We have to make up for that by coolin' the thing off quicker. That's the reason why all the other experimenters have failed. They've never been able to cool things off quick enough. But I got over that."

From under the wash-stand he dragged out a gadget which the Saint had not noticed before. To the callously uninitiated eye it might have looked rather like a couple of old oil-cans and some bits of battered gaspipe, but Louie handled it as tenderly as an anarchist exhibiting his favourite bomb.

"This is the fastest cooler that's ever been made," he said. "I won't try to tell you how it works, because you probably wouldn't understand, but it's very scientific. When I throw this nugget that's forming in the crucible into it it'll be cooled off quicker than anything's ever been cooled off before. From four thousand degrees Fahrenheit down to a hundred below zero, in less than half a second! Have you any idea what that means?"

Simon realized that it was time for him to show some rudimentary intelligence.

"I know," he said slowly. "It means—"

"It means," said Mr Fallon, taking the words out of his mouth, "that you get a pressure of thousands of millions of tons inside that nugget of molten iron, and when you break it open the diamond's inside."

He lifted the lid of his oil-can contraption, picked up the crucible with a pair of long iron tongs, and poured out a blob of luminous liquid metal the size of a small pear. There was a loud fizzing noise accompanied by a great burst of steam, and Louie replaced the lid of his cooler and looked at the Saint triumphantly through the fog.

"Now," he said, "in half a minute you'll see it with your own eyes."

The Saint opened his cigarette-case and tapped a cigarette thoughtfully on his thumbnail.

"How on earth did you hit on that?" he asked, with wide-eyed admiration.

"I used to be an assistant in a chemist's shop when I was a boy," said Louie casually.

As a matter of fact, this was perfectly true, but he did not mention that his employment had terminated abruptly when the chemist discovered that his assistant had been systematically whittling down the contents of the till whenever he was left alone in the shop.

"I always liked playin' around with things and tryin' experiments, and I always believed it'd be possible to make perfectly good synthetic diamonds whatever the other experts said. And now I've proved it."

This also, curiously enough, was partly true. Improbable as it may seem, Mr Fallon had his dreams—dreams in which he could produce unlimited quantities of gold or diamonds simply by mixing chemicals together in a pail, or vast stacks of genuine paper money merely by turning a handle.

The psychologist, delving into Louie's dream-life, would probably have found the particular form of swindle which Mr Fallon had made his own inexorably predestined by these curiously childish fantasies—a kind of spurious and almost self-defensive satisfaction of a congenital urge for easy money.

He rolled up his sleeves and plunged his bare arms into the cooling gadget with the rather wistful expression which he always wore when performing that part of his task. When he stood up again he was clutching a round grey stone glistening with water, and for a moment or two he gazed at it dreamily.

It was at this stage of the proceedings that Louie's histrionics invariably ran away with him—when, for two or three seconds, his imagination really allowed him to picture himself as the exponent of an earth-shaking scientific discovery, the genuine result of those futile experiments on which he had spent so much of his time and so much of the money which he had earned from the sham.

"There you are," he said. "There's your diamond—and any dealer in London would be glad to buy it. Here—take it yourself." He pressed the wet stone into Simon Templar's hand. "Show it to anyone you like, and if there's a dealer in London who wouldn't be glad to pay two hundred quid for it, I'll give you a thousand pounds. You can't say I'm not being fair."

He picked up his glass again, and then, as if he had suddenly remembered the essential tone of his story, his face recovered its expression of uncontrollable gloom. "And I'm the unhappiest man in the world," he said lugubriously.

Simon raised his eyebrows.

"But good God!" he objected. "How on earth can you be unhappy if you can turn out a two-hundred-pound diamond every half hour?"

Louie shook his head. "Because I haven't a chance to spend the money," he replied.

He led the way back dejectedly into the living-room and threw himself into a chair, thoughtfully refilling his glass before he did so.

"You see," he said, when Simon Templar had taken the chair opposite him with his glass also refilled. "A thing like this has got to be handled properly. It's no good my just making diamonds and trying to sell them. I might get away with one or two, but if I brought a sackful of them into a shop and tried to sell 'em the buyer would start to wonder whether I was trying to get rid of some illicit stuff. He'd want to ask all sorts of questions about where I got 'em, and as likely as not he'd call in the police. And what does that mean?"

"It means that either I've got to say nothing and probably get taken for a crook and put in prison—" Louie's features registered profound horror at this frightful possibility. "Or else I've got to give away my secret. And if I said that I made the diamonds myself, they'd want me to prove it; and if I proved it, everybody would know it could be done, and the bottom would fall out of the diamond market. If people knew that anybody could make diamonds for threepence a time, diamonds just wouldn't be worth anything any more. People only want what's scarce, you see."

Simon nodded. The argument was logical and provided a very intriguing impasse. He waited for Mr Fallon to point the way out.

"What this thing needs," said Louie, duly coming up to expectations, "is someone to run it in a business-like way. It's got to be scientific just like the way the diamonds are made." Mr Fallon had worked all this out for himself in his daydreams, and the recital was mechanically easy. "Someone would have to go off somewhere—not to South Africa, because that's too much controlled, but to South America maybe—and do some prospectin'.

"After a while he'd report that he'd found diamonds, and set up a mine. We'd set up a company and sell shares to the public, and after a bit the diamonds'd start comin' home and they could all be sold in the regular market quite legitimate."

"Why don't you do that?" inquired the Saint perplexedly.

"I've got no heart for it," said Louie with a sigh. "I'm not so young as I was, and besides, I never had any kind of head for these things. And I don't want to do it. I don't want to get myself tied up in a lot of business worries and office work. I've had that all my life. I want to enjoy myself—travel around and meet some girls and have a good time. Between you and I," said Mr Fallon with a catch in his voice, and tears glistening in his eyes, "the doctors tell me that I haven't long to live. I've had a hard life, and I want to make the best of what I have got left. Now, if I had a young fellow like yourself to help me . . ."

He leaned further back in his chair, with his eyes half-closed, and went on as if talking to himself: "It'd have to be a chap who could keep his mouth shut, a chap who wouldn't mind doing a bit of hard work for a lot of money—someone that I could just leave to manage everything while I went off and had a good time. He'd have to have a bit of money of his own to invest in the company, just to make everything square and above-board and legal, and in a year or so he'd be a millionaire ridin' around in a Rolls Royce with chauffeurs and everything.

"You'd think it'd be easy to find a fellow like that, but it isn't. There aren't many chaps that I take a likin' to—not chaps that I feel I could trust with anything as big as this. That's why when I took a fancy to you, I wondered . . ." Mr Fallon sighed again, a sigh of heartrending self-pity. "But I suppose it's no use. Here am I with the greatest discovery in modern science, and I can't do anything with it. I suppose I was just born unlucky, like I told you.'

The Saint was sublimely sure that Louie Fallon was unlucky, but he did not dream of saying so. He allowed his face to become illuminated with a light of breathless cupidity which was everything that Mr Fallon had desired.

"Well," he said hesitantly, "if you've really taken a fancy to me and I can do anything to help you—"

Louie stared at him for a moment incredulously, as if he had never dared to hope that such a miracle could happen.

"No," he said at length, covering his eyes wearily, "it couldn't be true. My luck can't have changed. You wouldn't do a thing like that for a perfect stranger."

During the conversation that followed, however, it appeared that Louie's luck had indeed changed. His newfound friend, it seemed, was quite prepared to do such a service for a perfect stranger. They talked for another hour, discussing ways and means, and occasionally referring in a gentlemanly way to terms of business; then they went out to lunch in an aura of mutual admiration and regard, and discussed the fortunes which they would assist each other to make. And when they finally separated, the Saint had agreed to meet Mr Fallon again the following day, bringing with him—in cash—the sum of four thousand pounds which he was to invest in the new industry, on an equal partnership basis, as a guarantee of his good faith.

Simon went off with Louie Fallon's diamond in his pocket. As a purely precautionary measure, he took it to a diamond merchant of his acquaintance who pronounced it to be unquestionably genuine, and then he proceeded somewhat lightheadedly to make some curious purchases.

The clouds of ill-starred melancholy seemed to have dispersed themselves from Mr Fallon's sky overnight, for when he opened the door to Simon Templar the next day he was beaming. The flat, Simon noticed, was in some disorder, and there were three freshly-labelled suitcases standing in the hall.

"I hope I'm not late," said the Saint anxiously.

"Only a minute or two," said Louie heartily. "It's my own fault that it seems longer. I was just nervous. I guess I couldn't believe that my luck had really changed, until I saw you on the step. You see, I've got my tickets and everything. I'm ready to go as soon as everything's fixed up."

The Saint believed him. As soon as everything had been fixed up in the way Louie intended, Mr Fallon would be likely to go as fast and far as the conveniences of modern travel would take him. Simon made vague noises of sympathy and encouragement, and followed his benefactor into the living-room.

"There's the contract, all drawn up already," said Louie, producing a large and impressive-looking document with fat red seals attached to it. "All you've got to do is to sign on the dotted line and put in your capital, and you're in charge of the whole business. After that, if you send me two or three hundred pounds a week out of the profits, I'll be quite happy, and I don't much care what you do with the rest."

With all the eagerness that was expected of him, Simon sat down at the table, glanced over the document, and signed his name over the dotted line as requested. Then he took out his wallet and counted out a sheaf of crisp new banknotes, and Louie picked them up and counted them again with slightly unsteady fingers.

"Well, now," said the Saint, "if that's all settled, hadn't you better show me your process?"

"I've written it all out for you—"

"Oh, yes, I'd want that. But couldn't we try it over now just to make sure that I understand it properly?"

"Certainly, my dear chap—certainly." Mr Fallon pushed up his sleeve to look at his watch, and appeared to make a calculation. "I don't know whether I'll have time to see the experiment right through to the end, but once you've got it started you can't possibly go wrong. It's absolutely foolproof. Come along."

They went into the bathroom and Simon poured out magnesium and iron filings into the crucible exactly as he had seen Louie doing the previous day. The composition of the powder from which the diamonds were actually made gave him more trouble. It was apparently made up of the contents of various other unlabelled bottles, mixed up in certain complicated proportions.

It was at this stage in the proceedings that the Saint appeared to become unexpectedly stupid and clumsy. He poured out too much from one bottle and spilt most of the contents of another on the floor.

"You'll have to be more careful than that," said Louie, pursing his lips, "but I can see you've got the idea. Well, now, if I'm going to catch my train—"

"I'd like to finish the job," said the Saint, "even if the mixture has gone wrong. After all, I may as well know if there are any other mistakes I'm likely to make." He put a match to his mixture and stepped back while it flared up. Louie watched this studiously.

"I don't expect you'll get any results," he said, "but it can't do any harm for you to get some practice. Now as soon as the thing's properly white hot—"

He supervised the tipping of the contents of the crucible into the cooler indulgently. He had no cause for alarm. The proportions of the mixture were admittedly wrong, which was a perfectly sound reason to give for the inevitable failure of the experiment. He puffed at his cigar complacently, while the Saint went down on his knees and groped around in the cooling tank.

Then something seemed to go wrong with the mechanism of Mr Fallon's heart, and for a full five seconds he was unable to breathe. His eyes bulged, and the smug tolerance froze out of his face as if it had been nipped in the bud by the same Antarctic zephyr that was playing weird tricks up and down his spine. For the Saint had straightened up again with an exclamation of delight, and in the palm of his hand he displayed three little round grey pebbles.

The chill wind that was playing tricks with Louie Fallon's backbone whistled up into his head and brought out beads of cold perspiration on his brow. For a space of time that seemed to him like three or four years, he experienced all the sensations of a man who has sold somebody a pup and seen it turn out into a pedigreed prize winner.

The memory of all the hours of time, all the pounds of hard-earned money, and all the tormenting daydreams, which he had spent on his own futile experiments, flooded back into his mind in an interval of exquisite anguish that made him feel faintly sick. If he had never believed any of the stories he told about his hard luck before, he believed them all now, and more also.

The smile of happy vindication on the Saint's face was in itself an insult that made Louie's blood ferment in his veins. He felt exactly as if he had been run over by a steamroller and then invited to admire his own remarkable flatness.

"Here, wait a minute," he said hoarsely. "That isn't possible!"

"Anyway, it's happened," answered the Saint with irrefutable logic.

Louie swallowed, and picked up one of the stones which the Saint was holding. He knew enough about such things to realize that it was indubitably an uncut diamond—not quite so big as the one which he himself claimed to have made, but easily worth a hundred pounds in the ordinary market nevertheless.

"Try it again," he said huskily. "Can you remember exactly what you did last time?"

The Saint thought he could remember. He tried it again, while Louie watched him with his eyes almost popping out of his head, and his mouth hungrily half open. He himself fished in the cooling tank as soon as the steam had dispersed, and he found two more diamonds embedded in the clinker at the bottom.

Louie Fallon had nothing to say for a long time. He paced up and down the small room, scratching his head, in the throes of the fastest thinking he had ever done in his life. Somehow or other, heaven alone knew how, the young sap who was gloating inanely over his prowess had stumbled accidentally upon the formula which Mr Fallon had sought for half his life in vain.

And the young sap had just paid over four thousand pounds, and received in return his portion of the signed contract which entitled him to a half-share in all the proceeds of the invention. By fair means or foul—preferably more or less fair, for Mr Fallon was not by nature a violent man—that contract had to be recovered. There was only one way to recover it that Mr Fallon could see; it was a painful way, but with so much at stake Louie Fallon was no piker.

Finally he stopped his pacing, and turned round.

"Look here," he said. "This is a tremendous business."

The wave of his hand embraced unutterably gigantic issues. "I won't try to explain it all to you, because you're not a scientist and you wouldn't understand. But it's . . . tremendous . . . It means . . ."

He waved his hand again. "At any rate it makes a lot of difference to me. I . . . I don't know whether I will go away after all. A thing like that's got to be investigated. You see, I'm a scientist. If I didn't get to the bottom of it all, it'd be on my conscience. I'd have it preying on my mind."

The pathetic resignation on Mr Fallon's countenance spoke of a mute and glorious martyrdom to the cause of science that was almost holy. He was throwing himself heart and soul into the job, acting as if his very life depended on it—which, in his estimation, it practically did.

"Look here," he burst out, taking the bull by the horns, "will you go on being a sport? Will you tear up that agreement we've just signed, and let me engage you as . . . as . . . as manager?"

It was here that the sportiness of Simon Templar fell into considerable disrepute. He was quite unreasonably reluctant to surrender his share in a fortune for the sake of science. He failed to see what all the fuss was about. What, he wanted to know, was there to prevent Mr Fallon continuing his scientific researches under the existing arrangement? Louie, with the sweat streaming down inside his shirt, ran through a catalogue of excuses that would have made the fortune of a politician.

The Saint became mercenary. This was a language which Louie Fallon could talk, much as he disliked it. He offered to return the money which Simon had invested. He did, in fact, actually return the money, and the Saint wavered. Louie became reckless. He was not quite as broke as he had tried to tell Mr Olomo.

"I could give you a thousand pounds," he said. "That's a quick profit for you, isn't it? And you would still have your salary as manager.

"I'll go to the bank and get it for you right away," he added.

He did not go to the bank, because he had no bank account, but he went to see Mr Olomo, who on such occasions served an almost equally useful purpose. Louie's credit was good, and he was able to secure a loan to make up the deficiencies in his own purse at a purely nominal thirty per cent interest. He hurried back to the flat where he had left Simon Templar and stuck the notes into his hand—it was the only time Mr Fallon had ever parted gladly with any sum of money.

"Now I shall have to get to work," said Mr Fallon, indicating that he wished to be alone.

"What about my contract as manager?" murmured the Saint.

"I'll ring up my solicitor and ask him to fix it right away," Louie promised him.

Five minutes after Simon Templar had left him, he was tearing back to Mr Olomo in a taxi, with the paraphernalia from his washstand stacked up on the seat, and his suitcases beside him.

"I've made my fortune, Ollie," he declared somewhat hysterically. "All this thing needs is some proper financing. Watch me, and I'll show you what I can do."

He set out to demonstrate what he could do, but something seemed to have gone wrong with the formula. He tried again, with equally unsatisfactory results. He tried three and four times more, but he produced no diamonds. Something inside him turned colder every time he failed.

"I tell you, I saw him do it, Ollie," he babbled frantically. "He mixed the things up himself, and somehow he hit on the proportions that I've been lookin' for all these years."

"Maybe he has the diamonds palmed in his hand when he puts it in the tin, Louie," suggested Mr Olomo cynically.

Louie sat with his head in his hands. The quest for synthetic wealth faded beside another ambition which was starting to monopolize his whole horizon. The only thing he asked of life at that moment was a chance to meet the Saint again—preferably down a dark alley beside the river, with a blunt instrument ready to his hand. But the world was full of men who cherished that ambition. It always would be.

PUBLICATION HISTORY

Of the fourteen tales in this book, the majority of them were written by Charteris for the latter part of his contract with the *Empire News*, a now long defunct English Sunday newspaper, which employed him to write a fresh Saint short story every week for twenty-five weeks. The tales in this book were first published between 1 October 1933 ("The Ingenuous Colonel," which was originally entitled "Keep an Eye on the Clock"), and 3 December 1933 ("The Tall Timber," which was originally published under the rather jolly title of "The Moustache and the Tea-Cup"). "The Art Photographer" and "The Mixture as Before" were written specifically for this book.

"The Man Who Liked Toys" is rather unique. It was written by Charteris in 1933 when he was in America and was trying to establish himself as a writer, not necessarily of just stories about Simon Templar. It was published by *The American Magazine* in September that year, and the original story did not feature Simon Templar but a couple of gentlemen called Andy Herrick and George Kestry. The story didn't get quite the reaction Charteris hoped for, so he rewrote it for this book with Andy Herrick becoming Simon Templar and George Kestry becoming Inspector Teal. For those interested in reading the original story it would be worth tracking down a copy of *The Mammoth Book of Great Detective Stories*, which was published in 1985 in the UK, for it includes the un-Saintly version.

The book itself was first published under the title of *Boodle* by Hodder & Stoughton in August 1934. The gap between US and UK editions was steadily narrowing, for Doubleday Crime Club debuted the book, under the title *The Saint Intervenes*, in October that same year. By 1950, with the advent of the Saint's adventures appearing in paperback, UK publishers had adopted that title.

Hodder & Stoughton declined to publish a story that was critical of a publisher, so "The Uncritical Publisher" has never been published in book form in the UK until now. For reasons unknown, "The Noble Sportsman" was left out of some notably later editions.

As you might expect from a collection of short stories, a few were adapted for Roger Moore's incarnation of *The Saint*. "The Noble Sportsman" was the thirty-fourth episode to be aired and was first broadcast on 9 January 1964, "The Loving Brothers" was the forty-sixth episode and first aired on 15 November 1964, and "The Man Who Liked Toys" followed it a week later on 22 November. "The Damsel in Distress" first aired on Sunday, 3 January 1965, whilst "The Impossible Crime" was retitled "The Contract" and first aired on 7 January 1965. Finally "The Newdick Helicopter" was a very loose inspiration for "The Checkered Flag," which first aired on 1 July 1965.

Foreign translations are a little harder to find, for short stories appeared to be a harder sell to international publishers. A Swedish translation appeared in 1952 under the title *Helgonet i farten* (which sadly translates as "The Saint on the go"). The Germans had to wait until 1963 when, no doubt due to the popularity of the Roger Moore series, *Der "Heilige" greift ein* was published. Similarly the Dutch published *Troef voor de Saint* in 1964.

ABOUT THE AUTHOR

I'm mad enough to believe in romance. And I'm sick and tired of this age—tired of the miserable little mildewed things that people racked their brains about, and wrote books about, and called life. I wanted something more elementary and honest—battle, murder, sudden death, with plenty of good beer and damsels in distress, and a complete callousness about blipping the ungodly over the beezer. It mayn't be life as we know it, but it ought to be.

—Leslie Charteris in a 1935 BBC radio interview

Leslie Charteris was born Leslie Charles Bowyer-Yin in Singapore on 12 May 1907.

He was the son of a Chinese doctor and his English wife, who'd met in London a few years earlier. Young Leslie found friends hard to come by in colonial Singapore. The English children had been told not to play with Eurasians, and the Chinese children had been told not to play with Europeans. Leslie was caught in between and took refuge in reading.

"I read a great many good books and enjoyed them because nobody had told me that they were classics. I also read a great many bad books which nobody told me not to read . . . I read a great many popular scientific articles and acquired from them an astonishing amount of general knowledge before I discovered that this acquisition was supposed to be a chore."[1]

One of his favourite things to read was a magazine called *Chums*. "The Best and Brightest Paper for Boys" (if you believe the adverts) was a monthly paper full of swashbuckling adventure stories aimed at boys, encouraging them to be honourable and moral and perhaps even "upright citizens with furled umbrellas."[2] Undoubtedly these types of stories would influence his later work.

When his parents split up shortly after the end of World War I, Charteris accompanied his mother and brother back to England, where he was sent to Rossall School in Fleetwood, Lancashire. Rossall was then a very stereotypical English public school, and it struggled to cope with this multilingual mixed-race boy just into his teens who'd already seen more of the world than many of his peers would see in their lifetimes. He was an outsider.

He left Rossall in 1924. Keen to pursue a creative career, he decided to study art in Paris—after all, that was where the great artists went—but soon found that the life of a literally starving artist didn't appeal. He continued writing, firing off speculative stories to magazines, and it was the sale of a short story to *Windsor Magazine* that saved him from penury.

He returned to London in 1925, as his parents—particularly his father—wanted him to become a lawyer, and he was sent to study law at Cambridge University. In the mid-1920s, Cambridge was full of Bright Young Things—aristocrats and bohemians somewhat typified in the Evelyn Waugh novel *Vile Bodies*—and again the mixed-race Bowyer-Yin found that he didn't fit in. He was an outsider who preferred to make his own way in the world and wasn't one of the privileged upper class. It didn't help that he found his studies boring and decided it was more fun contemplating ways to circumvent the law. This inspired him to write a novel, and when publishers Ward Lock & Co. offered him a three-book deal on the strength of it, he abandoned his studies to pursue a writing career.

When his father learnt of this, he was not impressed, as he considered writers to be "rogues and vagabonds." Charteris would later recall that "I wanted to be a writer, he wanted me to become a lawyer. I was stubborn, he said I would end up in the gutter. So I left home. Later on, when I had a little success, we were reconciled by letter, but I never saw him again."[3]

X Esquire, his first novel, appeared in April 1927. The lead character, X Esquire, is a mysterious hero, hunting down and killing the businessmen trying to wipe out Britain by distributing quantities of free poisoned cigarettes. His second novel, *The White Rider*, was published the following spring, and in one memorable scene shows the hero chasing after his damsel in distress, only for him to overtake the villains, leap into their car . . . and promptly faint.

These two plot highlights may go some way to explaining Charteris's comment on *Meet—the Tiger!*, published in September 1928, that "it was only the third book I'd written, and the best, I would say, for it was that the first two were even worse."[4]

Twenty-one-year-old authors are naturally self-critical. Despite reasonably good reviews, the Saint didn't set the world on fire, and Charteris moved on to a new hero for his next book. This was *The Bandit*, an adventure story featuring Ramon Francisco De Castilla y Espronceda Manrique, published in the summer of 1929 after its serialisation in the *Empire News*, a now long-forgotten Sunday newspaper. But sales of *The Bandit* were less than impressive, and Charteris began to question his choice of career. It was all very well writing—but if nobody wants to read what you write, what's the point?

"I had to succeed, because before me loomed the only alternative, the dreadful penalty of failure . . . the routine office hours, the five-day week . . . the lethal assimilation into the ranks of honest, hard-working, conformist, God-fearing pillars of the community."[5]

However his fortunes—and the Saint's—were about to change. In late 1928, Leslie had met Monty Haydon, a London-based editor who was looking for writers to pen stories for his new paper, *The Thriller*—"The Paper with a Thousand Thrills." Charteris later recalled that "he said he was starting a new magazine, had read one of my books and would like some stories from me. I couldn't have been more grateful, both from the point of view of vanity and finance!"[6]

The paper launched in early 1929, and Leslie's first work, "The Story of a Dead Man," featuring Jimmy Traill, appeared in issue 4 (published on 2 March 1929). That was followed just over a month later with "The Secret of Beacon Inn," starring Rameses "Pip" Smith. At the same time, Leslie finished writing another non-Saint novel, *Daredevil*, which would be published in late 1929. Storm Arden was the hero; more notably, the book saw the first introduction of a Scotland Yard inspector by the name of Claud Eustace Teal.

The Saint returned in the thirteenth issue of *The Thriller*. The byline proclaimed that the tale was "A Thrilling Complete Story of the Underworld"; the title was "The Five Kings," and it actually featured Four Kings and a Joker. Simon Templar, of course, was the Joker.

Charteris spent the rest of 1929 telling the adventures of the Five Kings in five subsequent *The Thriller* stories. "It was very hard work, for the pay was lousy, but Monty Haydon was a brilliant and stimulating editor, full of ideas. While he didn't actually help shape the Saint as a character, he did suggest story lines. He would take me out to lunch and say, 'What are you going to write about next?' I'd often say I was damned if I knew. And Monty would say, 'Well, I was reading something the other day . . .' He had a fund of ideas and we would talk them over, and then I would go away and write a story. He was a great creative editor."[7]

Charteris would have one more attempt at writing about a hero other than Simon Templar, in three novelettes published in *The Thriller* in early 1930, but he swiftly returned to the Saint. This was partly due to his self-confessed laziness—he wanted to write more stories for *The Thriller* and other magazines, and creating a new hero for every story was hard work—but mainly due to feedback from Monty Haydon. It seemed people wanted to read more adventures of the Saint . . .

Charteris would contribute over forty stories to *The Thriller* throughout the 1930s. Shortly after their debut, he persuaded publisher Hodder & Stoughton that if he collected some of these stories and rewrote them a little, they could publish them as a Saint book. *Enter the Saint* was first published in August 1930, and the reaction was good enough for the publishers to bring out another collection. And another . . .

Of the twenty Saint books published in the 1930s, almost all have their origins in those magazine stories.

Why was the Saint so popular throughout the decade? Aside from the charm and ability of Charteris's storytelling, the stories, particularly those published in the first half of the '30s, are full of energy and joie de vivre. With economic depression rampant throughout the period, the public at large seemed to want some escapism.

And Simon Templar's appeal was wide-ranging: he wasn't an upper-class hero like so many of the period. With no obvious background and no attachment to the Old School Tie, no friends in high places who could provide a get-out-of-jail-free card, the Saint was uniquely classless. Not unlike his creator.

Throughout Leslie's formative years, his heritage had been an issue. In his early days in Singapore, during his time at school, at Cambridge University or even just in everyday life, he couldn't avoid the fact that for many people his mixed parentage was a problem. He would later tell a story of how he was chased up the road by a stick-waving typical

English gent who took offence to his daughter being escorted around town by a foreigner.

Like the Saint, he was an outsider. And although he had spent a significant portion of his formative years in England, he couldn't settle.

As a young boy he had read of an America "peopled largely by Indians, and characters in fringed buckskin jackets who fought nobly against them. I spent a great deal of time day-dreaming about a visit to this prodigious and exciting country."[8]

It was time to realise this wish. Charteris and his first wife, Pauline, whom he'd met in London when they were both teenagers and married in 1931, set sail for the States in late 1932; the Saint had already made his debut in America courtesy of the publisher Doubleday. Charteris and his wife found a New York still experiencing the tail end of Prohibition, and times were tough at first. Despite sales to *The American Magazine* and others, it wasn't until a chance meeting with writer turned Hollywood executive Bartlett McCormack in their favourite speakeasy that Charteris's career stepped up a gear.

Soon Charteris was in Hollywood, working on what would become the 1933 movie *Midnight Club*. However, Hollywood's treatment of writers wasn't to Charteris's taste, and he began to yearn for home. Within a few months, he returned to the UK and began writing more Saint stories for Monty Haydon and Bill McElroy.

He also rewrote a story he'd sketched out whilst in the States, a version of which had been published in *The American Magazine* in September 1934. This new novel, *The Saint in New York*, published in 1935, was a significant advance for the Saint and Leslie Charteris. Gone were the high jinks and the badinage. The youthful exuberance evident in the Saint's early adventures had evolved into something a little darker, a little more hard-boiled. It was the next stage in development for the author and his creation, and readers loved it. It became a bestseller on both sides of the Atlantic.

Having spent his formative years in places as far apart as Singapore and England, with substantial travel in between, it should be no surprise that Leslie had a serious case of wanderlust. With a bestseller under his belt, he now had the means to see more of the world.

Nineteen thirty-six found him in Tenerife, researching another Saint adventure alongside translating the biography of Juan Belmonte, a well-known Spanish matador. Estranged for several months, Leslie and Pauline divorced in 1937. The following year, Leslie married an American, Barbara Meyer, who'd accompanied him to Tenerife. In early 1938, Charteris and his new bride set off in a trailer of his own design and spent eighteen months travelling round America and Canada.

The Saint in New York had reminded Hollywood of Charteris's talents, and film rights to the novel were sold prior to publication in 1935. Although the proposed 1935 film production was rejected by the Hays Office for its violent content, RKO's eventual 1938 production persuaded Charteris to try his luck once more in Hollywood.

New opportunities had opened up, and throughout the 1940s the Saint appeared not only in books and movies but in a newspaper strip, a comic-book series, and on radio.

Anyone wishing to adapt the character in any medium found a stern taskmaster in Charteris. He was never completely satisfied, nor was he shy of showing his displeasure. He did, however, ensure that copyright in any Saint adventure belonged to him, even if scripted by another writer—a contractual obligation that he was to insist on throughout his career.

Charteris was soon spread thin, overseeing movies, comics, newspapers, and radio versions of his creation, and this, along with his self-proclaimed laziness, meant that Saint books were becoming fewer and further between. However, he still enjoyed his creation: in 1941 he indulged himself in a spot of fun by playing the Saint—complete with monocle and moustache—in a photo story in *Life* magazine.

In July 1944, he started collaborating under a pseudonym on Sherlock Holmes radio scripts, subsequently writing more adventures for Holmes than Conan Doyle. Not all his ventures were successful—a screenplay he was hired to write for Deanna Durbin, "Lady on a Train," took him a year and ultimately bore little resemblance to the finished film. In the mid-1940s, Charteris successfully sued RKO Pictures for unfair competition after they launched a new series of films starring George Sanders as a debonair crime fighter known as the Falcon. But he kept faith with his original character, and the Saint novels continued to adapt to the times. The transatlantic Saint evolved into something of a private operator, working for the mysterious Hamilton and becoming, not unlike his creator, a world traveller, finding that adventure would seek him out.

"I have never been able to see why a fictional character should not grow up, mature, and develop, the same as anyone else. The same, if you like, as his biographer. The only adequate reason is that—so far as I know—no other fictional character in modern times has survived a sufficient number of years for these changes to be clearly observable. I must confess that a lot of my own selfish pleasure in the Saint has been in watching him grow up."[9]

Charteris maintained his love of travel and was soon to be found sailing round the West Indies with his good friend Gregory Peck. His forays abroad gave him even more material, and he began to write true-crime articles, as well as an occasional column in *Gourmet* magazine.

By the early '50s, Charteris himself was feeling strained. He'd divorced his second wife in 1943 and got together with a New York radio and nightclub singer called Betty Bryant Borst, whom he married in late 1943. That relationship had fallen apart acrimoniously towards the end of the decade, and he roamed the globe restlessly, rarely in one place for longer than a couple of months. He continued to maintain a firm grip on the exploitation of the Saint in various media but was writing little himself. The Saint had become an industry, and Charteris couldn't keep up. He began thinking seriously about an early retirement.

Then in 1951 he met a young actress called Audrey Long when they became next-door neighbours in Hollywood. Within a year they had married, a union that was to last the rest of Leslie's life.

He attacked life with a new vitality. They travelled—Nassau was a favoured escape spot—and he wrote. He struck an agreement with *The New York Herald Tribune* for a Saint comic strip, which would appear daily and be written by Charteris himself. The strip ran for thirteen years, with Charteris sending in his handwritten story lines from wherever he happened to be, relying on mail services around the world to continue the Saint's adventures. New Saint books began to appear, and Charteris reached a height of productivity not seen since his days as a struggling author trying to establish himself. As Leslie and Audrey travelled, so did the Saint, visiting locations just after his creator had been there.

By 1953 the Saint had already enjoyed twenty-five years of success, and *The Saint Detective Magazine* was launched. Charteris had become adept at exploiting his creation to the full, mixing new stories with repackaged older stories, sometimes rewritten, sometimes mixed up in "new" anthologies, sometimes adapted from radio scripts previously written by other writers.

Charteris had been approached several times over the years for television rights in the Saint and had expended much time and effort during the 1950s trying to get the Saint on TV, even going so far as to write sample scripts himself, but it wasn't to be. He finally agreed a deal in autumn 1961 with English film producers Robert S. Baker and Monty Berman. The first episode of *The Saint* television series, starring Roger Moore, went into production in June 1962. The series was an immediate success, though Charteris himself had his reservations. It reached second place in the ratings, but he commented that "in that distinction it was topped by wrestling, which only suggested to me that the competition may not have been so hot; but producers are generally cast in a less modest mould." He resented the implication that the TV series had finally made a success of the Saint after twenty-five years of literary obscurity.

As long as the series lasted, Charteris was not shy about voicing his criticisms both in public and in a constant stream of memos to the producers. "Regular followers of the Saint saga . . . must have noticed that I am almost incapable of simply writing a story and shutting up."[10] Nor was he shy about exploiting this new market by agreeing to a series of tie-in novelisations ghosted by other writers, which he would then rewrite before publication.

Charteris mellowed as the series developed and found elements to praise too. He developed a close friendship with producer Robert S. Baker, which would last until Charteris's death.

In the early '60s, on one of their frequent trips to England, Leslie and Audrey bought a house in Surrey, which became their permanent base. He explored the possibility of a Saint musical and began writing some of it himself.

Charteris no longer needed to work. Now in his sixties, he supervised the Saint from a distance whilst continuing to travel and indulge himself. He and Audrey made seasonal excursions to Ireland and the south of France, where they had residences. He began to write poetry and devised a new universal sign language, Paleneo, based on notes and symbols he used in his diaries. Once Paleneo was released, he decided enough was enough and announced, again, his retirement. This time he meant it.

The Saint continued regardless—there was a long-running Swedish comic strip, and new novels with other writers doing the bulk of the work were complemented in the 1970s with Bob Baker's revival of the TV series, *Return of the Saint*.

Ill-health began to take its toll. By the early 1980s, although he continued a healthy correspondence with the outside world, Charteris felt unable to keep up with the collaborative Saint books and pulled the plug on them.

To entertain himself, Leslie took to "trying to beat the bookies in predicting the relative speed of horses," a hobby which resulted in several of his local betting shops refusing to take "predictions" from him, as he was too successful for their liking.

He still received requests to publish his work abroad but had become completely cynical about further attempts to revive the Saint. A new Saint magazine only lasted three issues, and two TV productions—*The Saint in Manhattan*, with Tom Selleck look-alike Andrew Clarke, and *The Saint*, with Simon Dutton—left him bitterly disappointed. "I fully expect this series to lay eggs everywhere . . . the only satisfaction I have is in looking at my bank balance."[11]

In the early 1990s, Hollywood producers Robert Evans and William J. Macdonald approached him and made a deal for the Saint to return to cinema screens. Charteris still took great care of the Saint's reputation and wrote an outline entitled *The Return of the Saint* in which an older Saint would meet the son he didn't know he had.

Much of his time in his last few years was taken up with the movie. Several scripts were submitted to him—each moving further and further away from his original concept—but the screenwriter from 1940s Hollywood was thoroughly disheartened by the Hollywood of the '90s: "There is still no plot, no real story, no characterisations, no personal interaction, nothing but endless frantic violence . . ." Besides, with producer Bill Macdonald hitting the headlines for the most un-Saintly reasons, he was to add, "How can Bill Macdonald concentrate on my Saint movie when he has Sharon Stone in his bed?"

The Crime Writers' Association of Great Britain presented Leslie with a Lifetime Achievement award in 1992 in a special ceremony at the

House of Lords. Never one for associations and awards, and although visibly unwell, Leslie accepted the award with grace and humour ("I am now only waiting to be carbon-dated," he joked). He suffered a slight stroke in his final weeks, which did not prevent him from dining out locally with family and friends, before he finally passed away at the age of 85 on 15 April 1993.

His death severed one of the final links with the classic thriller genre of the 1930s and 1940s, but he left behind a legacy of nearly one hundred books, countless short stories, and TV, film, radio, and comic-strip adaptations of his work which will endure for generations to come.

> *I was always sure that there was a solid place in escape literature for a rambunctious adventurer such as I dreamed up in my youth, who really believed in the old-fashioned romantic ideals and was prepared to lay everything on the line to bring them to life. A joyous exuberance that could not find its fulfilment in pinball machines and pot. I had what may now seem a mad desire to spread the belief that there were worse, and wickeder, nut cases than Don Quixote.*
>
> *Even now, half a century later, when I should be old enough to know better, I still cling to that belief. That there will always be a public for the old-style hero, who had a clear idea of justice, and a more than technical approach to love, and the ability to have some fun with his crusades.*[12]

---

1 *A Letter from the Saint,* 30 August 1946

2 "The Last Word," *The First Saint Omnibus,* Doubleday Crime Club, 1939

3 *The Straits Times,* 29 June 1958, page 9

4 Introduction by Charteris to the September 1980 paperback reprint of *Meet—the Tiger!* (Charter), the last ever print edition.
5 *The Saint: A Complete History,* by Burl Barer (McFarland, 1993)
6 PR material from the 1970s series *Return of the Saint*
7 From "Return of the Saint: Comprehensive Information" issued to help publicise the 1970s TV show
8 *A Letter from the Saint,* 26 July 1946
9 Introduction to "The Million Pound Day," in *The First Saint Omnibus*
10 *A Letter from the Saint,* 12 April 1946
11 Letter from LC to sometime Saint collaborator Peter Bloxsom, 2 August 1989
12 Introduction by Charteris to the September 1980 paperback reprint of *Meet—the Tiger!* (Charter).

WATCH FOR THE SIGN

OF THE SAINT!

THE SAINT CLUB

And so, my friends, dear bookworms, most noble fellow drinkers, frustrated burglars, affronted policemen, upright citizens with furled umbrellas and secret buccaneering dreams that seems to be very nearly all for now. It has been nice having you with us, and we hope you will come again, not once, but many times.

Only because of our great love for you, we would like to take this parting opportunity of mentioning one small matter which we have very much at heart . . .

—*Leslie Charteris,* The First Saint Omnibus *(1939)*

Leslie Charteris founded The Saint Club in 1936 with the aim of providing a constructive fanbase for Saint devotees. Before the War, it donated profits to a London hospital where, for several years, a Saint ward was maintained. With the nationalisation of hospitals, profits were, for many years, donated to the Arbour Youth Centre in Stepney, London.

In the twenty-first century, we've carried on this tradition but have also donated to the Red Cross and a number of different children's charities.

The club acts as a focal point for anyone interested in the adventures of Leslie Charteris and the work of Simon Templar, and offers merchandise that includes DVDs of the old TV series and various Saint-related publications, through to its own exclusive range of notepaper, pin badges, and polo shirts. All profits are donated to charity. The club also maintains two popular websites and supports many more Saint-related sites.

After Leslie Charteris's death, the club recruited three new vice-presidents—Roger Moore, Ian Ogilvy, and Simon Dutton have all pledged their support, whilst Audrey and Patricia Charteris have been retained as Saints-in-Chief. But some things do not change, for the back of the membership card still mischievously proclaims that . . .

> *The bearer of this card is probably a person of hideous antecedents and low moral character, and upon apprehension for any cause should be immediately released in order to save other prisoners from contamination.*

To join . . .

Membership costs £3.50 (or US$7) per year, or £30 (US$60) for life. Find us online at www.lesliecharteris.com for full details.

Made in the USA
Monee, IL
01 September 2022

12953221R00173